TERROR TALES OF
THE LAKE DISTRICT

TERROR TALES OF THE LAKE DISTRICT

Edited by Paul Finch

TERROR TALES OF THE LAKE DISTRICT

First published in 2011 by Gray Friar Press.
9 Abbey Terrace, Whitby,
North Yorkshire, YO21 3HQ, England.
Email: gary.fry@virgin.net
www.grayfriarpress.com

Typesetting and design by Paul Finch and Gary Fry

ISBN: 978-1-906331-25-2

TABLE OF CONTENTS

LITTLE MAG'S BARROW
Adam L G Nevill

If you drive from Penrith to Windermere on the A592 and cut up towards Troutbeck, you won't see the house from the road. Head along the eastern shore of Ullswater and ask for directions in Wreay or Longthwaite, and they won't be able to help you. In Matterdale End, they will shake their heads. And you would think the local people of Glenridding know of the place. They don't.

But the cottage called Little Mag's Barrow does exist. On the first edition of 'Otley's District of the Lakes', published in 1827, the site of the house is even featured, though not named. It is given the symbol of a Site of Antiquity: a black cross.

Today, agricultural buildings obscure the cottage from the front, so it cannot be seen from the narrow lane from which the farm is accessed. A long low mound, above crags formed by the last ice age, protects the rear. But you can see the great Saurian spine of Helvellyn wreathed in snowy vapours from the upstairs room at the back of the cottage. The vast still waters of Ullswater are also within walking distance, if you know the way.

Little Mag's Barrow has never been let out to tourists. The last three postmen were never once required to deliver a letter to its black door. And the farmer's family have long stopped thinking about the small stone building with the slate roof spotted with milky green lichen, far out on the boundary of their land. From which it can be glimpsed through the trees bordering a distant corner of the field their sheep rarely bother with. They are no longer even sure who even owns the building on the tiny plot of stony ground. But the children of the farm remember throwing stones at the house once, when they were younger and roamed that way. And their mother occasionally recalls them coming home abnormally chaste and nervous, though none of them were able to explain why to her.

Standing before the front door, with a heavy key in the palm of her plump hand (a key that would fit no lock forged after 1850) Kitty Yew's relief and satisfaction at finding the cottage so easily, almost in error really, vanished and was replaced by the familiar heat of her temper. Before she'd even alighted from her car, into Kitty's mind had come an image of Morag Gascard's long face and lank hair and she'd torn her phone from her pocket to berate the idiot. And then paused, remembering the signal had vanished after Glenridding.

When the unfailingly meek and diffident Morag offered Kitty the place for a long weekend, Morag hadn't described her family's holiday cottage in terms like *miserable*, or *uninviting*, which this squat hovel appeared to be.

Revenge would be served soon enough when she made Morag, and another two of her colleagues in Children's Books, redundant on her return to London. Kitty nearly didn't accept Morag's surprise offer of the cottage. Making use of the place had seemed inappropriate. Long before Morag gave Kitty the old key, taped to a hand-drawn map, "to getaway for a few days", Kitty Yew had already made the decision to place the long-serving and earnest Senior Editor on a one month consultation period, with statutory minimum terms of severance.

Outside Little Mag's Barrow, Kitty forced herself to breathe and then recite the cognitive exercise learnt at the anger management course she had been sent to by the Board. It was still fresh in her mind; she'd sat through eight hours of counselling and group exercises each day the previous week. Making today the beginning of the second week of her Leave of Absence. Which directly followed the last of three tribunals she had attended, as the accused, in as many years running NPD Books. *Into the ground*, the last sales director had said to her, ten minutes before she fired him by email. There had been two charges against her of unfair dismissal, and a third for bullying. She'd lost all three cases, which was almost unheard of for an employer. That is unless the plaintiffs were really determined to address unfair treatment, and it appeared that all three of them had been.

The legal setbacks left Kitty wondering whether she would survive the impending buyout of NPD Books by a corporate publishing giant. But then the Board of Directors needed someone to take care of the due diligence in the takeover. And, of course, once you are at the top it's very hard to be toppled.

It was the psychiatrist at the centre who insisted she get away from London to spend time alone examining her behaviour. How had he put it? To alleviate her "hypomania" with reflection, to temper her "compulsions" with solitude, far away from the social and professional "situations that triggered her obsessive need for control and adulation", and her "inability to empathise" followed by her "defensive short circuits into blame, denial, and rage".

No one had dared speak to her like that for a long time; certainly not in a professional capacity, and not socially or romantically either; though she readily admitted that was due to a lack of participation in these arenas. Nonetheless, the accusations from the psychiatrist had fallen like blows. In recent times, the only thing angering her as much as the psychological profile (the doctor had even said her personality disorder was "probably pathological and potentially disabling") was the insistence of the Board that she "seek help" in the first place.

But all of them were mistaken about her. She knew that without recourse to solitude and reflection. Ethics and scruples were luxuries for those not charged with turning over seven million pounds each year. And what use would a week away from her desk be in this wretched ruin? A horseshoe had even rusted to dust against the peeling wood of the front door; an entrance so small, she would be forced to duck her head to get inside.

"You have got to be joking," Kitty said out loud, after struggling with the door. Pungent with neglect and the woody-camphor fragrance that huddles about preserved antiquity, the unaired and unappealing space seemed to suddenly exhale into her face the very moment Kitty pushed the door inward, scraping itself with a groaning recalcitrance across the slate floor.

A low ceiling created a pressure of darkness inside a cluttered room that served as the ground floor of the building. A tiny and dingy annex containing a chaotic kitchen appeared on the far side, separated from the solitary ground floor room by a tatty curtain. Opposite the front door, a flight of open-sided stairs led up to the next floor. There were no lights; no electricity.

Kitty immediately thought of returning to the car, and then driving all the way back to London in one furious epic journey. Her chest tightened. She felt dizzy and leant against the doorframe. Exhausted by the long drive, she'd further worn herself down with a rotation of anger and dismay the moment her car jerked into sight of Little Mag's Barrow. A familiar cycle. Now hunger burned inside her stomach too. She was going nowhere tonight and knew it. And felt herself mocked by the grin of the stuffed fox, poised upon a shelf hectic with old books and small ornamental bells.

Kitty passed into the cool dim interior. Was pleased, at least, to be out of the sun. She dropped herself into the ancient armchair beside the grubby hearth, its mantle a riot of iron candlesticks, desiccated sprigs of heather, and miniatures of what might have been saints from the suggestions of the wan, beatific faces, all greenish with age and appealing for her sympathy from out of their wooden frames.

3

She sneezed from the dust that puffed up from the seat cushions. What looked like a tuft of human hair poked from one worn armrest. She removed her freckled forearm from it. "Oh, Morag. You little bitch ... We'll see. We'll see," she said to herself, nodding her head vigorously so her mass of red curls made her Chanel sun glasses bob up and down upon her head.

With what felt like a colossal personal defeat, Kitty acknowledged the disingenuous nature of Morag's offer of the cottage. Because Morag had obviously gotten wind of her looming redundancy and decided to trick her boss into driving from London to the Lake District only to be confronted by this dump, huddled behind the rocky mound. She might even be showing photos of the unpleasant property in the pub after work. Perhaps even right now. Kitty checked her wristwatch and confirmed the hunch. They'd all be laughing and congratulating Morag on her subterfuge. And into Kitty came such an urgent heat of rage she grew light-headed, and was forced to close her eyes and regulate her breathing, again.

And she sat alone and in silence while her eyes groped about the cramped and gloomy room. A single window, screened with grubby nets, allowed a thin dusty light to fall inside. A tiny piano painted white and patterned with gaudy red flowers had been positioned under the sill. An instrument that made her think of a circus monkey wearing a little bellhop suit; she'd seen one as a child, plinking and plonking away upon something similar. Before the piano was a small stool, with a red velvet seat, that must have been intended for a child.

The other framed prints on the walls were dim and dusty, but featured variations of the same theme; suggestions of round-faced peasants with grubby cloths bound about their heads, from which their hollow eyes and open mouths leered as they toiled in wintry Medieval scenes. Whether it was the oafish faces or the patched and peeling plaster around the picture frames, she wasn't sure, but Kitty found her scrutiny of the walls an unsettling experience. A little black shovel for the ashes in the grate leant against a wicker basket, filled with cobwebbed wood.

When the light outside dimmed, as if a lone cloud had just crept under the waning sun, she made to rise from the armchair to fetch her bags from the car. But paused and looked up at the ceiling. Ever so faintly, she was sure she had just heard the sound of small feet landing upon a hard floor. As if a cat had leapt from a bed.

Frowning, Kitty stood up. Walked to the bottom of the staircase. Peered upwards at the cramped landing, and the solitary door she could see in shadow. She nearly called out a challenge, but felt foolish. Straining her hearing up and into the first floor rooms, she surmised that in such a small building, there couldn't have been more than two rooms and a bathroom up there.

Silence.

Squashing her body against the wall, because there was no railing on the other side overlooking the downstairs room, she went up. Her feet boomed on the steep steps.

The small landing featured two closed doors. The first opened on to a bathroom, with an ancient toilet shoved up against a bathtub so small an adult would have struggled to sit inside it with their knees bent. It was more of a large deep sink than a bath. One look at it confirmed her purpose to leave the following morning, early. Which meant the second door led to a solitary bedroom. So how could a family have ever lived here? One must have done, and perhaps they'd all crowded into a single bed to keep warm. There were no radiators in the property, only fireplaces.

The bedroom was mostly filled with the bed; an ancient looking thing with dark wooden panels at the sides of the frame. A rectangular box in effect with a mattress fitted inside it. Big enough for one short adult. The ceiling sloped down on either side of the room to match the slant of the roof. One window, inside a deep casement, filtered a weak grey light through the nets. Mercifully, the walls were unadorned.

Kitty stepped inside the room to peer through the window and see what kind of view might present itself beyond the ugly mound of rock and earth. But a figure sitting upright inside the room, on her left, snatched at her attention. She turned her head, then started. "Jesus!" Slapping both hands to her chest, she staggered backward until the base of the bedframe indented the rear of her legs, bringing her to an ungainly stop.

In relief, Kitty closed her eyes and slowly exhaled. It was only a doll.

On a small chair. One so perfect for the dimensions of its diminutive occupant, it suggested it had actually been made for the little scruffy figure. Kitty hadn't seen it from the landing, because the door had obscured the position of the chair propped against the wall opposite the foot of the bed.

Kitty stared at it with an instant loathing, and what she also identified as anxiety. But what was it about the figure that unnerved her? Because it wasn't the round face of plain silk with indifferent features embroidered so roughly upon it with red wool. Nor was it the blank unappealing glare of the mother-of-pearl button eyes. Or

5

the long wooden arms and legs, painted in flesh tones, but chipped; the latter appendages ending in little lace-up ankle boots. And even though the limbs had the appearance of having been removed from another doll, or even a disabled child to add an unwelcome realism where they poked out from the stained and ragged christening gown that fell to its knees, it still wasn't the limbs that repelled her. No, the most unsettling facet of the doll was its hair. The heavy chestnut curls, reminiscent of Charles I's luxuriant wig, were undoubtedly cut from a real human head. But their incongruity about the crude cloth face gave the impression that the doll was an actual child wearing a fabric mask.

She would not sleep a minute with it sitting upright on a chair at the foot of her bed.

Kitty seized the doll by a wooden wrist and raised it from the chair. It flopped and drooped from her hand as she went back down the stairs to the kitchen. The sense that she was dragging a surly child by force to some destination where it would serve a penance, for the doll was as easily as big as the average four year old, did not escape her. In fact, that very suggestion grew until she'd dumped it in the kitchen's tin sink and yanked the little frayed curtain along its rattling rail to seal the kitchen annex from the main room.

A quick inspection of the disorderly surfaces and dusty little cupboards inside the kitchen area, had also made her realise she wouldn't be preparing food in the kitchen for the duration of her short stay. The stove even required a gas bottle. She'd be gone by morning and, until then, would make do with the cake, crisps, biscuits, chocolate and wine she'd brought with her.

Kitty collected her bags from the car. She put the box of food and wine on the armchair, and headed upstairs with her holdall. By the time the task was complete, she dropped heavily on to the bed and covered her face with her hands. The enormity of Morag's deception, and the atmosphere of the ugly cottage, weighed so heavily upon her spirits, she felt a terrible inertia settle upon her; but the apathy did not relax her, it seemed to weaken her instead, and profoundly too. And with such a tired mind it became hard to define what additional, almost unrecognisable ailments, also assailed her. She didn't feel well. Physically uncomfortable, if not drained, but also fatigued with what felt like remorse. *Condemned.*

Nothing stirred her from her resignation and misery and rancour, until a curious series of sounds outside made her raise her weary face from her hands. She heard something similar to a flock of birds rising suddenly. Though the cries that issued from them were reminiscent of the sounds heard from a distant school playground.

Children?

She rose from the bed and bent over to peer through the tiny slot of a window. The glass was grimy and she could only make out the hump of the large black hillock standing between the sinking sun and the cottage. The sky behind the hill was a bright white screen, too painful to look at for long. Kitty turned away, blinking. And went downstairs instead to investigate the noise.

From the rear of the cottage, any kind of vista typical of the area was blocked by the long mound of earth; or maybe it was merely a sharp rise in the terrain. But whatever it was, the hill cast the house into partial shadow. And although it was a hot day, the outside of her arms goosed.

The sun was low and cast itself through the metallic clouds to blast over the summit. She could see little from behind the cottage, besides a blinding white light and the black silhouette of the hill's curving summit within the light, like the curve of an eclipse. And so bright was the sun, she shielded her eyes with a hand and gasped from the sudden pain in her eyes.

Morag had said something about *walking up the hill to see the view* that was, presumably, beyond it. Kitty showed the landscape her shuttered eyes. And her capped teeth bared in a grimace, encircled by the bright oval of her pink lips. *I'd like to see that boneless cow get up the hill.* A person would have to go up in a crouch, or on their hands and knees; the sides were too steep, too uneven, for anything but indignity. And when was the last time the grey-faced spinster, Morag, had even been here?

Kitty turned her head away, but a curious physical sensation lingered; the darkness of the hill continued to stain her eyes, while the lingering brightness of the sky above smarted and flashed even deeper inside her skull. She tottered. The blood in her head ebbed. For a moment of complete disorientation, Kitty was no longer sure which way was up or down, or which way she was even facing. And when she clamped her eyes tightly shut, she even felt as if she were hanging upside down, perhaps suspended by an ankle. The sudden vertigo nearly brought the contents of her stomach roaring up her throat.

Random medicalised phrases sounded in her thoughts: *blood pressure, deep vein thrombosis*. She was overweight and terribly unfit, and had been behind the wheel for six hours. Then she desperately hoped the faint spell was connected to low blood sugar

7

... She panicked. Heard herself cry out. But it was as if she had called from far away and outside her own blindness. An echo perhaps, because the cry also sounded as if it were rushing, if not being dragged, up the hill and away from her.

Falling more than sitting down, her large body thumped and then quivered in an ungainly protest at the suddenness of its collapse. Beneath her the ground was cold and smelled unpleasantly peaty. Was wet too, soaking through her thin dress and underwear and into her flesh. The earth also drew the heat from her body and replaced it with a chill that ached inside the bones of her legs and spine.

A moment of vanity surfaced and she feared the nearby presence of a laughing crowd. Had farm workers or ramblers seen the fat lady slip and fall? Yes, or at least someone had seen her, because you can't be mistaken about the boisterous rushing presence of ... maybe it was an animal. A sheep, cow, or dog ... Coming in close and quick like that. No, not an animal, because there was a sudden swish of garment and a perceptible whisk of air parting about two quick legs. Perhaps there was even the casting of a darker shadow than the one already filling her eyes, and a cooling of the air now too, as a small body came between her and the sky.

"Fallen," she said, to whoever was there. Probably a child from the farm or a nearby holiday cottage.

And then such considerations about her pride vanished, and she was overwhelmed by the business of trying to blink and wipe the terrible darkness of the hill from her face. It needed to be done immediately, even before she got back to her feet, because it seemed persistent and reluctant to be blinked away. It clung, as if on the inside of her face.

In her half-blinded state, she sensed the rise of the house over her head, like it had suddenly animated and grown, yearning for the sky, but also losing its balance and now about to fall heavily upon her body while she floundered in the damp grass before it.

She was next stricken with a nausea. And a sudden onset of despair, futility, and a crushing comprehension of her own insignificance invaded her frantic mind. An incongruous, but vital and pressing desire to apologise – to beg forgiveness – from the house instinctively flared up inside her and she nearly muttered a string of loud entreaties.

But stopped herself, realising the emotion was ridiculous and that she had merely been sun-blinded, lost her balance and fallen. Kitty turned on to her front and pushed herself up to her knees.

The ground stilled, her vision returned and she found herself facing the aged walls of the cottage on all fours, in a position of sublimation so offensive to her, she was back on her feet in one great surge of determination. She twisted around to confront the witness, the voyeur, who had come up close to leer at her disgrace.

No one there. She swatted her skirt down at the back. Kept her eyes lowered to avoid the brightness above her, but scanned her surroundings under a hand held up like the peak of a cap. Down to the far dry-stone walls that marked the end of the rocky plain, and all across the grey stones breaking through the uncut grass, there was no one and nothing moved. Not even a bird.

With some shock, she realised what must have caused the confusion; this sudden lapse in coordination and her impaired balance. She hadn't taken a Xanax that morning because of the long journey. My God, she'd been dropping them for so long that eight hours withdrawal from the mood stabilizers had rendered her helpless. Feeble and panic-stricken and practically hallucinating, like an addict. It explained everything, and the explanation settled her nerves enough for her to regain the presence of mind to snatch up her keys and race for her car.

*

"No one has lived there for years, besides Ragdalena. And I don't think she will tolerate you."

"What? What did you say?" Kitty's voice rose and carried up the street, seeming to propel a white paper bag into a frenetic dance along the curb.

After her fall outside, Kitty had driven into Glenridding to get a phone signal and to put a call into Morag. Who was in a pub, as she had correctly surmised. It was noisy at Morag's end. Music was playing. A white noise of chatter grew and ebbed around the speaker. A bad connection because Morag's meek voice would be clear for seconds, and then suddenly distant as if underground.

"I said no one has lived there for years. Only Ragdalena. And she won't mind you being there. I bet she's glad of the company."

"You never mentioned her … Who is she? What are you saying? Someone lives in there? Who is – "

"You sound surprised with what you found, Kitty. But people have bit their tongues. Looked away as their friends and colleagues were marched out the door."

"What?"

"The view is wonderful from the barrow. You must try and get up it. I'd rather be up it than inside it."

"What? What did you just say? Before – "

"Have you seen the barrow yet? It's very picky, but if it gets inside you, I'd say we'll be very lucky to see you again."

"What are you saying? I can't hear you."

"Sam had a nervous breakdown. You bullied poor Mary onto anti-depressants. Lisa miscarried, but even then you never took your foot from her throat."

"Now you listen to me!"

"Do you hear things from where you sit on that throne all day?"

"How dare you!"

"But you'll hear the music tonight, girl. For whom the bell tolls, eh. There's still ways to bury a queen, my girl. Old ways. Little Mag was the first laid deep by those who take up strange raiment and dance." Morag giggled.

"Morag!"

"It'll take some getting used to. I doubt you've been anywhere like the barrow before, Kitty. But do try and make the most of it. Because *she* will."

Kitty stood, stunned into silence, as Morag's tone switched from casual and assuring, into something brittle and spiteful she didn't recognise at all. And all the time the woman's voice, that wasn't making any real sense, swept from the distance to a horrible clarity in the foreground. Had she even heard Morag correctly?

"Now you listen to me, you wet bitch!' But had there been a dialling tone on her mobile phone, Kitty would have been talking to it.

Three people coming out of the Spar shop stopped talking to stare at her, shouting in the street.

*

Kitty woke in darkness. Wondered where she was. Was certain she was buried under something, enclosed within …

She was in the horrible cottage; she remembered now. Recalled her arrival at the wretched place, her feeling unwell outside, the phone call to Morag, coming back to the cottage and lying down for a few minutes on the bed; it all rushed into her mind.

She must have dozed off. For hours.

It was so dark now.

Her reason scrabbled for solutions: there was only a tiny window and there was no ambient light pollution up here. Her hands scrabbled for her phone; she'd placed it on the floor beside the bed. What was the time?

The screen of her phone threw a weak green underwater light about the bed, pushing shadows like retreating bystanders back to the walls and silhouetting the unoccupied chair at the foot of the bed.

One in the morning. She'd slept for hours. She tried to count them: seven to eight to nine to ten to eleven to twelve to one. How many was that? More than she usually got back home any night of the week.

Downstairs something metallic struck the slate floor. A clang and rattle before silence returned to the little house. Kitty sucked in her breath.

The kitchen. It was under the bedroom; someone was coming in through the tiny window and had disturbed the implements around the sink.

But the window was tiny; how would they get through it?

Kitty lay rigid, hardly breathing. Doubted she had the courage or the strength to even get off the bed, let alone rush for the front door downstairs.

A single flat note from the piano rang out from below.

Kitty sat up and screamed.

Silence.

It had been muffled through the floor, but she was not mistaken; the little white piano had made a sound.

"Oh God," she said, and whimpered when she heard it again. This time several keys rang out their tuneless chimes as if a fist had struck them, as opposed to a single selective finger.

Her breath panting in and out of her, Kitty shifted her position and placed her feet upon the floor. It groaned under her weight.

Silence.

If she heard the piano again, her heart would stop, she just knew it. Its beating sped up, but her pulse certainly didn't fail, when she heard the little bell.

Now she was crying and could not stop. She tried to move, but fell sideways and snatched at the wall she could not see in the darkness. Missed her footing and ended up on her hands and knees, between the bed and the wall, in the cold lightless room.

But the bell ringing downstairs did not stop. Instead, it became furious. She placed its location at the bottom of stairs, as if someone were standing down there looking upwards at the door of her room, and furiously shaking one of the little brass bells she had seen on the shelf by the horrid fox.

On all fours, Kitty crawled at where she remembered the door to be. Dragged the little chair across the floor and shoved it under the door handle.

She ran for the window. Smashed her knee into the bedframe. Her head lit up with white pain. Staggering around the bed frame, her hands slapping at the bedclothes for guidance, she reached the little window and yanked it open. And screamed. Cried out for help. Threw her distinctive bellow out there; the timbre that so many had withered under in publishing meetings and in the dreaded confines of her office. But it was like shouting into a hole dug into wet ground. Outside her window existed a total absence of light. Not so much as a single star or slither of moon illumined the ground or the air above it. In fact, as she paused for breath, her senses were assailed by a great wet peaty odour and, for a moment, she even wondered if the house had slipped entirely under the rocky turf as she slept. But then she was also sure the side of the nearby hill was currently pressed against the side of the building.

What had Morag said about burying a queen?

But it was the infernal chaotic hammering of that little bell, rising up the stairs now, that prevented her from saving her thoughts from a rout of panic, terror and unreason. The din stalled her attempts to account for the suffocating miasma of wet black earth, that poured into the room like gas, and the terrible chill of great stones she uncharacteristically imagined crowding all about the outside of the house, looking upwards.

She only turned from the window and fled back through the darkness to the bedroom door, when what sounded like small hard hands and feet began an insistent banging and knocking on it, as if a child in the midst of a violent tantrum were throwing itself against the wood from outside.

"What do you want? … Please stop! … Oh God help me!" Her words disintegrated into sobs, and then whimpers. And it was only when she thought of the horrible doll, and how she had dumped it in the sink, and it was only when she remembered her unease and mystification at the sight of the small piano and stool, that she began the desperate witless panting, like a tired dog, down there within the darkness close to the floor, on her hands and knees, pressed against the little chair. And all the time the bell was rung out shrilly by a small untiring arm, on the other side of the door upon the tiny landing.

12

The bell stopped its incessant ringing at two. And all was silent again in the cottage called Little Mag's Barrow.

At four, Kitty gathered the courage to rise to her feet and remove the chair from beneath the door handle, but she kept her body pressed against the inside of the door.

At four-thirty, she could wait for dawn no longer, and opened the door. Just a crack. And stared into total darkness. The vague light of her telephone screen showed her that there was no one on the little landing, or stairs. She opened the bedroom door halfway in the frame. And didn't dare breathe. Stood like that for a long time, just listening and unable to move.

Just before five, she ventured out to the little landing, paused and waited for her head to stop spinning. Leant forward and peeked down and into the ground floor room she could see from the side of the open staircase. In the phone screen's meagre glow, she saw the silhouettes of the piano, stool, armchair, hearth and cluttered walls, but no sign of any kind of life. Even the little curtain was still pulled across the opening of the kitchen alcove. It was all as she had left it the previous evening. And this gave her hope.

Breathing out, Kitty eased herself down two steps.

And it was only then, in the tense lightless air of neglect, surrounded by the frail gleam of her phone's screen, that she heard the little bathroom door swing open and bang against the wall. But she never looked behind her, because she couldn't bear to. Though she possessed the wits to start a rapid descent away from the sudden *tap tap tap tap* of little boots upon the floorboards, and the jangle of a bell not shaken, but carried in the hand of one moving swiftly, and close by in the darkness.

She was struck as much as pushed, and hard too, behind the knees. And whatever had come at her with such force from the rear, toppled her.

*

By morning as the red sun began to rise, all was quiet again inside the cottage called Little Mag's Barrow. Downstairs, the front door was locked from the inside, the key visible inside the lock. The little windows were latched.

In the thinnest light that fell around the net curtains, Kitty began to peer about herself, without moving her neck from where she lay

13

towards the foot of the staircase; she was lying at an angle with her head below her feet, which were still up above her somewhere on the staircase that she was too afraid to look back at. When she dared take anything but the shallowest of breaths, a terrible pain came out of her right side: her ribs. Her right arm was trapped beneath her weight.

She'd fallen hard. Had been knocked out cold by the edge of a wooden step. But once her senses reoriented and she'd blinked the judder from her wide open eyes, and when she began to recall the events leading up to her current dilemma, Kitty tried to move. But in the exact moment of her recovery, as she raised her head, the tatty drape across the front of the kitchen shrieked along its rail.

And Kitty screamed at the same time the small silhouette marched into the living room from where it had been hiding. In the dimness, luxuriant curls bounced upon the small head of what was not much more than an outline. Stiff unarticulated limbs swivelled in hidden sockets and little arms were thrown up towards the ceiling in what appeared to be triumph.

When the figure confirmed that she was awake upon the stairs, by turning a dim oval face of what might have been cloth in her direction, it began capering with a jerking side-to-side motion across the living room floor. And on little clicking heels its ungainly dance sped up with excitement, or even anticipation, perhaps both at once, as it came across to her so swiftly.

THE MAD CLOWN OF MUNCASTER

Muncaster Castle, near Ravenglass, is still regarded as the most haunted house in England. It certainly has the credentials for it because it is very ancient. The site was first occupied by a Roman garrison, who built a fortress there to guard the mouth of the River Esk. In the great tradition of English history, this fort was later taken over by British and then Saxon forces. In the year 1208, it was granted to the Anglo-Norman baron, Alan de Penitone, who built the first stone castle at Muncaster, and made it into his ancestral home. His direct descendents, the Pennington family, still occupy the castle, though of course it has changed shape many times.

Demolished in some parts, extended in others, demolished again, rebuilt again, and so on, fragments from all periods of British history, both in terms of architecture and family heirlooms, are now to be seen at the castle. However, Muncaster is in a remote spot. Despite being close to Ravenglass, it is located on a bleak stretch of the Cumbrian coast, far from any administrative centre. For this reason, it only had one period of major political influence – during the Wars of the Roses, when the Lancastrian king, Henry VI, driven mad by his defeat at the battle of Hexham in 1464, wandered there on foot, a broken, desolated man. Henry's sad ghost is only one of many now said to wander the castle's gloomy halls and corridors.

Ironically, Henry did not die at Muncaster, but in the Tower of London, where he was smothered by his Yorkist captors. But there have been many other violent deaths here, a significant number attributed to a sinister character called Tom Skelton, better known as 'Tom Fool'.

Tom Fool, whose eerie portrait can still be seen at the end of a long passage in the castle, was employed as a jester at Muncaster during the time of William Shakespeare, and in fact was believed to have met the Bard of Avon, and maybe inspired some of his comic characters – though in truth there was nothing comical about Fool himself. On the surface he was a clown, but his real task in the service of his lord and master, Sir Ferdinand Pennington, was assassination. Fool first murdered a young carpenter, who had seduced Helwise, Sir Ferdinand's daughter. Fool killed the unfortunate man by severing his head, which he then took to Sir Ferdinand as a gory prize. It was also said that Fool would lead unwanted guests at the castle astray on the marshy banks of the

15

River Esk, and sit beneath his favourite chestnut tree, chuckling, as they drowned in the quicksand.

In a strange twist of fate, Fool himself fell victim to this horrible trick. In the year 1600, while stumbling home from a drunken night in a local tavern, he too lost his way, wandered into the marshes and sank without trace.

His ghost is now reputed to be by far the most powerful of all those residing at Muncaster. Long after his death, it was whispered that Fool still delighted in leading unwary travelers into the treacherous marshes, though in recent times he appears to have confined himself to playing rude and nasty pranks on the ghost-watch societies who occasionally are allowed to hold all-night vigils there.

In the 21st century, magnetic disturbances and other scientific phenomena have provided explanations for why Muncaster appears to be so alive with spirit activity, but not everyone is convinced. The Pennington family believes that Tom Fool's malignant ghost still haunts their family home, but are unconcerned by it because they feel he is loyal to them. Visitors to the castle are less relaxed. Many have reported an overwhelming sensation that an unseen something has accompanied them on their journeys around the ancient edifice, and that its aura is cold and menacing.

THE *CONISTON STAR* MYSTERY
Simon Clark

From The Cumbria Herald
30th August, 1910

DRAMATIC SINKING OF STEAMSHIP!
SENSATIONAL ESCAPALOGIST FEARED DEAD!

T*he screams of horrified onlookers rang out across Coniston Water yesterday as what had been billed as 'The Spectacle of the Century' ended in most dreadful tragedy.*

Mister Iskander Carvesh, the renowned escapologist, had been shackled to the bright yellow funnel of the Coniston Star by prison guards so ably trained in such methods of restraint. The vessel was then anchored on the lake without another soul on board. Meanwhile, hundreds of people had been carried by a flotilla of small craft to a vantage point where they could view the terrifying spectacle of Mr. Carvesh's devising.

Witnesses report that Mr. Carvesh's dramatic entertainment was running to plan until just before the hour of seven o'clock when a terrifying thunderstorm burst across the face of lake. In a matter of moments, the storm had sent both the Coniston Star, and Iskander Carvesh, with the Wizard of the Keys', to their cold, watery grave.

*

Coniston Water. The present day.

Three people stood in back of the dive boat. On that bright Saturday afternoon in April they were donning their scuba gear in readiness for what promised to be an eerie glide down through ice-cold waters to the bed of the ancient lake.

From a distance, the divers' preparations looked calm and methodical as they zipped up black rubber suits and checked air cylinders. However, in reality, the tempers of two of the divers were fiery, and another violent argument was just about to explode on the deck of the *Lottie Hass*.

The man stared hard at the woman. He was a towering grizzly bear of a guy, with dark hair that was as sharply spiked as his personality. She was perhaps twenty-five years of age, blue-eyed, and had the delicate prettiness of a porcelain doll. Her blonde hair was so fine that it almost seemed to fade away at the tips, as if trying hard to become nothing more than pale mist.

He snarled, "Did you know that the wreck is haunted? There are things down there would turn your hair white."

She didn't answer. Instead, she pulled up the zip of her neoprene diving suit.

The man's eyes flashed with anger. "Did you hear me, Spud? There's something terrifying down there. So watch out." He gave a harsh laugh. "And be careful of the pike. The bloody things are all teeth."

Andrew Harvey realised that there was more than anger in the big man's glare. Andrew had been Blake Kellet's diving buddy for ten years. And he knew that stare meant that Blake was boiling with lust. The woman was extremely pretty in a fragile, elfin kind of way. The black wetsuit clung to her slim body. It revealed the breathtaking curve of her hips and smooth mounds of her breasts.

Only there was more than lust firing up Blake Kellet's blood. He and Andrew had been arguing for hours. Blake constantly nagged Andrew to commit himself to becoming a professional diver. *"There's good money to be made in wreck salvage. Far bloody more than you'll ever make teaching Wordsworth to spotty twerps."* Andrew Harvey couldn't disagree about the money. Yet he loved being a schoolteacher. And he didn't teach spotty twerps. They were decent kids that lived in the suburbs of Sheffield. Andrew knew that education mattered. Knowledge is the new gold.

And so when the guy's sexual tension manifested itself as a bullying attack on a woman that both men had only met yesterday, that was when Andrew's patience evaporated.

He'd been sitting in the doorway of the cabin to pull on his flippers when he'd heard Blake trying to frighten the woman with stories about the wreck being haunted. All this was normal diver banter. Other divers would take the joke in their stride. Only this fragile-looking girl began to stare at the water in real, heart-pounding fear. As if she could see ghostly faces emerging from the waves.

"Spud. Hey, Spud. Did I tell you about the monster eel down there?" Blake's face took on an oily expression of glee. "They coil around your neck, then they start gnawing at your face. Are you listening, Spud?"

Andrew had heard enough. "She's not interested in your stories, Blake."

"But I'm only warning her what's down there, aren't I Spud?" Blake spoke with mock concern. "I don't want her to be shocked if she comes face-to-face with the evil phantom of the wreck."

"Blake. Shut up."

"Oh, so you're going to make me shut up, Andrew?"

"You're frightening her."

Blake pantomimed surprise. "Spud? I'm not frightening you, am I?"

"He's joking," Andrew told her. "Pay no attention."

"She's got to listen. She's got to know the danger." Blake hammed up his role as the predictor of doom. "Coniston Water's a dangerous place. They've pulled lots of corpses out of here. Accidental drowning. Murder victims. Divers who died of fright when they saw the phantom of the wreck."

"You're sick," Andrew snapped. "Do you know that?"

"You're a coward, Andrew Harvey, do you know that?" He'd mimicked Andrew's voice. "You know something, Spud? I've tried to persuade Andrew here to go into the very lucrative business of being a professional diver. He tells me all he wants to do is teach twerps for a living."

"For the last time, Blake, shut up."

"So you're going to shut me up, right?"

A charge of hostility crackled through the air.

"Blake …"

"Okay, come on, schoolteacher, sir. See who's got the balls. *Sir!*"

"You're behaving like an idiot."

Blake lunged at Andrew. The two men in the wetsuits went sprawling onto the boat deck. A compressed air cylinder fell over in the struggle, making a terrific clanging sound.

The grizzly bear of a man soon had the upper hand. He straddled Andrew, then raised his balled fist, ready to deliver a bone-cracking punch. With a violent roar, he slammed his hand down onto the wooden boards. After that, he climbed off Andrew, headed to the cabin, and slammed the door shut behind him.

Andrew sat up. He was panting. In the confines of the rubber suit perspiration trickled down his chest. The day was turning out to be not only unpleasant, but dangerous, too. Undertaking a dive when two of the participants are at war isn't a good idea.

Andrew sucked in a deep breath of cold air. The lake encircled them in placid silence. He allowed his gaze to rest on the hill known as the Old Man of Coniston. Even though it was April, the snows of winter still painted white lines along its summit. This was a landscape he loved. He recharged the tired batteries of his heart here after a long, hard week of teaching. The Lake District is nourishment for the soul. He let it work its unique magic on him right now.

Andrew realized that the woman gazed at him as if hypnotized.

He tried to shrug off the confrontation. "Blake's not normally like that." He glanced in the direction of the cabin. The door was firmly closed. "He's had a tough time of it lately. His father's engineering company went bust a couple of months ago." She continued to gaze in that expressionless way at him, and he found the words slipping from his lips as easily as if they'd been dipped in warm olive oil. "Blake's decided that the only way to help his parents is by him and me going into business as professional divers. Last week he sold his car so he could buy new gear – aqualungs, state-of-the-art electronics, the works. But I'm happy being a schoolteacher." He shrugged. "And sometimes teachers talk too much." He smiled. "Then we get a lot of practice. A captive audience, you see."

He anticipated that the woman would comment on Blake's bad temper. Instead, what she said was so unexpected and so strange it took him by surprise.

"There's something about this lake," she told him. "It keeps drawing me back. I paddle a canoe out here, then I sit with my fingers in the water. Sometimes it feels as if a hand reaches up to me from down there. It holds onto my fingers. I have a sense of overwhelming loneliness. They are crying out for a companion."

She'd spoken in an understated way. There was nothing hysterical about that unsettling statement: *Sometimes it feels as if a hand reaches up to me from down there.* The way she talked was all so matter-of-fact.

A breath of cold air passed over the water. Waves whispered against the flanks of the boat. There was something about that breeze that seemed so unusual. Andrew had felt nothing like it before. That cold breath of air seemed to pass through the thick rubber of the wetsuit, through his skin and into his veins. The woman sat just opposite him. Within touching distance. Only she was *not there* in a way he couldn't explain. Her blonde hair seemed to fade away into a yellow mist. And the centre of her eyes contained the darkness of the lake at midnight.

At that moment, he wanted to be back in class. One full of noisy boys and girls. Only he wasn't in a warm classroom. He was out on Coniston Water. And at that moment he knew his life would never be the same again.

20

Bang! The door of the cabin was kicked open from the other side. The burly, grizzly of a man strode out onto the deck.

"You stinking dog, Andrew Harvey!" Blake shoved a tray at him. On it were three steaming mugs. "Hot tea. Rum. Two sugars." His face creased into a smile. "It's the nearest thing I've got to a bloody peace offering." He handed Andrew a mug. "Get this down you, then we'll dive. It's time we found the great magician's bones."

Blake handed the woman a mug of tea. She took it. Even so, she stared at the big man in such a strange way, as if she saw some omen of disaster in his face.

"What's wrong, Spud? Didn't Andrew tell you that we're hunting for the bones of Iskander Carvesh? The great escapologist? Surely, you've heard what happened out here?" When she didn't reply he took a meaty slurp of his tea, then nodded at Andrew. "You're good at telling stories. Tell Spud about how the famous wizard met his doom."

*

Maybe Blake had been hitting the rum in the boat's galley as he'd brewed the tea, because it wasn't like him to reveal details of a wreck he'd found to strangers. They'd only met the woman yesterday. She'd simply appeared on the beach to watch them loading scuba gear onto the boat. In fact, Andrew couldn't be absolutely certain how she'd come to be invited along today. Even more extraordinary was the fact that Blake had asked her to join them on the dive.

Clearly Blake lusted after the woman. Maybe carnal desire overruled his mercenary nature. After all, there could be valuable artifacts on the wreck. Divers kept their discoveries secret for as long as they possibly could. Otherwise, rivals would strip a wreck bare.

"Go on, mate," Blake said as he checked the aqualungs. "Tell Spud the grisly tale."

Andrew shrugged. "If it's okay by you, then it's okay by me." He sat on the seat opposite to the woman in her clingy wetsuit. That slim body in figure-hugging black rubber gave him tingles. Nevertheless, he took a deep breath, and launched into the story: "A hundred years ago there was a famous escapologist called Iskander Carvesh. He was also known as Wizard of the Keys, because he could conjure keys out of thin air to open locks on any chain that shackled him."

"No doubt the keys were tucked away into some cranny of his body," Blake said cheerfully. "Also, during the act, he'd wear a

21

black leather hood. So even if he'd hidden a key in his mouth people wouldn't see it. Sorry Mr. Harvey, please continue."

"Anyway. The year's 1910. Iskander Carvesh had fallen on hard times. His audiences deserted him. They were bored of seeing him escaping from the same old handcuffs night after night. So he planned to turn his fortunes round with a huge, spectacular stunt. It would take place here on Coniston Water. Carvesh had himself chained to the funnel of a pleasure steamer called the *Coniston Star*. It was moored out on the lake with only him on board. People paid sixpence each to be rowed out to watch him make his death-defying escape. To make it more exciting for the audience he fixed a rifle to a frame on the boat's deck. On the stroke of seven o'clock the rifle would be automatically triggered by a timing device, and a bullet would be fired into his heart. All went according to plan, but there was something that Iskander Carvesh, Magician of the Keys, couldn't control. The weather. A terrific thunderstorm broke just before seven. The waves were the biggest people had ever seen on Coniston Water. Because there was only Carvesh on board, and he was chained to the funnel, there was nobody to close the hatches. Water gushed over the deck, then down into the hull – and down the boat went, too. It sank in three minutes flat.

"Taking Iskar Carvesh with it." Blake grinned. "What do you think to Andrew's dramatic tale, Spud?"

"My name's not Spud." She spoke in a matter-of-fact voice. "It's Enid Carvesh."

*

Blake Kellet erupted. This revelation that the stranger on their dive boat was somehow related to Iskar Carvesh sent the man into a fury. He accused Andrew of colluding with Enid Carvesh. That they planned to swindle Blake in some way.

"I don't want to rob you of anything," Enid told him softly. "I only know that I have to go down to the wreck."

"You can forget making the dive." Blake unzipped his neoprene suit. 'I'm cancelling, do you hear? You're not going down there with us.'

"I must," she whispered. "I have to."

"No way." Blake pointed at Andrew. "Weigh anchor. We're taking Miss Carvesh back to shore."

Enid's eyes had such a beseeching intensity that Andrew felt a shiver run down his spine.

"Please," she said. "Ever since I learned about what happened to my ancestor I haven't been able to get him out of my mind. At night I dream that I'm standing there on the deck of the steamer. The thunder is deafening. Lightning is striking the water. These strange splashes of light are all around the boat. I watch Iskander struggling. He wears the black hood on his head. The chains bind him to the funnel. He has one arm free. There's a key to the padlock in his fingers. Only it's too late. The water rushes over the deck and the boat sinks." Her voice possessed the same whispery quality as the cold breeze blowing across the lake. "And, in the dream, I'm still there on-deck as the boat falls through the water. And it's all black … there's a blackness flowing all around me, and through me, and right inside my heart." She closed her eyes. "And I watch as my flesh-and-blood ancestor fights to escape the chains. His head lashes from side-to-side. He manages to free another arm. He only need slip the chain from his waist, then he can swim back to the surface …" Her chest rose and fell as emotion overwhelmed her.

Blake told her firmly, "I'm not letting you onto that wreck just because you have nightmares."

"Let her dive with us." Andrew picked up his aqualung. "I'll look after her."

"No." Blake fiercely shook his head. "We're taking her back to shore. For one thing, it's way too deep and too risky for a beginner."

"I'm not a beginner," Enid said, still with that cool, detached air: her mind was in another place. "I've dived many times before. And I told Andrew a secret."

"I don't want to know." Blake sounded angry.

"I come out here often." Her elfin face turned to the lake. It seemed as if someone called to her. "I sit here in a canoe, so I can put my fingers into the water. Soon I feel another hand reach out to mine. I sit here on the lake and I'm holding hands with someone just below the surface. My great, great grandfather."

"You need help," Blake snarled. "Lots of pills. And men in white coats."

"Please," she said. "You don't know how important this is."

"No."

"I need to see for myself if Iskander Carvesh is down there."

"We won't know ourselves until we've raised the funnel," Andrew told her. "We think the bones lie in the mud under the funnel itself."

Blake snapped, "Andrew, I told you to pull up that bloody anchor."

Then Enid Carvesh said the words that stopped everything dead. "If you let me come, I'll tell you about the treasure that Iskander took to the bottom of the lake."

Blake stared. He was most definitely interested in this statement. "What treasure?"

"Iskander Carvesh had something with him when the boat sank." Her pale eyes fixed on Blake's face. "Allow me to make the dive ... I'll tell you what to look for."

Blake whirled on Andrew. "Don't just sit there, lummox." A massive grin transformed his face. "Get the lady an aqualung. It's time we got into the water."

*

Coniston always reminded Andrew Harvey of black coffee. And always before making a dive, he'd find himself gazing down into the lake. Daylight penetrated its dark waters by a foot or so to reveal shreds of leaf floating there. The wreck of the *Coniston Star* lay ninety feet beneath his feet, entombed in the mud and the darkness where not so much as a gleam of daylight reached.

Down there was another world. Andrew knew that death lay on the other side of the glass of the diver's face mask. Submerged branches, discarded fishing lines complete with barbed hooks. The jagged remains of the wreck added to the danger. It's so easy for a diver to be snared by underwater debris. The only air that prevented them drowning was contained in a pair of steel cylinders on his or her back. That supply was limited to minutes, not hours. Once the needle entered the meter's red zone death wasn't far away.

Don't do this. The part of his brain that contained the instinct for self-preservation was most insistent. *Don't make the dive today. Say that you're sick. Make any excuse. Just don't go into the water. It's not safe. Something isn't right.*

Against his better instincts he ignored the voice.

The three of them stood on the platform at the back of the boat. It was so close to the surface of the water that waves broke over it. Ripples flowed around their fins. All three wore wetsuits zipped up to the chin. Aqualungs were strapped to their backs.

Blake gave the last words of instruction. "You might not be familiar with this kind of mask. It's a full face mask. You don't have a mouthpiece. The air flows from these vents in the side. The black bead just beneath the glass face plate is a microphone. I paid a bloody fortune for these, so they better work. Just talk as you would on dry land. We should be able to hear each other. Got that?"

Andrew and Enid nodded. The woman gazed at the water. She was eager to reach the *Coniston Star*. Maybe the thing called her name, Andrew thought. Or, perhaps, *something* on the wreck called her name.

There was a dangerous grin on Blake's face as he caught the woman by the arm. "Before I let you into the water. Tell me what we're going to find down there. You said Carvesh took treasure to the bottom with him when the boat sank?"

The woman's elfin features were expressionless. "Iskander Carvesh was known as the Wizard of the Keys."

"We already know that."

"What you don't know," she said, "is that he wore twenty keys on a cord around his neck."

He shrugged. "We know he hid keys on his body. That's how he opened the locks during his act."

"As well as keys being his trademark, these keys were also his life savings," she told him. "The twenty keys around his neck were made of solid gold. The scrap value will be worth thousands. And there are collectors who will pay *tens of thousands*." She pulled on the mask.

"Wait," Andrew shouted. "Something's wrong. I'm not going down there!" But Blake and Enid had already leapt from the platform. Coniston Water swallowed them in a single gulp.

Don't go. Don't follow them. Stay on the boat. The voice inside his head begged him not to jump. But he'd face Blake's eternal scorn if he chickened out. Reluctantly, he pulled down the mask. Then he dropped into the lake. He'd crossed the threshold from one realm to another. The world of air and light vanished. He was sinking fast towards the wreck. Andrew Harvey had passed the point of no return.

*

The two men and the woman swam downwards into the dark embrace of Coniston Water. They switched on powerful electric lights fixed to the top of the face masks. Three cones of light sought out the wreck of the steamer that sank during the thunderstorm over a hundred years ago.

When Andrew Harvey made out the iron funnel lying half-embedded in the silt he pictured Carvesh chained to it as lighting blazed across angry skies. He also recalled what Enid Carvesh had said. That she repeatedly dreamed she stood on the deck of the *Coniston Star* as it foundered. And as her ancestor, Iskander Carvesh, Wizard of the Keys, hooded and chained, struggled to free himself.

Andrew could hear the respiration of his diving companions in his earpiece.

Blake's voice suddenly barked, "Is everyone alright? Are the radios working?"

Andrew gave a thumbs-up; he wasn't used to the luxury of being able to speak to other divers underwater.

Enid's voice, on the other hand, came as a faint sigh. "I can hear you. Is that all there is of the boat?"

By this time they were thirty feet above the wreck. Their lights revealed a misty outline of the timber ribs of the *Coniston Star*, and the cylinder shape that was the funnel.

Andrew said, "There's not much left of the hull. Most of the wooden parts have rotted away. We managed to retrieve some of the brass portholes."

"What about Iskander?" she asked. "Where is the body?"

"There's no body, Spud." Blake spoke in that hearty way of his that could be so inappropriate at times like this. "We dug away the mud near the funnel and found the bones of a foot. The rest of the skeleon is trapped under the funnel itself."

"Then we must move the funnel." She spoke in that peculiarly distant way of hers. "We must bring his bones to the surface."

"Slow down there, Spud." Blake's laugh sounded harsh in Andrew's earpiece. "The funnel is made from cast iron. It weighs half a ton, at least."

Then she spoke again. To Andrew it sounded slyly manipulative. "If the main part of the skeleton is under the funnel, then the gold keys will be, too. They were around Iskander's neck."

Blake's fins moved faster. "Pay attention to the lady, Andrew. Let's get that skeleton out from under the funnel."

"Wait. You said yourself it weighs at least half a ton. We need floatation bags."

"You're supposed to be the brains of the outfit, Mr. Schoolteacher, sir." Blake laughed. "See that mud? It's as soft as your mother's porridge. We'll dig under it."

"With our bare hands?" Andrew hovered over the wreck. Red danger signs pulsated in his head. "It's too risky. How are we going to stop the sides of a hole from caving in?"

"I was right," Blake told him. "You are a coward."

Blake dived downwards to attack the soft mud with his bare hands. Even with no tools other than his fingers, he soon scooped a hollow beside the funnel. Mostly the environment at the bottom of Coniston Water was black. Black mud. Black water. Black wreckage. Then all that blackness changed. Suddenly, a glint of white bone. Iskander Carvesh's skull.

That's when the insanity began. Blake furiously clawed at the black mud. Even through clouds of sediment, Andrew could make out the gleaming white dome of Carvesh's skull. Blake stabbed his fingers through the eye sockets, then dragged it from the lake bed.

Blake's voice exploded in Andrew's ears. *'Gold! There's gold, Andrew! I can see it!'*

There it was. The treasure the woman had told them about. A dozen or more gold keys, each the size of a finger, shone against the black dirt. They looked like a constellation of stars shining against the darkness of infinity.

Blake hurled the skull aside.

"No!" screamed Enid. "Show some respect!"

"They're only moldy old bones. We'll get 'em later!" Blake shouted so loudly that the microphone distorted the sound into an electronic scream.

He was now burrowing his way down in dog-like fashion, clawing out a crater so large that he could insert his entire body into it, which even in normal circumstances would have seemed a crazy thing to do beneath ninety feet of water.

"Blake!" Andrew protested, but Blake could no longer hear him.

He was almost out of sight, wrenching bones from the muck like he was ripping weeds from an overgrown garden border. The human remains meant nothing to him. Only the gold mattered. Those brilliant nuggets of yellow. No doubt he saw himself on the front page of newspapers. The heroic diver who found Iskander Carvesh's gold. The prestige. The fame. The money. *For God's sake, think of the money!*

Enid kicked her feet, swimming down to protect the bones of her ancestor. Andrew saw another problem. Currents at the bottom of the lake had scooped the silt into mounds around the wreck. Now that Blake had disturbed the silt, the nearest mound began to slip down into the hole he'd made.

"Blake! Get out of there! You're going to be buried alive!"

"No way! Not until I've got the gold."

Blake smashed what remained of the magician's ribcage in order to get his hands on the other gold keys that were trapped beneath the bones.

Enid sobbed, "Oh no, oh no." Pathetically she tried to gather the bones to her breast. Andrew found it harder to see. The silt had been stirred up so much it turned the water into a black fog. Bubbles streamed from the aqualungs. Enid and Blake hyper-ventilated as one tried to rescue her ancestor's mortal remains, and the other fought to retrieve the golden keys as the mudslide began to fill the hole.

Blake used both hands to grab at the gold artifacts, which he then stuffed inside his partly unzipped diving suit. Andrew saw a huge object looming above them begin to move. For a moment, he wondered if the legends of the monster eel in the lake were true. Because there, in the mist of dirt and silver bubbles, a vast cylindrical body had turned over, as if the monster's slumber had been disturbed.

Then Andrew saw what it really was. The steamer's funnel had begun to roll. Blake had now excavated a big enough hole to disturb the resting place of that half ton of iron. Gravity dictated that the funnel should roll downwards into the pit that Blake had dug.

Blake was still down in the hole. He clawed out Iskander's bones, throwing them out behind him. His attention had been nailed to the gold keys. Nothing else mattered. Gold. It's what he needed. What he lusted after. That gold would right so many wrongs in the man's life.

Andrew had no doubt those were the thoughts that filled his friend's head right then. Not the precarious nature of his position. Or the surrounding mounds of silt that grew more unstable by the second. He probably didn't even know that the funnel rolled in slow motion towards him.

Enid Carvesh still sobbed as she tried to gather the broken remains of her ancestor.

Andrew swam downwards to save his friend. The voices, the deafening roar of respiration filled his ears. Yet even at that moment some small part of him fixed on the image of Enid Carvesh riding her canoe out across the lake. There she'd sit with her hands trailing in the water. Eventually, fingers would reach up from beneath. She'd sit in the canoe and hold hands with her dead ancestor as the shadows of the clouds passed over the Lakeland hills. At least, that's what she believed. That the man who was more than a hundred years dead reached out to her.

28

The woman's belief was utter insanity. But no less of an insanity than Blake Kellet's desperate attempt to rescue the gold as the funnel threatened to roll down on top of him. An iron tombstone for his grave. Andrew Harvey knew what he must do. He'd grab hold of his friend and drag him to safety. That's all that mattered.

Andrew reached the funnel as it rolled towards the pit that Blake had excavated. Here there was a swirling vortex of mud and tiny pieces of Carvesh's skeleton. Blake had just four golden keys left to pick from the mud.

Andrew shouted, "The sides of the pit are collapsing!" He put both hands up to push at the funnel. He managed to stop it rolling down over Blake. "Get clear!"

"Just one more minute. I've nearly got them all."

"Blake! Leave them!"

"No, I'll never find them again."

There were three gold keys left on the lake bed. They each had a large round fob. The barrel of the key was fully the length of a finger. They were enchanting as they lay there. Like nuggets of sunlight. They seemed to radiate a promise of great value. Andrew pictured himself on television as he told the story of how the keys had been found. About how he and his friend had been both ingenious and brave. Those gold keys were rightfully theirs. They deserved them. They deserved the wealth and fame that they would bring. Rival diving teams would be in awe of Andrew Harvey and Blake Kellet.

A voice in Andrew's head screamed *Danger!* It begged him to swim clear of the half ton cylinder that tried with its all its iron soul to roll over the pit.

"Andrew!" Blake shouted. "I can't reach the one nearest your foot."

"Leave it!"

"It's the biggest one. We must have it."

Andrew took the chance. He swam down headfirst into the pit. His friend patted his shoulder.

"I knew you wouldn't let me down." Blake sounded so pleased that his diving buddy hadn't deserted him in the end.

Then it happened. So quickly. So inevitably. The soft sides of the pit gave way. Silt flooded into the void. The funnel rolled over the top of the cavity. Half a ton of iron. Over a hundred years ago Iskander Carvesh had been chained to the funnel. It had pulled him down into Coniston Water.

And now, here at the bottom of the lake, its dead weight sealed the two men into the hole. Silt flowed from the mounds around the shipwreck. The lake bed returned to being an undulating realm of slick blackness.

The electric light revealed the skull of Iskander Carvesh to the two men trapped in the grave-sized void beneath the funnel. The skull sat on the mud. A rounded dome of old bone. One that had contained the magician's brain, which had been so alive with thoughts of miraculous escape. The twin orbits had once held eyes that watched the thunderstorm approach across the lake. Now they were twin pools of shadow. Beneath the open nasal passage was the cold snarl of teeth. They had lost their covering of flesh decades ago. Just like the rest of the skeleton that Blake had torn to pieces when gold fever took possession of his soul.

In the time he had left, Andrew could only stare at the skull. His chest grew tighter and tighter as the air stopped flowing into his mask. *When the end comes,* he told himself. *I hope I don't start screaming. I really don't...*

A moment later, Blake did start to scream. Andrew Harvey switched off his radio. There was nothing but silence now. Silence everlasting.

*

Coniston Water. One year later.

Enid Carvesh let the canoe drift above the spot where she knew the *Coniston Star* lay ninety feet beneath her. The dark waters were tranquil. Light and shade played catch on the emerald green hills that surrounded the lake. She rested the paddle across the canoe's fibreglass shell. Then she allowed her fingers to trail in the water. She waited patiently for what would come next.

And here it comes...

She felt the light touch of fingertips against her own fingers. Presently a hand slipped into hers.

"I've met another team of divers." She smiled to herself. "They told me they've found the wreck of the *Coniston Star*. And they're going to let me dive with them." The hand gave *her* hand a loving squeeze. "I know I can never bring you back, Iskander. But I'm going to make sure that you're never alone down there."

The fingers tightened around hers for a moment. They seemed to signal their approval of her plans. Oh – and did she have plans. She waved to the men in the dive boat as they made their way across the lake towards her.

"Here they come, Iskander," she murmured happily. "Your new friends. Your new friends forever and ever."

THE CROGLIN VAMPIRE

One of the most celebrated supernatural mysteries of the Lake District concerns the so-called Croglin Vampire.

Croglin Low Hall, ten miles north of the Neolithic stone circle called 'Long Meg and Her Daughters', was once known as Croglin Grange. It had been a country seat dating from the late Middle Ages, but had often had difficulty attracting long-term tenants – which might explain why, unusually for England, it had only been constructed to the height of one storey. Rumours abounded that this had been a troubled spot for some time, though no specific tales were told.

The Grange stood a couple of miles from the village of Croglin, and was only several hundred yards from a country church, which was destroyed during a fierce action in the English Civil War. Some thirty years after the war had finished, in the 1680s, a family comprising two brothers and their younger sister, leased the property for a period of seven years, either unaware that it had a troubled history or unafraid by it.

Their first winter there passed uneventfully and by spring the family had settled comfortably, enjoying the scenic location and the Grange's handsome furnishings. However, one night in early summer, the sister was in bed when she glanced through the mullioned glass of her window and saw a curious object approaching from the direction of the ruined churchyard. It was the tall, thin figure of a man, and it appeared to be carrying some kind of reddish light in front of its face. When it came closer, she realised to her consternation that the light emanated from its red, piercing eyes.

The figure came right up to her bedroom window and peered through the glass at her. It was a true vision of horror. Though its eyes glowed, its flesh was brown and shriveled as though it had been mummified. Struck dumb with fear, the girl could only watch as it began to unpick the lead at her window. At length a panel fell out, and the thing entered her bedroom. Only then did she find the strength to scream. Her brothers were lodging in distant parts of the building, but they heard her and came running. By this time, the apparition had grabbed the girl by the hair, hauled her from her bed and bitten her on the throat with a foul, broken-toothed mouth. When her brothers entered the room, it fled into the darkness outside.

The unfortunate girl was in a dreadful state, and her brothers had to take her right out of the country, to Europe, before she could recover her shattered nerves. She never wanted to return to Croglin Grange again, but because of their lease they had no option. Several months passed before they made the journey back. On the way, the girl became steadily more fearful. Once there, the brothers tried to ease her worries by fixing boards across her bedroom window so that nothing could enter. However, during the course of that first night, she was awakened by a scratching sound. To her disbelief, the boards were yanked away and again the ghastly, mummified form climbed in, its eyes glowing like hot coals.

She shrieked for help, and this time her brothers were ready. They burst in and discharged their pistols while the figure was still in the window frame. Struck in the leg, it turned and began hobbling away. The brothers gave chase to the graveyard, but there it stumbled out of sight among the aged sepulchres.

The next morning they brought their dogs, which followed a scent to a broken-open vault. Inside, there was a chilling scene. Numerous ancient coffins had been smashed, and their contents mangled, mutilated and thrown all around the moldering chamber. Only one remained intact, with its lid half open. They looked inside and found the creature that had attacked their sister, apparently in a deep sleep. Part of its leg had been blown off by a pistol ball. Enraged, the brothers dragged it outside and burned it on a pyre.

No further reports of this nature, or disturbances of any sort, were heard at Croglin Grange again. In 1720 it was rebuilt, a second storey added, and renamed Croglin Low Hall. It remains occupied to this day.

DEVILS OF LAKELAND
Paul Finch

E ven Killington Lake services on the M6 motorway had an air
of familiarity. As Graham locked his car and walked to the
lodge, he looked up at the great hump of Brant Fell and saw it
as he had that summer day all those years ago when he and Timmy
had bought comics and sweets. Its great patchwork sides had been
green and gold, dotted all over with sheep, its rounded summit misty
and dappled with sunlight.

When he got back to his car, he sat behind the wheel to eat his
sandwiches and looked up again at Brant, savouring the memory of
that happiest holiday of all, even though now the fell was hidden in
cloud and his windscreen spattered with February rain. There was
still an atmosphere of peace. The Lake District would always have
this effect on him, he supposed. Even here in its foothills. Even at a
time of tragedy, like this.

After he'd eaten he drove on, taking the A684 west to Kendal,
then the A591 to Windermere. Everything he saw on the way, he
recalled vividly: the pine-clad hills and deep river valleys littered
with boulders, the quaint hamlets with their rock-built walls and slate
cottages, the ever-distant mountains, and of course the lakes, dark
and glimmering through the black trees – Windermere, Grasmere,
Rydal Water, Thirlmere. There was no off-season in Lakeland, so
even in this weather the lanes were lined with walkers in bright
cagoules, the pub car parks full. Graham found it hard to believe
he'd only been up here once before. Everything seemed so familiar.

He drove down into Keswick late afternoon, negotiating the
complex, narrow streets with surprising ease despite the bustle of
shoppers, and was soon out on the B5299, heading south along the
wooded shore of Derwent Water. Folk seemed to agree this was the
most scenic lake of them all, steel-grey and rolled out smooth as
glass between the granite ridges of the Catbells and High Seat.

However, as he followed the winding road, dark woods rose
steeply on his left, hemming him to the water, and Graham felt his
first pang of unease. Exactly what did he hope to achieve? Was it
really worth taking unpaid absence from work and driving all the
way here when the police had closed the case? Like so many men
Graham knew, his brother Tim had bottled up most of his cares.

Who could say what state he'd been in beneath that calm exterior? Who knew what could have caused him to do the thing he'd done?

Around the next bend, the shore-line trees gave out briefly to a shingle beach and timber jetty. Graham gazed at it as he cruised past, but then felt a sudden chill. Baffled, he braked and pulled up. This was the sort of place which in summer would be teeming, but now was quite dreary. The jetty looked unsafe; it was covered in green moss and leaned at an angle. The shadows of dusk were thick in the surrounding trees, and across the water an ebbing mist had blocked out the farther shore.

Graham shivered and drove on. Five minutes later he had by-passed the Lodore Falls at the southern end of the lake and was heading towards Borrowdale village. The gigantic valley was still as bleak and grand as he remembered it. More so now, with the dark stains of evening creeping down the rugged flanks of the mountains.

The High View hotel was off the road at the top of a steep drive, and enclosed by tall pines. As a structure it was very handsome, made from local slate and covered in green and purple ivy, but there didn't seem to be many lights shining out of it, and the parking area to the front was strangely empty.

Graham collected his sports bag from the boot and was about to go in, but first glanced up at the central window on the third floor. The 'Tower Room', as the hotel management used to refer to it. Not in a tower as such, but the one with the best view. The one they'd taken all those years ago for that wonderful holiday. This too was in darkness.

Inside, the hotel was even less welcoming, all low beams, dark wood and sombre paintings. The one or two lamps switched on in Reception were heavily shaded and gave out minimal light. There was a smell of dust, as if renovation work was going on.

Nobody was on duty at the desk, so Graham rang the bell and waited. As he did he glanced around. The layout was vaguely familiar. The staircase serving the upper floors was central, while to the right of that were the double-doors to the restaurant. At present they were closed and probably locked. Left of the staircase was the door to the bar. That too was closed.

A blonde receptionist slipped out from a back office. She wore an immaculate blue uniform and a practised smile, which faltered badly when she saw Graham. For a moment she seemed stunned.

Graham understood. "I'm the brother. I booked yesterday."

The receptionist nodded, suddenly embarrassed. "Of course ... it's just, well you look so similar."

"There was only a year between us," he said.

She seemed unable to reply, and handed over a room-key as he filled in the register. Then, furtively, she crept away. There was some quiet conversation in the back office and a second later a man appeared in a pin-striped suit. He had wooden features, a beak-like nose and thinning grey hair. A gold tab pinned to his breast pocket revealed that he was 'Mr. Summers, Manager'.

He seemed awkward and unsure of himself, only coming to the counter when Graham finally looked up. "On behalf of the staff, Mr. Foster," he began. "I'd ... I'd like to offer our deepest condolences. Such terrible news."

Graham closed the register and picked up his key. "I don't suppose any of your staff spoke to my brother?"

Mr. Summers shrugged helplessly. "Not that I know of. We had all this with the police, of course. Nobody remembers anything. Your brother was in very high spirits when he arrived here – that I do remember. He said it was a holiday he'd been looking forward to. It did seem odd that he suddenly cut it short like that. I mean he was due to be with us the whole week."

For the thousandth time, Graham mulled over what he knew about the incident. None of it made sense. Mr. Summers watched him unhappily. Clearly the manager was wondering why Graham had come up, and viewed the whole thing as an ordeal which he hoped would soon end. "Could it have been an accident?" he suddenly asked. "Perhaps your brother got lost and didn't realise the cliff was there?"

Graham shook his head. "I'd love to believe that, Mr. Summers. I really would."

When he went up to Room 22, he carried his own bag. There was no porter at *The High View*. Apparently there never had been, though Graham seemed to remember smiling, helpful staff everywhere when he'd been here as a child.

It would have been nice to think that Tim had died in an accident on the way home, but as the Cumbrian Traffic sergeant had said at the inquest, you can't drive off Black Sail Drop by accident. It's sixty yards from the road, and to get to it you've first got to crash through a perimeter fence, which Tim had done. As if that wasn't enough, the place was miles out of his way. He must have driven for hours to get there.

Room 22 stood alone on a dark landing on the second floor. There was a spiral stair opposite, leading up into shadow. Graham was puzzled. He had specifically asked for the Tower Room, the third floor room where he'd stayed as a youngster. He sighed and let himself in. It would probably be the same design. Couldn't have half the same atmosphere though.

It didn't. And neither was it as cosy. Spartan would have been a better way to describe it. It was furnished with a single bed and side-table, a desk, a chest of drawers, a wardrobe and an armchair, but the walls were unimaginatively papered and the bathroom was cold. The fact that it was quite spacious made it feel emptier.

Graham dumped his bag and went to the window. Beyond it, through the trees, was the distant blue haze of the lake; at its far end the rolling black hummock of Skiddaw. The lights of Keswick twinkled at the mountain's feet. It was almost the same view he remembered, though not quite because now he was one storey down and having to gaze *through* branches rather than over them. It still brought memories rushing back. Him and Timmy snug under their massive quilt while Dad went down to dinner; having pillow fights every evening; enjoying milk and sandwiches; reading comics and telling jokes.

After he'd unpacked, he called Reception and expressed mild disappointment that he hadn't been given the Tower Room. He was surprised however when the receptionist said that she didn't know of any Tower Room. When he explained which room he meant, she recognised it as No. 32, the one directly above him, but apologised and said that it was unavailable.

He hung up feeling disgruntled, but a minute later heard the scampering of tiny feet somewhere above his head. More than one pair too. It pricked his conscience. He'd been selfish, wanting that room for himself purely for nostalgic purposes. Why not let another young family enjoy it the way he and Timmy had?

After he'd put his things away, Graham lay down on the bed and glanced through the two paperbacks of Tim's that he'd brought along with him. They were collections of horror stories. Rare ones apparently, which his brother had sent for from abroad. Graham shook his head. He'd never been able to understand Tim's obsession with such garbage. It had been going on for as long as he could remember, easily since they'd been at school. First it had been the usual stuff, the popular titles gleaned from high street stores; then the works of antiquity found in second hand shops; finally the really obscure material, purchased through literary fairs, specialist dealers or book-finding services. The collection had grown and grown over the years. The expenditure that had gone into it must have been phenomenal. But it had only really struck Graham how infatuated his brother had become a month before his death, when he'd unexpectedly announced that he was off to the Lakes to find the book that had originally sparked his interest. It was a special little tome called 'Devils Of Lakeland'; a collection of ghost stories with a Lake District atmosphere. He'd only thumbed through it, but even then he'd realised its value. Didn't Graham remember? They'd seen it in a poky little bookshop in Keswick all those years ago, during that wonderful holiday. At the time, Tim had wanted to buy it desperately, but Dad had said it wasn't suitable.

Graham hadn't remembered at all. How could he after three decades? Tim had been resolute though. He'd been determined to track it down, and Keswick was the obvious place to start. Only when he possessed that priceless book would his collection be complete.

*

Dinner that evening was not as pleasant an experience as Graham had anticipated. There were few other diners in the restaurant, and the windows were heavily draped in purple, which, along with the dark paneling, had a sombre effect. The food was of only average quality as well: the vegetables were dry, his steak bloody when he'd asked for it well-done. He ordered a bottle of house red with his meal, but found it vinegary, and ended up leaving it only half-drunk.

The restaurant staff were mostly young and seemed uninterested in the guests, bringing dishes and taking them away again with robotic indifference. There was one of them who Graham recognised, however: a Cockney waiter who on their previous visit they'd known affectionately as 'Tel'. Graham remembered him as a short cheerful man with cobalt blue eyes, sharp cheekbones and a head of ginger curls. Now he was bald, with grey wrinkled cheeks. His red tunic was crumpled and buttoned incorrectly, while he walked with a stoop and could only carry trays of food precariously. Graham watched him sadly.

After dinner, he went over to the bar, but half way there noticed a long corridor which he didn't remember. He stopped to look at it. It was located behind the staircase, thus hidden from the main vestibule, and ran off into darkness. It was clearly for public use; there was no 'Private' or 'Staff Only' notice above it, and closer inspection revealed that it was decorated all the way down with paintings and display cases containing Lake District crafts. Graham presumed it had been added since his visit. It probably connected with the hotel gardens or a walk to the fells. He put it from his mind and went into the bar, ordering himself a scotch and soda.

"I was sorry to hear about your brother, sir," the barman said, as he attended to it.

Graham glanced up. The man was quite young, but very smart in a shirt and bow-tie. He nodded politely as Graham handed him the money.

"You didn't have any conversation with him, I don't suppose?" Graham wondered.

"None at all I'm afraid," the barman said. "Neither him nor the young lady."

It took a moment for the words to sink in. Graham looked up again. "Excuse me ... young lady?"

"That's right, sir. The young lady he was in here with. Brunette, she was." Graham gazed at him, and suddenly the barman blushed. "Oh dear sir, I hope I haven't compromised somebody."

"No, it's alright. Tim wasn't married. It's just that ... he never said anything."

The barman was now pouring drinks for the next customer. "Perhaps he met her here, sir?"

"And she was a brunette, you say?"

The barman thought about it. "That's right. But you know, it's a bit funny. She had this white dress on. Looked a bit formal, it did. Knee-length. Like a uniform. Like she was a nurse or something."

"A nurse?"

"That's right. Couldn't have been though. I mean she was in here at the bar with him."

Graham puzzled over it for the next hour or so, downing one scotch and soda after another. It was possible that Tim had met a woman here but it seemed out of character. Graham's brother had never been particularly interested in women or sex. His obsessive hobby had taken up most of his spare time. It could have been that there was a secret side to him, but Graham was sure that he'd have known about it.

Later, close on one o'clock, when he stumbled out of the bar, he glanced back into the darkened corridor – and went rigid with surprise. Just for a split-second then, he'd fancied he'd seen a woman walking away down it. A woman in a knee-length white dress. He stared into the shadows at the far end. Finally, he took a tentative step towards them. Then another. A moment later he was making his way unsteadily down the passage. It grew dark quickly, and almost immediately he blundered into a glass display case, rocking it noisily. He moved back, cursing. The darkness had gripped him completely. Briefly, he didn't know where he was or what he was doing.

"Excuse me, sir!" someone said.

Graham turned. A silhouette was approaching from a blur of light, which he supposed must have been the bar area. "Excuse me, sir," the figure said again, in a distinct Cockney accent.

Fuddled as he was, Graham recognised the chalky tones. He wondered if the old Londoner would recognise him. "Tel ... how are you, mate?"

"'Fraid you must have got me mistaken for somebody else, sir," the waiter said. Graham's eyes attuned to the half-light as the waiter came up close – it was clearly Tel. "I'm John," he added.

Graham slurred as he spoke. "You ... you were called Tel, though."

The waiter shook his head. "Not as I recall, sir."

Graham was baffled. Why should the man lie? "You are that London bloke who was here thirty years ago?"

The waiter eyed him curiously. "Well yes I am, sir. But I've never been called Tel." Graham pondered this, and as he did, the waiter took him gently by the elbow. "Thing is, sir ... there's nothing down this passage. This wing's being renovated. I was wondering if you might be lost or something?"

Graham glanced over his shoulder as he was steered back towards the light. "I thought I saw someone go down there."

"Couldn't have, sir. It's all boarded up down there. Leads nowhere."

Graham allowed himself to be led back to the stairs and then up to his room. Inside it, the walls began to spin around him. He toppled over as he stripped off his shirt and tie, and fell onto the bedclothes. Sleep stole over him with astonishing speed, but before it took him completely he heard the youngsters upstairs again – two pairs of scampering feet and muffled giggling.

*

He dreamed about Timmy and himself as they had been on their first arrival at *The High View*, tearing out of Dad's green Morris 1100, dashing to the main doors in a frenzy of excitement. Behind them, framed on an azure sky, Dad was getting luggage out from the boot. Not Dad as he was now: hairless, gammy-eyed and drooling in his wheelchair; but Dad as he had been then, looking like Elvis with his quiff and laughing eyes, shouting at them not to knock anyone down. Finally out of his shell again, after the months and months of mourning for Mum.

When Graham woke up, his head was splitting and he was sick to the pit of his stomach. He lay helpless, dazed and shivering in the milky light of dawn. His cheeks were wet with tears.

It took hours to get himself together, though he had no plans to even attempt to eat breakfast. By ten he'd dressed in jeans, trainers and a thick sweater, and was ready to face the world. He closed the door behind him and was just locking it when he thought about the Tower Room and the youngsters. He glanced at the narrow stair spiralling upwards. A pale light was shining down it. He considered, and then, deciding that it couldn't do any harm, crept up to have a look. When he reached the top, he found the door to the Tower Room standing ajar and daylight streaming through.

Graham peeped in. Then, perplexed, he opened the door properly and entered. The room was bare of carpet and furniture, and thickly layered in dust. The wallpaper, faded and brownish, hung off in strips. Not only was Room 32 not in use, it had not been in use for what looked like years. He strode aimlessly around it, finally moving to the window and gazing out. At least the stunning vista was still the same, though at present it was buried in rain-clouds. Below, a car was pulling away down the hotel drive. Within a second it vanished, but Graham had the distinct impression it had been a green Morris 1100.

He went downstairs. Inevitably, his feet led him back to the corridor where he thought he had seen the woman in the white dress. Now he wasn't sure what he remembered from the previous night, but the passage still stood empty and in darkness. As old John had said, it was awaiting restoration. There wasn't a lot in the *High View* that wasn't, Graham thought sourly. He wondered if they'd bothered telling this to Tim when he'd booked himself in so excitedly a few weeks ago.

*

Later that morning, he drove to Keswick. As he followed the lakeside road, he thought again about the woman in white and puzzled over who she might be. If she was local and he could get to speak to her, it might at least help in his understanding of what Tim had done. It wouldn't bring him back, but there was a mystery here and this woman was the only lead.

41

The local police were as helpful as they had been previously, but seemed bewildered that Graham had come up to see them. He spoke to a uniformed inspector in a side office in the station, and, over several cups of tea, had it reiterated to him that Tim had driven his car off Black Sail Drop in Copeland Forest, a point only accessible by the most primitive back roads. And in broad daylight too. An accident was out of the question. It had to have been suicide. They'd even found a road map beside the body, folded open on that page.

When Graham mentioned the woman in white and wondered if anyone had reported her to them, the inspector simply shrugged. As gently as he was able, he reminded Graham that the case was now closed. Tim Foster had committed suicide. Only new evidence of ground-breaking significance could change that verdict. The fact that Tim had been seen talking to a woman in a bar did not alter anything.

Outside the station, Graham found the weather changing for the worse. The temperature had plummeted and the spitting rain was turning to sleet. Beyond the high roofs of the town, the mountaintops were capped with snow. He huddled into his thin jacket. He couldn't have prepared less for February in the Lakes if he'd consciously tried. A spot of lunch in a fish and chip bar didn't help, so he called in to the boutique next door and bought himself a scarf and a pair of suede gloves.

While he was in there, he asked about local bookshops. How many were there? Were there any particularly good second-hand ones? The proprietor was delighted to tell him that they had lots of bookshops in their town, and some especially good second-'anders. Graham thanked him, then went to search for them.

As always, the centre of Keswick, around its information bureau and medieval moot-hall, was thronging with people, but away from it, out of view, its various narrow courts were quieter than Graham had expected. They ran back and forth between jumbled buildings of grey slate, winding up and down from one level to the next. Many were cobbled and now greasy with rain.

Graham traversed them for an hour, and found plenty of 'poky little shops', to use Tim's own description, but invariably they sold either antiques or cream teas. He didn't seriously expect to stumble across that little bookshop from so long ago, but felt certain that Tim would have looked for it. Five minutes later however, he came upon an arch clustered with ivy and, inexplicably, he felt that he knew it.

As he walked towards it, he remembered running under the arch as a child. Timmy had been in front and shouting something about "the cyclops' cave", because it reminded them of a Sinbad movie that Dad had taken them to see.

Now Graham passed under the arch again, followed a curved tunnel and came out at a crossroads of passages. Instinctively he went left, and to his surprise began to feel a tingle of excitement. It became a positive surge when he rounded the next bend and saw, tucked away at the end of the alley, a poky little shop that was undeniably familiar. It was 'olde worlde' in style, with mullioned windows and a shield hanging over its front door.

Graham hurried towards it, almost breathless with anticipation – *only to stop in his tracks.* The windows were not filled with books, as he'd expected, but with old toys. He went slowly forward and pressed his face against the glass. Stuffed teddy bears were propped up in heaps, all ragged and filthy. In the middle stood a decrepit rocking-horse, without a flake of paint left on it and only wisps of string for a mane. Graham gazed at it, recalling how its eyes had once flashed sapphire blue, how its scarlet lips had drawn back on a set of strong white teeth, how its flanks had been a brilliant orange with large green polka-dots on them.

Then he wondered how he remembered all that, and he stepped back, alarmed. He was touched by something cold, the way he had been at the jetty on the lake, and briefly he was mesmerised. Slowly, he came round and looked up.

Above his head, the shield read:

Second Hand – Bought & Sold

The wrong shop. That was all. Probably the wrong side of town. He turned to walk away – but was immediately confronted by another shop directly behind him. He hadn't noticed it before, but it hit him full force now. This one was equally as dingy as the other, and equally poky. And its sign read:

Books Books Books

Graham approached it warily. Again he felt a tingle of anticipation. A moment later he was inside. A thousand memories swam back to him: the dark cave-like interior, racked on every wall with old volumes; the musty smell; the thick carpet under his feet. The shop was manned by a red-haired man in tweeds. He was reading a book himself, and smoking a pipe. On Graham's entry, he

43

looked up from behind his till in surprise as if this was a startling event. "Anything I can help you with, sir?" he asked cheerfully.

Still entranced, Graham waved him into silence and drifted through the foyer into the back room, where he knew he would find various passages leading off into the rabbit warren of a building, each one lined with books.

For minutes on end, Graham searched, going spine by spine along the creaking shelves, emptying boxes onto the floor, working his way though one untidy pile after another. It seemed that every book ever printed was to be found there, most stiff and cracking and assembled in no logical order. However, Graham knew that he would find what he was looking for. And he did. In a narrow space at the back of the shop – a type of conservatory in fact, with a roof of stained glass – he crouched down and placed his finger on a single dusty volume. On its spine, in gold leaf, it was inscribed:

Devils of Lakeland

Almost giddy, he drew it out and opened it. He expected it to be ludicrously expensive, but could find no price-tag. Puzzled, he flipped through several pages.

Then he flipped through several more.

It was impossible to believe what he was seeing. A feeling of dismay grew steadily inside him. Frantically, he began to race through the book, but it was the same from beginning to end: a collection of creepy stories with a local flavour, just as Tim had described. *But they were stories for children!* Printed in a large type-face and interspersed with nursery rhyme-type pictures. Graham's brow beaded with sweat as he stared down at the yellow pages, from which pixies, elves and sprites gazed innocently back.

Only then did he hear the feet scraping somewhere above his head.

He glanced up sharply. To his astonishment, he saw two misted shapes through the stained glass, clambering over it like spiders and with no great care. Heavy boots came down hard on the glass panels, dust trickling from the leaden joists. Graham supposed they were workmen involved in some job or other, though surely they'd be more careful than this?

He wondered why he hadn't heard them before.

And then, with a shock, he realised.

At first they'd been silent because they'd been watching him. As in fact, they were still watching him. Their faces were blurred and

44

misshapen through the glass, but were clearly fixed on him. And now they were making a noise because they were trying to find a way down. *A way down to him!*

Graham dashed out, stumbling along darkening passages filled with books but twisting back and forth, constantly returning him to the conservatory. On several occasions he passed under skylights, and imagined dark shapes above them, peering through. At last, he made it to the front of the shop and stood there quaking, ears straining. From above, there was still a faint scraping of feet. It was muffled and distant, but getting closer.

"That'll be two pounds fifty, please, sir," a voice said.

Graham started. It was the shopkeeper, sitting up behind his till, smiling.

Graham glared at him. "Are you mad? I don't want this! Why the hell would I want this?"

He thrust the book into the startled man's hands and fled outside, hurrying down the nearest alley and not stopping or looking back until he was in the town centre.

He crossed it quickly, and took another entry down to the car park. The sweat was now cooling on his brow and he felt a little more relaxed. As he dug into his pocket for his keys, he glanced over his shoulder – and saw two men slouching down the alley about forty yards behind. Workmen in fact, clad in heavy coats and dust-caked boots. Their hands were stuffed into their pockets and they were staring at him hard, from livid red faces.

Graham began to run. He crossed the slip-road without looking and vaulted the barrier into the car park. Again he glanced around. The workmen were still coming, but only slowly. He started to run again, staggering down the lanes of parked cars, at first unable to find his Ford Fiesta. When at last he did, his hands were shaking so badly that he dropped the key twice before he could insert it.

He leaped into the vehicle and drove out of the car park in a rush, swerving onto the slip-road. Only when it was too late did he remember that this road would actually take him back around the perimeter of the car park before feeding him into the main traffic. Which meant that he'd pass right by the two workmen. Within touching distance.

Graham felt his blood freeze, but then he swore and jammed his foot down hard. He'd get past them! Damn right he would! But what if they were blocking the road?

They weren't however. As he bore round one curve after another, the passage remained clear. There was no sign of anyone at all. Even the car park was deserted. Gasping with relief, Graham reached the next junction and cut out sharply into the traffic.

*

The first thing he did when he got back to the hotel was totter into the bar and order himself a stiff whisky. He drank it in a gulp, and ordered another. The young barman watched him with faint alarm. Graham swallowed only half of the second one, then stood erect, breathing hard, eyes tightly closed. He could still feel the sweat on his neck and shoulders.

Eventually, the barman asked him if he was alright. Graham wasn't sure himself. He opened his eyes, glanced around, and was just about to answer when he saw two diminutive shapes walk past the door. It rooted him to the spot.

Two young boys, they'd been.

In t-shirts and short pants.

Walking hand-in-hand.

He laid the whisky on the bar and crossed to the door. There was no sign of the youngsters now, but he knew where they'd gone. Across the hall from him, the black mouth to the unused corridor gaped invitingly. Graham could imagine them, innocent and happy, toddling hand-in-hand towards the shadows at its deepest end.

He walked over and gazed down it, seeing only darkness. Then he realised that somebody was standing at his shoulder. He turned – it was old John, uniformed up for another evening of duty. The waiter was watching Graham with a kindly but concerned expression. "A bit fascinated with that corridor, aren't we, sir?"

Graham wiped the sweat from his brow. "I know where it leads to now. It goes down to the old nursery, doesn't it? Where the parents used to leave their children while they went off gallivanting."

John seemed surprised that Graham knew. "We haven't used it as a nursery for a very long time," he said.

Graham gazed into its depths. "What ... what happened to that rather attractive young nanny you used to have working there?"

The old waiter seemed even more surprised. "Miss Anne ... well, there's an old story. And a sad one. Almost finished us off, that did."

"How?"

John frowned. "Well, nice young girl she was, but I guess she didn't have the dedication. Terrible, what happened. Absolutely terrible. I think she was more interested in the young men than their nippers, sir. After what happened, it was no wonder she threw herself off that jetty into the lake."

But Graham was no longer listening. At least, not to old John. Because behind him, in the bar, he could hear the loud drunken laughter of a man and a woman. Hysterical drunken laughter in fact. It was ridiculous to get so pissed at this early hour. Ridiculous and shameless. If only their voices didn't sound so familiar. *Dear God ...*

Without looking back, Graham turned and ran. He took the stairs three at a time and reached his room in seconds. It was filled with late afternoon shadows, and he had to fumble for the light switch before finding it. He flung his belongings into his bag haphazardly, all the time singing to himself. Singing as loudly as possible so that he wouldn't hear any more sounds from above, any more sounds that might suddenly move out from the Tower Room and come hurriedly down the spiral stair.

He scrambled down to Reception without even checking that he'd got everything. The woman on duty was astonished. She asked him if everything was alright. But he told her to hurry up please, just hurry up. He had to go!

She didn't seem particularly upset by this, but still took ages to tot up his bill and process his credit card, almost as if she was deliberately delaying him. And as she did, Graham became aware of the figure approaching down the darkened corridor from the old nursery. A figure in a white dress. Coming right towards him.

He clenched his teeth, unwilling to look round, and the second the receptionist handed him his receipt, left the hotel at a staggering run, crossing the drive and throwing himself into his car. He gunned the engine furiously and, before he knew what was happening, he was speeding down the narrow drive and onto the winding lane to Keswick. He had to put *The High View* behind him.

Behind him.

Behind him ...

Graham stiffened. The hair prickled on his neck.

There hadn't been a nanny called Miss Anne in that nursery of course. Not that afternoon at least, when she'd found a liquid lunch with Dad preferable to tedious hours watching Graham and Timmy kick around the teddy bears and play on the rocking horse. That glorious holiday afternoon, when the two workmen, who'd been watching them through the window all morning, had finally come in.

There *was* a nanny now though. Graham didn't need to glance into the rear-view mirror and see who was sitting in the back seat, to know that. There was a nanny now. And she'd never make the mistake of leaving him alone again. Not ever again.

He wondered how long he'd be able to take it, before he headed for the nearest cliff.

THE MUMPS HALL MURDERS

Mumps Hall is a listed building and tea-room near Gilsland in east Cumbria, but records show that it was once a roadside inn and hostelry. Walter Scott's popular novel 'Guy Mannering' made it infamous, but records show that it had a ghoulish reputation in real life.

The landlady of the inn was a certain Meg Teasedale, and despite the unattractive name of her establishment – Mumps Hall meant Beggar's Hall – she was a popular and respected figure in the district. By all accounts, she served good ale and baked good pastry – and if the occasional stranger or traveler stayed at her house overnight and was never seen again, nobody seemed to notice.

At least, nobody noticed at the time.

The shocking revelations about what had really been happening at Mumps Hall only came out after Meg Teasedale's death in 1777, when she was ninety-eight. Supposedly, she murdered a number of her guests in order to steal their goods and money. The method by which she carried out these acts was quite horrific. She would creep up to the bedroom where the unfortunate guest was residing, and once he was sound asleep, place beside him the Hand of Glory. This was the pickled left hand of a hanged man, which, when treated with virgin wax and sesame oil, could be used as a candle. The poisonous fumes emitted would be sufficient to render the guest deeply unconscious. Meg would then go through his belongings, taking anything of value, before dragging his inert form down the stair, out of the inn and across the road to a deep pond, into which she would weigh him with stones

Just how many victims were claimed is open to debate. The view has been expressed that Meg might have been continuing a family business, and that her mother – who held the inn before her, and died at the age of sixty-six in 1711 – might also have robbed and murdered her passing trade, but there is no proof of this. The researcher, Marjorie Rowling, wrote that, after Meg's death, when the extent of her crimes became apparent, her property was examined by the local authorities, and, among various items found, was the skeleton of a child and a shriveled hand, which suggested that she had indeed used the Hand of Glory, but that she had also practiced witchcraft as well.

Ms. Rowling regarded the epitaph on Meg's gravestone as a clue to Satanic practice:

> *What I once was, some may relate,*
> *What I am now is each man's fate;*
> *What I may be, none can explain,*
> *Till He that called me, calls again.*

Of course, this could also be read as an ordinary Christian epitaph, and it has to be acknowledged that unfounded legends about murderous landlords and landladies are common throughout the British Isles. But, on the evidence thus far, it does seem that something rather unpleasant was once going on at Mumps Hall.

THE MORAINE
Simon Bestwick

The mist hit us suddenly. One moment we had the peak in sight; the next, the white had swallowed up the crags and was rolling down towards us.

"Shit," I said. "Head back down."

For once, Diane didn't argue.

Trouble was, it was a very steep climb. Maybe that was why we'd read nothing about this mountain in the guidebooks. Some locals in the hotel bar the night before had told us about it. They'd warned us about the steepness, but Diane liked the idea of a challenge. All well and good, but now it meant we had to descend very slowly; one slip and you'd go down the mountainside, arse over apex.

That was when I saw the faint desire-line that led off, almost at right angles to the main path, running sideways and gently downwards.

"There, look," I said, pointing. "What do you reckon?"

Diane hesitated, glancing down the main path then up at the fast-falling mist. "Let's try it."

So we did.

"Look out," I said. Diane was lagging a good four or five yards behind me. "Faster."

"I'm going as fast as I bloody can, Steve."

I didn't rise to the bait, just turned and jogged on. The gentler slope meant we could run, but even so, we weren't fast enough. Everything went suddenly white.

"Shit," Diane said. I reached out for her hand – she was just a shadow in the wall of white vapour – and she took it and came closer. The mist was cold, wet and clinging, like damp cobwebs.

"What now?" Diane said. She kept her voice level, but I could tell it wasn't easy for her. And I couldn't blame her.

Don't be fooled by Lakeland's picture-postcard scenery; its high mountains and blue tarns, the boats on Lake Windermere, the gift shops and stone-built villages. You come here from the city to find the air's fresher and cleaner, and when you look up at night you see hundreds, thousands more stars in the sky because there's no light pollution. But by the same token, fall on a slope like this and there'll be no-one around, and your mobile won't get a signal. And if a mist like this one comes down and swallows you up and you don't know

51

which way to go – it doesn't take that long, on a cold October day, for hypothermia to set in. These fells and dales claimed lives like ours each year.

I took a deep breath. "I think…"

"You OK?" she asked.

"I'm fine." I was a little nettled she'd thought otherwise; she was the one who'd sounded in need of reassurance, but I wasn't going to start bickering now. It occurred to me – at the back of my head, and I'd have denied it outright if anyone had suggested it to me – that this might be a blessing in disguise; if I could stay calm and lead us to safety, I could be a hero in her eyes. "We need to get to some lower ground."

"Yes, I *know*," she said, as if I'd pointed out the stupidly obvious. Well, perhaps I had. I was just trying to clarify the situation. Alright, I wanted to impress her, to look good. But I wanted to do the right thing as well. Honestly.

So I pointed down the trail – the few feet of it we could see where it disappeared into the mist. "Best off keeping on. Keep our heads and go slowly."

"Yes, I worked that bit out as well." I recognised her tone of voice; it was the one she used to take cocky students down a peg. There'd been a time when I used to slip into her lectures, even though I knew nothing, then or now, about Geology; I just liked hearing her talk about her favoured subject. I couldn't remember ever seeing her in any of *my* lectures – not that she was interested in Music. Maybe it had never been what I'd thought it was. Maybe it had never been for either of us.

Not an idea I liked, but one I'd kept coming back to far too often lately. As had Diane. Hence this trip, which was looking less and less like a good idea all the time. We'd spent our honeymoon here; I suppose we'd hoped to recapture something or other, but there's no magic in places. Only people, and precious little of that; less and less the older you get.

And none of that was likely to get us safely out of here. "OK then," I said. "Come on."

*

Diane caught the back of my coat and pulled. I wheeled to face her and swayed, off-balance. Loose scree clattered down into the mist; the path had grown rockier underfoot. She caught my arm and steadied me. I yanked it free, thoroughly pissed off. "What?"

52

"Steve, we're still walking."

"I noticed. Well, actually, we're not just now, since you just grabbed me."

She folded her arms. "We've been walking nearly twenty minutes." I could see she was trying to stop her teeth chattering. "And I don't think we're much closer to ground level. I think we might be a bit off course."

I realised my teeth had started chattering too. It was hard to be sure, but I thought she might have a point; the path didn't look like it was sloping down any longer. If it'd levelled off, we were still halfway up the damned mountain. "Shit."

I felt panic threatening, like a small hungry animal gnawing away inside my stomach, threatening to tear its way up through my body if it let it. I wouldn't. Couldn't. Mustn't. If we panicked we were stuffed.

At least we hadn't come completely unprepared. We had Kendal Mint Cake and a thermos of hot tea in our backpacks, which helped, but they could only buy a little more time. We either got off this mountain soon, or we never would.

We tried our mobiles, but it was an exercise; there was no reception out here. They might as well have been bits of wood. I resisted the temptation to throw mine away.

"Should've stayed on the main path," Diane said. "If we'd taken it slow we'd have been OK."

I didn't answer. She glanced at me and rolled her eyes.

"What?"

"Steve, I wasn't having a go at you."

"Fine."

"Not everything has to be about that."

"I said, fine."

But she wouldn't leave it. "All I said was that we should've stuck to the main path. I wasn't saying this was all your fault."

"*Okay.*"

"I wasn't. If I'd seen that path I would've probably done the same thing. It looked like it'd get us down faster."

"Right."

"I'm just saying, looking back, we should've gone the other way."

"Okay. Alright. You've made your point." I stood up. A sheep bleated faintly. "Can we just leave it now?"

"*Okay.*" I saw her do the eye roll again, but pretended not to. "So now what? If we backtrack …"

"Think we can make it?"

"If we can get back to the main path, we should be able to find our way back from there."

If we were very lucky, perhaps; our hotel was a good two miles from the foot of this particular peak, and chances were the mist would be at ground level too. Even off the mountain we'd be a long way from home and dry, but it seemed the best choice on offer. If only we'd taken it sooner; we might not have heard the dog bark.

But we did.

We both went still. Diane brushed her dark hair back from her eyes and looked past me into the mist. I looked too, but couldn't see much. All I could see was the rocky path for a few feet ahead before it vanished into the whiteout.

The sheep bleated again. A few seconds later, the dog barked.

I looked at Diane. She looked back at me. A sheep on its own meant nothing – most likely lost and astray, like us. But a dog – a dog most likely had an owner.

"Hello?" I called into the mist. "Hello?"

"Anybody down there?" Diane called.

"Hello?" A voice called back.

"Thank god for that," Diane whispered.

We started along the rattling path, into the mist. "Hello?" called the voice. "Hello?"

"Keep shouting," I called back, and it occurred to me that we were the ones who sounded like rescuers. Maybe we'd found another fell-walker, caught out in the mists like us. I hoped not. What with the dog barking as well, I was pinning my hopes on a shepherd out here rounding up a lost sheep, preferably a generously-disposed one with a warm, nearby cottage complete with a fire and a kettle providing hot cups of tea.

Scree squeaked and rattled underfoot as we went. I realised the surface of the path had turned almost entirely into loose rock. Not only that, but it was angling sharply down after all. Diane caught my arm. "Careful."

"Yeah, okay, I know." I tugged my arm free and tried to ignore the long sigh she let out behind me.

The mist cleared somewhat as we reached the bottom. We could see between twenty-five and thirty yards ahead, which was a vast improvement, although the whiteout still completely hid everything beyond that point. The path led down into a sort of shallow ravine between our peak and its neighbour. The bases of the two steep hillsides sloped gently downwards to a floor about ten yards wide. It was hard to be certain as both the floor and those lower slopes were covered in a thick layer of loose stone fragments.

The path we'd followed petered out, or more into accurately disappeared into that treacherous surface. Two big, flat-topped boulders jutted out of the scree, one about twenty yards down the ravine floor, the other about fifteen yards on from that, at the mouth of a gully that gaped in the side of our peak.

The mist drifted. I couldn't see any sign of man or beast. "Hello?" I called.

After a moment, there was a click and rattle somewhere in the ravine. Rock, pebbles, sliding over one another, knocking together.

"Bollocks," I said.

"Easy," Diane said. "Looks like we've found some low ground anyway."

"That doesn't mean much. We've lost our bearings."

"There's somebody around here. We heard them. Hello?" She shouted the last – right down my earhole, it felt like.

"Ow."

"Sorry."

"Forget it."

There was another click and rattle of stone. And the voice called out "Hello?" again.

"There," said Diane. "See?"

"Yeah. Okay."

There was a bleat, up and to our left. I looked and sure enough there was the sheep we'd heard, except it was more of a lamb, picking its unsteady way over the rocks on the lower slopes of the neighbouring peak.

"Aw," said Diane. "Poor little thing." She's one of those who goes all gooey over small furry animals. Not that it stops her eating them; I was nearly tempted to mention the rack of lamb in red wine jus she'd enjoyed so much the night before. Nearly.

The lamb saw us, blinked huge dark eyes, bleated plaintively again.

In answer, there were more clicks and rattles, and an answering bleat from further down the ravine. The lamb shifted a bit on its hooves, moving sideways, and bleated again.

After a moment, I heard the rocks click again, but softly this time. It lasted longer too, this time. Almost as if something was moving slowly, as stealthily as the noisy terrain allowed. The lamb was still, looking silently up the ravine. I looked too, trying to see past where the scree faded into the mist.

The rocks clicked softly, then were silent. And then a dog barked, twice.

The lamb tensed but was still.

Click click click, went the rocks, and the dog barked again.

The lamb bleated. A long silence.

Diane's fingers had closed round my arm. I felt her draw breath to speak, but I turned and shushed her, fingers to her lips. She frowned; I touched my finger back to my own lips and turned to look at the lamb again.

I didn't know why I'd done all that, but somehow knew I'd had to. A moment later we were both glad of it.

The click of shifting rocks got louder and faster, almost a rustle, like grass parting as something slid through it. The lamb bleated and took a few tottering steps back along the slope. Pebbles clattered down. The rock sounds stopped. I peered into the mist, but I couldn't see anything. Then the dog barked again. It sounded very close now. More than close enough to see, but the ravine floor was empty. I looked back at the lamb. It was still. It cocked its head.

A click of rocks, and something bleated.

The lamb bleated back.

Rocks clattered again, deafeningly loud, and Diane made a strangled gasp that might have been my name, her hand clutching my arm painfully, and pointed me with her free hand.

The ravine floor was moving. Something was humped beneath the rocks, pushing them up as it went so they clicked and rattled in its wake. It was like watching something move underwater. It raced forward, arrowing towards the lamb.

The lamb let out a single terrified bleat and tried to turn away, but it never stood a chance. The humped shape under the scree hurtled towards it, loose stone rattling like dice in a shaken cup, and then rocks sprayed upwards like so much kicked sand where the lamb stood. Its bleat became a horrible squealing noise – I'd no idea sheep could make sounds like that. The shower of rubble fell back to earth. The lamb kept squealing. I could only see its head and front legs; the rest was buried under the rock. The front legs kicked frantically and the head jerked about, to and fro, the lips splaying back horribly from the teeth as it squealed out its pain. And then a sudden, shocking spray of blood spewed out from under the collapsing shroud of rocks like a scarlet fan. Diane clapped a hand to her mouth with a short, shocked cry. I think I might have croaked 'Jesus', or something along those lines, myself.

The lamb's squeals hit a new, jarring crescendo that hurt the ears, like nails on a blackboard, then choked and cut off. Scree clattered and hissed down the slope and came to rest. The lamb lay still. Its fur was speckled red with blood; its eyes already looked fixed and unblinking, glazing over. The rocks above and around it glistened.

With any luck it was beyond pain. I hoped so, because in the next moment the lamb's forequarters were yanked violently, jerked further under the rubble, and in the same instant the scree seemed to surge over it. The heaped loose rock jerked and shifted a few times, rippled slightly and was still. Even the stones splashed with blood were gone, rolled under the surface and out of sight. A few glistening patches remained, furthest out from where the lamb had been, but otherwise there was no sign that it'd even existed.

"Fuck." I definitely said it this time. "Oh fucking hell."

There was a moment of silence; I could hear Diane drawing breath again to speak. And then there was that now-familiar click and rattle as something moved under the scree. And from where the lamb had been a voice, a low, hollow voice called "Hello?"

*

Diane put her hand over my mouth. "Stay quiet," she whispered.

"I know that," I whispered back, muffled by her hand.

"It hunts by sound," she whispered. "Must do. Vibration through the rocks."

There was a slight, low hump where the lamb had been killed, and you had to look hard to see it, and know what it was you were trying to spot. A soft clicking sound came from it. Rock on rock.

"It's under the rocks," she whispered.

"I can *see* that."

"So if we can get back up onto solid ground, we should be okay."

"Should."

She gave me an irritated look. "Got any better ideas?"

"Okay. So we head back?"

"Hello?" called the voice again.

"Yes," whispered Diane. "And very, very slowly, and carefully and quietly."

I nodded.

The rocks clicked and shifted, softly. Diane raised one foot, moved it upslope, set it slowly, gently gown again. Then the other foot. She turned and looked at me, then reached out and took my hand. Or I took hers, as you prefer.

I followed her up the slope. We climbed in as near silence as we could manage, up towards the ravine's entrance, towards the solidity of the footpath. Rocks slid and clicked underfoot. As if in answer, the bloodied rocks where the lamb had died clicked too, knocking gently against one another as something shifted under them.

"Hello?" I heard again as we climbed. And then again: "Hello?"

"Keep going," Diane whispered.

The rocks clicked again. With a loud rattle, a stone bounced down to the ravine floor. "John?" This time it was a woman's voice. Scottish, by the accent. "John?"

"Fucking hell," I muttered. Louder than I meant to and louder than I should have, because the voice sounded again. "John? John?"

Diane gripped my hand so tight I almost cried out. For a moment I wondered if that was the idea– make me cry out, then let go and run, leave the unwanted partner as food for the thing beneath the rocks while she made her getaway, kill two birds with one stone. But it wasn't, of course.

"Shona?" This time the voice was a man's, likewise Scottish-accented. "Shona, where are ye?"

Neither of us answered. A cold wind blew. I clenched my teeth as they tried to start chattering again. I heard the wind whistle and moan. Shrubs flapped and fluttered in the sudden gale and the surrounding terrain became a little clearer, though not much. Then the wind dropped again, and a soft, cold whiteness began to drown the dimly-glimpsed outlines of trees and higher ground again.

Stones clicked. A sheep's bleat sounded. Then a cow lowed.

Diane tugged my hand. "Come on," she said, "let's go."

The dog barked two, three times as we went, sharp and sudden, startling me a little and making me sway briefly for balance. I looked at Diane, smiled a little, let out a long breath.

We were about nine feet from the top when a deafening roar split the silence apart. I don't know what the hell it was, what kind of animal sound – but even Diane cried out, and I stumbled, and sending a mini-landslide slithering back down the slope.

The broken slate heaved and rattled, and then surged as something flew across, under, *through* the ravine floor towards us.

"Run!" I heard Diane yell, and I tried, we both did, but the shape was arrowing past us. We saw that at the last moment; it was hurtling past us to the edge of the scree, the point where it gave way to the path.

Diane was already starting back down, pushing me behind her, when the ground erupted in a shower of stone shrapnel. I thought I glimpsed something, only for the briefest of moments, moving in the hail of broken stone, but when it fell back into place there was no sign of anything – except, if you looked, a low humped shape.

Diane shot past me, still gripping my hand, pelting along the ravine. Behind us I heard the stones rattle as the thing gave chase. Diane veered towards the nearest of the boulder – it was roughly the size of a small car, and looked like pretty solid ground.

"Come on!" Diane leapt – pretty damned agile for a woman in her late thirties who didn't lead a particularly active life – onto the boulder, reached back for me. "Quick!"

The shape was hurtling towards us, slowing as it neared us. Its bow-wave of loose stones thickened, widened; it was gathering speed. I could see what was coming; I grabbed Diane and pushed her down flat on the boulder. She didn't fight, so I'm guessing she'd reached the same conclusions as me.

There was a muffled thud and the boulder shook. For a moment I thought we'd both be pitched onto the scree around it, but the boulder held, too deeply rooted to be torn loose. Rocks rained and pattered down on us; I tucked my head in.

I realised I was clinging on to Diane, and that she was doing to the same to me. I opened my eyes and looked at her. She looked back. Neither of us said anything.

Behind us, there were clicks and rattles. I turned slowly, sliding off Diane. We both sat up and watched.

There was a sort of crater in the layer of loose rocks beside the boulder, where the thing had hit. The scree at the bottom was heaving, shifting, rippling. The crater walls trembled and slid. After a moment, the whole lot collapsed on itself. The uneven surface rippled and heaved some more, finally stopped when it looked as it had before – undisturbed, except of course for the low humped shape beneath it.

Click went the stones as it shifted in its tracks, taking stock. Click click as it moved and began inching its way round the boulder. "John? Shona? Hello?" All emerged from the shifting rocks, each of those different voices. Then the bleat. Then the roar. I swear I felt the wind of it buffet me.

"Christ," I said.

The rocks clicked, softly, as the humped shape began moving, circling slowly round the boulder. "Christ," my own voice answered me. Then another voice called, a child's. "Mummy?" Click click click. "Shona?" Click. "Oh, for god's sake, Marjorie," came a rich, fruity voice which sounded decidedly pre-Second World War. If not the First. "For God's sake."

Click. Then silence. The wind keened down the defile. Fronds of mist drifted coldly along. Click. A high, thin female voice, clear and sweet, began singing 'The Ash Grove.' Very slowly, almost like a dirge. "*Down yonder green valley where streamlets meander...*"

Diane clutched my wrist tightly.

Click, and the song stopped, as if a switch had been thrown. Click click. And then there was a slow rustling and clicking as the shape began to move away from the boulder, moving further and further back. Diane gripped me tighter. The mist was thickening and the shape went slowly, so that it was soon no longer possible to be sure exactly where it was. Then the last click died away and there was only the silence and the wind and the mist.

*

Time passed.

"It's not gone far," Diane whispered. "Just far enough that we've got some freedom of movement. It wants us to make a move, try to run for it. It knows it can't get us here."

"But we can't stay here either," I pointed out in the same whisper. My teeth were already starting to chatter again, and I could see hers were too. "We'll bloody freeze to death."

"I know. Who knows, maybe it does too. Either way, we'll have to make a break for it, and sooner rather than later. If we leave it much longer we won't stand a chance."

"What the hell do you think it is?" I asked.

She scowled at me. "You expect me to know? I'm a geologist, not a biologist."

"Don't suppose you've got the number for a good one on your mobile?"

She stopped and stared at me. "We're a pair of fucking idiots," she said, and dug around in the pocket of her jeans. Out came her mobile. "Never even thought of it."

"There's no signal."

"There wasn't before. It's worth a try."

Hope flared briefly, but not for long; it was the same story as before.

"Okay," I said. "So we can't phone a friend. Let's think about this then. What do we know about it?"

"It lives under the rocks," Diane said. "Moves under them."

"Likes to stay under them, too," I said. "It was right up against us before. *That* far from us. It could've attacked us easily just by coming up out from under, but it didn't. It'd rather play it safe and do the whole waiting game thing."

"So maybe it's weak, if we can get it out of the rocks. Vulnerable." Diane took off her glasses, rubbed her large eyes. "Maybe it's blind. It seems to hunt by sound, vibration."

"A mimic. That's something else. It's a mimic, like a parrot."

"Only faster," she said. "It mimicked you straight away, after hearing you once."

"Got a good memory for voices, too," I whispered back. "Some of those voices …"

"Yes, I think so too. And that roar it made. How long's it been since there was anything roaming wild in this country, could make a noise like that?"

"Maybe a bear," I offered, "or one of the big sabre-toothed cats."

Diane looked down at the scree. "Glacial till," she said.

"What?"

"Sorry. The stones here. It's what's called glacial till – earth that's been compressed into rock by the pressure of the glaciers coming through here." She looked up and down the ravine.

"So?"

The look she gave me was equal parts hurt and anger. "So… nothing much, I suppose."

Wind blew.

"I'm sorry."

She shrugged. "S'okay."

"No. Really."

She gave me a smile, at least, that time. Then frowned, looked up at the way we'd come in – had it only been in the last hour? "Look at that. You can see it now."

"See what?"

She pointed. "This is a moraine."

"A what?"

"Moraine. It's the debris – till and crushed rock – a glacier leaves behind when it melts. All this would've been crushed up against the mountainsides for god knows how long …"

I remembered Diane telling me about the last Ice Age, how there'd have been two miles of ice above the cities we'd grown up in. How far down would all this have been? And would – *could* – anything have lived in it?

I was willing to bet any of our colleagues in the Biology Department would have snorted at the idea. But even so ... life is very tenacious, isn't it? It can cling on in places you'd never expect it to.

Maybe some creatures had survived down here in the Ice Age, crawling and slithering between the gaps in the crushed rock. And in every food chain, something's at the top- something that hunted blindly by vibration and lured by imitation. Something that had survived the glaciers' melting, even prospered from it, growing bigger and fatter on bigger, fatter prey.

The lost lamb had saved us by catching its attention. Without that, we'd have had no warning and would've followed that voice – no doubt belonging to some other, long-dead victim – into the heart of the killing ground.

Click click click, went the rocks in the distance, as the creature shifted and then grew still.

And Diane leant close to me, and breathed in my ear: "We're going to have to make a move."

*

To our left was the way we'd come, the scree-thick path sloping up before blending with the moraine. Twenty yards. It might as well have been ten miles.

The base of the peak was at our backs. It wasn't sheer, not quite, but it may as well have been. The only handholds were the occasional rock or root; even if the fall didn't kill you, you'd be too stunned or injured to stand a chance. The base of the opposite peak – even if we *could* have got past the creature – was no better.

To our right, the main body of the ravine led on, thick with rubble, before vanishing into the mist. Running along that would be nothing short of suicide, but there was still the gully we'd seen before. From what I could see the floor of it was thickly littered with rubble, but it definitely angled upwards, hopefully towards higher ground of solid earth and grass, where the thing from the moraine couldn't follow. Better still, there was that second boulder at the gully mouth, as big and solidly rooted-looking as this one, if not bigger. If we could make it that far – and we might, with a little luck – we had a chance to get out through the gully.

I looked at the boulder and back to Diane. She was still studying it. "What do you reckon?" I breathed.

Click click click, came softly, faintly, gently in answer.

62

Diane glanced sideways. "The bastard thing's fast," she whispered back. "It'll be a close thing."

"We could distract it," I suggested. "Make a noise to draw it off."

"Like what?"

I nodded at the rocks at the base of the boulder. "Pick a spot and lob a few of them at it. Hopefully it'll think it's another square meal."

She looked dubious. "S'pose it's better than nothing."

"If you've got any better ideas."

She looked hurt rather than annoyed. "Hey …"

"I'm sorry." I was, too. I touched her arm. "We've just got to make that boulder."

"And what then?"

"We'll think of something. We always do."

She forced a smile.

Reaching down to pick up the bits of rubble and rock wasn't pleasant, mainly because the thing had gone completely silent and there was no knowing how close it might be now. Every time my hands touched the rocks I was convinced they'd explode in my face before something grabbed and yanked me under them.

But the most that happened was that once, nearby, the rocks clicked softly and we both went still, waiting, for several minutes before reaching down again after a suitable pause. At last we were ready with half a dozen good-sized rocks apiece.

"Where do we throw them?" Diane whispered. I pointed to the footpath; we'd be heading, after all, in the opposite direction. She nodded.

"Ready?"

Another nod.

I threw the first rock. We threw them all, fast, within a few seconds, and they cracked and rattled on the slate. The slate nearby rattled and hissed as something moved.

"Go," Diane said; we jumped off the boulder and ran for the gully mouth.

Diane'd often commented on my being out of condition, so I was quite pleased that I managed to outpace her. I overtook easily, and was soon a good way ahead. The boulder was two more strides away, three at most, and then –

The two sounds came together; a dismayed cry from Diane, and then that hiss and click and rattle of displaced scree, rising to a rushing roar as a bow wave of broken rocks rose up behind Diane and bore down on her.

63

I screamed at her to run, covering the rest of the distance to the boulder and leaping onto it, turning, holding my hands out to her, as if that was going to help. But what else could I have done? Running back to her wouldn't have speeded her up, and –

Oh. Yes. I could've tried to draw it off. Risked my own life, even sacrificed it, to save hers. Yes, I could've done that. Thanks for reminding me.

It got to her as I turned. There was an explosion of rubble, a great spray of it, and she screamed. I threw up my hands to protect my face. A piece of rock glanced off my forehead and I stumbled, swayed, losing balance, but thank God I hadn't ditched my backpack – the weight dragged me back and I fell across the boulder.

Rubble rained and pattered about us as I stared at Diane. She'd fallen face-down on the ground, arms outstretched. Her pale hands, splayed out on the earth, were about three feet from the boulder.

I reached out a hand to her, leaning forward as far as I dared. I opened my mouth to speak her name, and then she lifted her head and looked up. Her glasses were askew on her pale face, and one lens was cracked. In another moment I might have jumped off the boulder and gone to her, but then she screamed and blood sprayed from the ground where her feet were covered by a sheet of rubble. Her back arched; a fingernail split as she clawed at the ground. Red bubbled up through the stones, like a spring.

Diane was weeping with pain; she tried to twist round to see what was being done to her, but jerked, shuddered and cried out before she could complete it. She twisted back to face me, lips trembling, still crying.

I leant forward, hands outstretched, but couldn't reach. Then I remembered the backpack and struggled out of it, loosening the straps to give the maximum possible slack, gripping one and holding the backpack as far out as I could, so that the other dangled closer to her. "Grab it," I whispered. "I'll pull you in."

She shook her head hard. "No," she managed at last. "Don't you get it?"

"What?" We weren't whispering anymore. Didn't seem much point. Besides, her voice was ragged with pain.

"It wants you to try. Don't you see? Otherwise it would've dragged me straight under by now."

I stared at her.

"Steve... it's using me as bait." Her face tightened. She bit her lips and fresh tears leaked down her pale cheeks. Her green eyes squeezed shut. When they opened again, they were red and bloodshot. "Oh God. What's it done to my legs? My feet?"

"I don't know," I lied.

"Well, that's it, don't you see?" She was breathing deeply now, trying to get the agony under control. "I've had it. Won't get far, even if it did let me go to chase after you. Can't get at you up there. So stay put."

"But... but..." Dimly I realised I was crying too. This was my wife. My *wife*, for Christ's sake.

Diane forced a smile. "Just stay put. Or try... make a getaway."

"I'm not leaving you."

"Yes, you are. It'll go after you. Might be able... drag myself there." She nodded at the boulder. "You could go get help. Help me. Might stand a chance."

I looked at the blood still bubbling up from the stones. She must have seen the expression on my face. "Like that, is it?"

I looked away. "I can try." My view of the gully was still constricted by my position. I could see the floor of it sloping up, but not how far it ultimately went. If nothing else, I could draw it away from her, give her a chance to get to the boulder.

And what then? If I couldn't find a way out of the gully? If there wasn't even a boulder to climb to safety on, I'd be dead and the best Diane could hope for was to bleed to death.

But I owed her a chance of survival, at least.

I put the backpack down, looked into her eyes. "Soon as it moves off, start crawling. Shout me when you're here. I'll keep making a racket, try and keep it occupied."

"Be careful."

"You too." I smiled at her and refused to look at her feet. We met at University, did I tell you? Did I mention that? A drunken discussion about politics in the Student Union bar. More of an argument really. We'd been on different sides but ended up falling for each other. That pretty much summed up our marriage, I supposed. "Love you," I managed to say at last.

She gave a tight, buckled smile. "You too," she said back.

That was never something either of us had said easily. Should've known it'd take something like this. "Okay, then," I muttered. "Bye."

I took a deep breath, then jumped off the boulder and started to run.

*

65

I didn't look back, even when Diane let out a cry, because I could hear the rattle and rush of slate behind me as I pelted into the gully and knew the thing had let her go – let her go so that it could come after me.

The ground's upwards slope petered out quite quickly and the walls all around were a good ten feet high, sheer and devoid of handholds, except for at the very back of it. There was an old stream channel – only the thinnest trickle of water made it out now, but I'm guessing it'd been stronger once, because a mix of earth and pebbles, lightly grown over, formed a slope leading up to the ground above. A couple of gnarled trees sprouted nearby, and I could see their roots breaking free of the earth – thick and twisted, easy to climb with. All I had to do was reach them.

But then I noticed something else; something that made me laugh wildly. Only a few yards from where I was now, the surface of the ground changed from a plain of rubble to bare rock. Here and there earth had accumulated and sprouted grass, but what mattered was that there was no rubble for the creature to move under.

I chanced one look behind me, no more than that. It was hurtling towards me, the huge bow-wave of rock. I ran faster, managed the last few steps, and then dived and rolled across blessed solid ground.

Rubble sprayed at me from the edge of the rubble and again I caught the briefest glimpse of something moving in there. I couldn't put any kind of name to it if I tried, and I don't think I want to.

The rubble heaved and settled. The stones clicked. I got up and started backing away. Just in case. Click, click, click. Had anything ever got away from it before? I couldn't imagine anything human doing so, or men would've come back here with weapons, to find and kill it. Or perhaps that survivor hadn't been believed. Click. Click, click. Click, click, click.

Click. A sheep bleated.
Click. A dog barked.
Click. A wolf howled.
Click. A cow lowed.
Click. A bear roared.
Click. "John?"
Click. "Shona? Shona, where are ye?"
Click. "Mummy?"
Click. "Oh, for God's sake, Marjorie. For god's sake."
Click. *"Down yonder green valley where streamlets meander…"*
Click. "Christ." My voice. "Christ."
Click. "Steve? Get help. Help me." Click. "Steve. Help me."

I turned and began to run, started climbing. I looked back when I heard stones rattling. I looked back and saw something, a wide shape, moving under the stones and heading away, back towards the mouth of the gully.

"Diane?" I shouted. "Diane?"

There was no answer.

*

I've been walking now, according to my wristwatch, for a good half-hour. My teeth are chattering and I'm tired and all I can see around me is the mist.

Still no signal on the mobile. They can trace your position from a mobile call these days. That'd be helpful. I've tried to walk in a straight line, so that if I find help I can just point back the way I came, but I doubt I've kept to one.

I tell myself that she must have passed out – passed out from the effort and pain of dragging herself onto that boulder. I tell myself that the cold must have slowed her circulation down to the point where she might still be alive.

I do not think of how much blood I saw bubbling out from under the stones.

I do not think of hypothermia. Not for her. I'm still going, so she still must have a chance there too, surely?

I keep walking. I'll keep walking for as long as I can believe Diane might still be alive. After that, I won't be able to go on, because it won't matter anymore.

I'm crawling, now.

We came out here to see if we still worked, the two of us, under all the clutter and the mess. And it looks like we still did.

There's that cold comfort, at least.

THE TAWNY BOY

In the year 1650, a curious case was reported from a farm at Overthwaite in the parish of Beetham, near Kirkby Lonsdale. It concerned an elderly but well-to-do farmer and his wife, who were receiving nightly visits from a small boy covered head to foot in very fine, tawny hair. The boy would knock at the farm door each night, and ask – in a strange, unidentifiable accent – if the couple had any chores they would like him to perform.

The first time this happened, the elderly couple were alarmed. They thought this was some 'Gypsy rascal', as they later said, and that it might be the prelude to an attack on their home. But no such thing happened. The farmer asked 'the tawny boy', as they referred to him, if he would clear up the stable yard. And in the morning, the stable yard was cleaner and tidier than they'd ever seen it. In the words of the farmer's wife, they could have eaten their breakfast from its sparkling flagstones.

Each night from this point on, the tawny boy asked if they had any chores, and they provided him with work, for which he never requested payment but which he had always completed by morning. The farm and its environs, which, in truth, had become a little much for the elderly couple, were soon spick and span. When there were no more chores to be done around the house, there was work on the farm itself – in the fields, orchards and vegetable patches. There were walls to be repaired, trees to prune, cows to milk, and so on. All of these tasks were performed to the farmer's full satisfaction. It seemed there was nothing the tawny boy could not turn his hand to.

Several months into these strange events, a friend of the farmer's wife came to stay, and was witness to the arrival of the tawny boy. She was stunned when the farmer and his wife sent him down to the river to spend the night netting fish for their following day's repast. When the tawny boy had gone about his task, the farmer's wife explained to her friend what had been happening, and how fortunate they were as the farm was in the best condition ever, and they themselves hadn't needed to lift a finger. The friend immediately scolded her, telling her that, though it was one thing to look a gift horse in the mouth, clearly this tawny boy was some demented child who had been living wild in the forest. It was outrageous and unchristian to exploit him this way. Feeling guilty, the farmer and his wife waited for the tawny boy the next night, and when he arrived, they seized him, forced him into a bathtub, shaved off his hair – to find a thin, pallid creature underneath – and provided him with a suit of clothes, which they had purchased from a market that very day. The tawny boy was so frightened that he fled from the house. They sought to follow, but were of such an age that wandering around in darkness was not to their liking. At which point they heard the boy speaking to someone in the shadows under the trees.

"Daddy, they clipped me and made me bare," he said. "Daddy, I am well, but I am sore".

Frightened, the couple closed the farm and shuttered the windows. A few minutes later, there was a furious banging on the door as if someone was striking it with a great club. The same treatment was meted to all the shuttered windows. A heavy figure stamped around outside the house for several hours, grunting, breathing hoarsely. There were repeated attacks on the doors and shutters, which at length had suffered considerable damage, though none had actually broken.

The following morning, the elderly couple, terrified, confessed everything to their pastor, who chided them for not confiding in him sooner. The tawny boy was not some demented child, he told them, but a brownie. The brownies were helpful beings who lived so deep in the wood that they could never be seen by day. However, if they were to assist you in any way it was the worst possible insult to offer them something in return, be it food, new clothes or even a haircut.

The couple feared this might mean they would now receive nightly visitations of a more malign sort, but the pastor assured them they would not. From this point on they would have no more dealings with the brownies. And this was true. The elderly couple never heard from the tawny boy, or his Daddy, again.

THE CLAIFE CRIER
Carole Johnstone

It was the ferryman. Afterwards she wasn't glad he'd put the thought into her head – not glad at all – but at the time it was little more than a story. A story and an excuse.

As soon as they had driven onto the small boat and her dad had turned off the engine, the rain obscured any view in flat, twisting ribbons of grey. It drummed against the roof; made echoless tattoos on the glass. Her dad tried on a hopeful smile that she might have tried to reciprocate had she not felt so hemmed in – trapped inside this grey, noisy space, seen by none. She didn't want to be here.

She jumped when the shadow fell across her lap and knocked hard against her window. She looked at her dad, watched the familiar suspicion cross his face. He nodded, and she wound the window down.

The ferryman was old, older than her dad. He was wearing a fluorescent windbreaker, its hood flapping wild, white beard with it. He didn't have a lot of teeth. The wet wind roared in after him.

"Weather's a pig on a stick, ain't 't?"

Her dad laughed the laugh he used on strangers. She tried to smile again.

"Thu folks ain't fixin' on goin' up t' Heights?"

Her dad leaned across her, passing the ferryman the fare. She was still trying to smile; still trying to remember what she had promised her mum. A stupid promise. *Try.*

"Well, we were," her dad said.

The ferryman was giving her a strange, sidelong look. She realised that she was holding her breath and let it out in a long exhale.

"Mebbe gee't up for a bad job, folks. Get thiseenn o'er t'oth' Sawrey Hotel; does a reet great tater 'ash. Good Hawkshead ale on tap in t' Claife Crier bar. Shandy for t' yung lass." He winked at her, and this time she managed a better smile back.

Her dad visibly bristled; she could feel the spiked hairs of his forearm where it brushed against hers. "Kerry's far too young to drink."

The ferryman's eyes were bloodshot, his eyelashes wet and dark with rain. He leaned close and her dad pulled back on her a little, his grip as overprotective as ever. Kerry felt something then – something she hated herself for – a pang, a memory of how her dad had once loved her. And then her mum saying, *just try, Kerry. This time, just try.*

"Tha ever hear t' story of t' Claife Crier, lass?"

"No."

"I don't think we need –"

Again, the ferryman gave her dad a long, considered look. "Story goes on stormy nights, t' ferrymen at Ferry Nab yuse to hear cries from t' heights at Claife for a boat to come across t' lake. They was awlus too scared to answer." He winked at Kerry, showed his gums. "Course, my mam's mam was nowt but a twinkle in 'er mam's eye back then, else it'd have bin a different story."

Kerry could still feel her father's angry arm against her own. She pretended that she couldn't. "But someone did go across?"

"Aye, that they did. A brave 'un rowed across, nobbut a yung lad. When he returned, he was so pig-afeart that he couldn'a tell a soul what he'd seen and dee'd the next day."

"Well, that's a bloody lovely story."

"Locals had a monk exorcise t' ghost of the Claife Crier and bind it to a quarry, so they say, but e'en today walkers report hearin' his cries and bein' followed at dusk by a hoodit figure on t' heights of Claife."

And there it was. The excuse.

"Oh for God's sake. Kerry, wind the window up, the rain's getting in."

The ferryman narrowed those bloodshot eyes. "If tha didno' want to hear no ghost stories, tha shudn't hev come to Lake Windermere. Story's true, an' thad I'll swear be king or prince." Pocketing the fare, he took his hand from the window, flashing yellow. "Head t'ord t' Sawrey Hotel. B5285 sou'west of t' Ferry Heawse." He glanced quick at Kerry, and the rain that ran off his eyelashes and onto his white, stubbled cheeks looked almost silver. His voice was low. "Gae yung fer a lot o' things."

*

There hadn't been many other passengers on the ferry, but the car park had completely emptied by the time the rain started to go off. Kerry looked out at the blurred signpost for Far Sawrey.

"Dad, can't we just go to the hotel like the ferryman said?"

Her dad continued to stare out of the windscreen, where the squeaked thump of the wipers now outmatched the dwindling rain.

His smile dimpled his cheeks just like hers did. "The walk only takes three hours at most. They say the view from the Heights over the lake is spectacular." He turned in his seat to face her. "C'mon, Carrot-top. I know things have been –" he dropped his gaze. "I know we haven't been getting on like we used to. That's why I wanted us to do this trip together."

That pang again. That horribly confusing, horribly mournful pang. And her mum's voice. *You only get one dad, honey. Only one.*

"But, Dad, what the ferryman said ..."

His smile disappeared and he managed to look both angry and sad at the same time. "Kerry, you're not a child anymore." An exhale; Kerry could see him struggling to keep his emotions in check, and the sudden love she felt for him caught her by surprise. When he took her hand, he smiled a better smile. "And that's something we both have to get used to."

They got out of the car, and Kerry thought better of complaining about the ugly cagoule and walking boots that her dad handed to her from the boot. It was cool, not cold, and the rain was now little more than a drizzle. While her dad checked his rucksack, she looked out across the lake. It was beautiful. Blue-grey and sparkling calm, long and narrow like a ribbon. At the visitor centre at Brockhole she'd read that it had been formed by melting glaciers more than 13,000 years before during the last major ice age. She liked to imagine things like that: an ancient, quiet space, untouched and breathing. There was a yacht out towards Bowness, gliding into the shadow of Belle Isle. On the opposite shore, the low foothills of the Lake District rose in green/brown steps towards the high fells in the north. The lazy rain obscured those higher moorlands; even if she squinted she could see nothing but grimy sky. Some of that claustrophobia slunk back – some, but not all. She shouldn't have been surprised that her excuse hadn't worked. They never did. And it was only three hours.

"Come on, Kerry!"

She turned her back on the lake and followed her dad to the edge of the woods. Close to the B5285 sign for Far Sawrey, a rusted marker had fallen on its side.

Quarry Car Park

"Dad, look!"

He looked at both her and the fallen sign, and then back at his map. "There's a trail through here."

72

The forest was damp and gloomy, though the track at first only skirted inside its fringes. Another signpost, this colonised by moss and dirt: The White Post Route. The trees were mainly pine and oak, their branches bowed low by rain. The track was narrow, muddy. A blackthorn dressed in white blossom dripped cold water onto Kerry's head as she passed under it, and she stopped to pull up the hood of her cagoule.

They came to a steep set of steps. Kerry watched the yellow back of her dad's cagoule as he began to climb, and followed after, knowing better than to complain. Not this early on at least. Head down, hood up, she kept her eyes on her wet, already dirty boots instead of the summit. By the time she reached it, her breath was choppy and her throat dry. Her dad was looking down at her with an old grin that she'd almost forgotten.

"Look at that, would you? It's bloody brilliant."

What it *was* was a ruin. An ugly, brownstone building with great holes for eyes looking out over the lake. "What is it?"

"Claife Station, built in the 18th century." He grinned his young smile again. "A Victorian viewpoint. It's huge! Can you imagine what it must have looked like then?"

Kerry didn't really care. A lake formed from 13,000 year old glaciers was one thing. A clapped out Victorian viewpoint was quite another. Her cold feet squelched, slipping on wet leaves.

"C'mon then, Philistine. Onward and upwards."

*

The path wound back into the woods and steadily climbed. The wind began to pick up, whispering through silver birch and ash. Bracken slapped at her thighs and knees. Every once in a while, her dad would stop, turn around and point out a plant or fern, and she would dutifully recite its name: primrose, wood anemone, snowdrop, meadowsweet, yellow flag. Her dad was a gardener, chiefly of Council parks and green spaces, but he'd tried to instill in her the kind of passion for flora and fauna that he'd long cultivated for himself. And Kerry remembered all of the names. Though it had been a long while since they'd been on a trip like this, Kerry remembered. Her stubborn memory had always let her down.

After half an hour they stopped at a viewpoint to catch their breath. Kerry's dad looked out over the lake, and in his profile she also remembered her mum calling him *my own Johnny Castle* whenever they snogged after too much wine. Her cheeks hot, she looked back into the forest. The sloped shouldered, upright pines, the dark wet branches and sleek wide overcoats of their neighbours, and then underneath, the brown/white, shadowed stretch away of their skeletons into gloom. The ugly, sun-starved forest floor, hidden from anyone who didn't want to look. She shivered. It reminded her too much of herself.

Then onward again. Further, higher, easing as they arrived at a place called Mitchell Knotts, passing a battered sign for Far Sawrey, which Kerry's dad turned away from, cutting right at a third white-painted post towards Hawkshead. Uphill again.

They had a very late lunch in an open grassy pasture close to the edge of the wood. A tarn bogged down with weeds and broken branches trickled sadly past flattened mats of bluebell in the becks. As Kerry drank tepid coffee from a thermos cup, she followed her dad's pointed finger out towards the pastures' carpet of spiked yellow flowers and blade-like leaves.

"Sundew?" It was a deliberate mistake; she didn't want him to think that she'd remembered them all. She took another sip, looked at his profile again, its jaw set. She relented. "Bog asphodel."

"Yep," he smiled. "And marsh marigold." Kerry found his forced joviality harder to stomach than his disapproval. "It's a mire out there alright. The rain will have made it soggier than your mum's spinach roast."

Clouds rolled in over their heads. The wind picked up, scattering clingfilm and kitchen towels. Kerry glanced back at the strangled river and at the mauve butterwort flowers carried high above the sticky leaves that trapped and digested any insects which flew into their path. She shuddered, looked back at the forest's darkening reach.

"C'mon, Dad. I think it's going to rain again."

*

It did. They'd been back on the forest path for less than half an hour when the rain resumed in earnest, battering against leaf, bark and stone in a restless scale of drumbeats, none louder than the flat fingered taps against the hood of Kerry's cagoule. The path zigzagged through the trees, and instead of white posts there was now only the occasional daub of white paint on a rock or a tree.

"Maybe we should go back, Dad!" She had to shout, and then pull the sodden sides of her hood from her ears to hear his answer.

"We're over halfway! It's just as easy to keep going."

But she could still hear the disappointment in his voice. Disappointment in the weather or in her. It hardly mattered. When they came to a clearing with a wooden footbridge over a stream, Kerry took advantage of the small respite to come alongside her dad and ask the question again.

"Kerry, we're going on. A wee short climb and we'll be at the top."

She looked at the moving fringes of the forest on the other side of the bridge. It was dark and breathing, readying itself to come against her like the oaks of Birnam Wood. "The Heights?"

He gave her an indulgent, condescending smile that made her feel sick and happy all at the same time. "You're not still thinking about what that mad old bastard on the ferry had to say, are you?" He chuckled, already crossing ahead of her. "A hooded figure, for God's sake. How many of them are said to be roaming the countryside at any one time? I'd have been more inclined to believe him if he'd said that *the Crier* wore dungarees and a flat cap."

When Kerry didn't immediately follow, he turned back, splayed his hands wide. "We're *already* in the Heights, Kerry. Have been for hours." He pointed towards the looming forest. "Up there's the summit at High Blind How, that's all. Then we can head back down the other side." His voice moved off as he struggled over the bridge. "And then we can go to Beatrix Potter's house; buy some bloody jam or something."

Kerry followed. There wasn't ever any choice.

This part of the forest did seem much thicker, darker, *alive*. Part of that was doubtless the clouds and the still relentless rain and wind; part of that was also doubtless her mood and perhaps her angry need for it to be. The way quickly became steep again. Her boots slipped and slid in the growing mud, and on more than one occasion she had to grab hold of ferns or branches to keep from falling down or sliding backward. Either side of her, the trees swayed and creaked in the rising wind. Leaves rustled. Coniferous and broadleaf. Laminar, lobular, compound and simple. Short and fat; long and thin. Linear and obtuse – just like people.

"Dad, I don't like this. I don't like this." But of course, she didn't expect him to hear her.

Something dark passed her by – deep in the forest, but seeing her nonetheless, she was sure of it – and she dropped to her knees, squinting left and low. Nothing but that brown/white naked underbrush stretching away into gloom. The feel of a breath on her wet cheek, a hand on her neck. In the instant before she screamed, she heard it. *She heard it.*

Her dad pulled her up. "Kerry? Jesus Christ, Kerry, are you alright?"

She clung to him just long enough for comfort. "I heard him – no, I did, Dad, I heard him!"

"No, you didn't."

She looked off into the forest. "And I saw something." Her dad was looking at her with that same patronising sympathy that he'd reserved for her as a child. Now that look made her a lot of things, but mainly angry. "For fuck's sake, Dad, I saw something!"

He didn't have a go at her for the language, which scared her a little, but that look disappeared in favour of an angry smile. "A deer, you probably saw a bloody deer."

"There's deer here?" Despite herself, she giggled.

"Yes, Kerry, there are deer here. I've seen their fraying marks on the trees."

Kerry had no idea what that meant, but the shadow could have been a deer. That was enough. When her dad said no more and turned around to resume his dogged march up the narrowing path, Kerry followed equally dogged suit. Besides, it wasn't dusk. It wasn't dusk, so it had to have been a deer.

*

Dusk. Definitely dusk. The rain had tapered to a fine drizzle again and the path had dwindled to something less than a track. Kerry's feet ached, their toes blistered inside her new boots. She shivered inside her damp jumper and jeans. The trees either side of the path crowded and jostled for shrinking space, she hadn't been able to even glimpse the lake through them for perhaps more than an hour, and a little voice inside her – a little voice that she hadn't heard from in a long time – said: *It's dusk. It's definitely dusk.*

Her dad hadn't said anything for a long time either. Too long a time. He wasn't even looking at the map anymore. Eventually, she couldn't stand it.

"Dad?"

Up ahead, he stopped. His shoulders slumped. He turned around. "I know. We should be there by now." He ran a hand through his wet hair. "There's a stone trig column just off the main path at the summit, but we must have missed it." That hand ran through his hair again. "I dunno, we must have wandered off the fucking main path at some point though, 'cause we sure as hell aren't still on it."

"Dad?"

"Hey, no, don't worry, Carrot-top. It's a round trip; you can't get lost for long." He smiled at her in the growing gloom.

That little voice now said: *You're going to have to spend the night here. You're going to have to spend the night here in the dark with your dad and the trees and the Crier.*

"Dad, I want to go home! You promised me we'd go back home tonight!"

She couldn't see his face anymore, but she could still make out the bright yellow of his cagoule – and the snap of annoyance that had crept back into his voice.

"And we will. Come on."

They kept on going. Her dad had a torch, but he only switched it on for a couple of minutes. Kerry could understand why. It wasn't yet dark and the torch's dancing spotlight only animated growing shadows. Kerry was frightened. The little voice knew why, but this time stayed quiet. When the rain finally went off completely, the wind swiftly died with it. And all the noises – the noises that they hadn't been able to hear or had attributed to the weather – started making a bad predicament a lot worse. Low creaking, as if the trees were talking to one another. Rustling, scuttling, snapping. The eerie song of birds calling others back to roost. The predators were coming out.

"What was that?"

"It wasn't anything, Kerry, shush."

And then a cry. Definitely a cry.

"Dad, what was *that*?"

She saw her dad stop on the path a few feet ahead. "An animal."

It came again. *Not an animal*, the little voice said, and Kerry was forced to agree. A man. A man standing high, his hands cupping his face. Calling. Not words as such – none she could make out anyway – just calling. For a boat to come across the water? *Stop it.* A joke; a joke for the tourists. Drunk lads at Bowness, maybe even Ferry Nab. Perhaps they had heard her earlier scream. At least it sounded far away. She shivered. Not on the Heights.

"It's someone playing silly beggars, Kerry."

"Yeah."

Her dad began moving again, his boots slapping in and out of the mud. "Fucking ferryman."

Kerry wondered if they would be too late to get a ferry back across now. She thought of the Sawrey Hotel. It no longer seemed quite so appealing; not now they might have to spend the night there.

The echoing call came again – maybe even further away this time.

"Dad, can we stop? Just for a little while. I'm thirsty."

They hunkered down under the vast arms of an old oak tree. Kerry wondered how long it had been alive. Her dad passed her a soggy stack of biscuits and a bottle of water.

"Be careful with that, it's our last." He smiled a bit unsteadily. "It's been raining all bloody day, and we've less than half a bottle between us."

The call came again. Three long bursts of echoing sounds, a little like the shouts of men coming home from the pub while she lay in her bed unable to sleep and looking out at orange stuttering streetlights. Was it closer now?

Her dad reached up and pulled a wet leaved branch down. It shook a little. "Latin name?"

"Dad …"

Again. This one a low, drawn out appeal. More plaintive. *Closer now*, the little voice said.

Kerry drank the water, tried not to choke. "Quercus petraea."

"Kerry, are we okay? I want us to be okay."

"Yes, Dad. I'm just scared. I just want to go home." What she didn't ask was what he meant by 'okay'. Momentarily, the question became bigger than that eerie far off caller – *Crier* or no. Because okay could be one of two very different things. And which did she want? She didn't know anymore. She'd become a teenager and he'd withdrawn his love for her. Did she want it back? Would it be the same? Did she want it to be? And that was the real question that she couldn't answer. The question that she couldn't even ask. Not because she didn't know, but because she thought she did.

And then a movement close behind them – too close behind them. Her dad scrambled forward on his hands and knees, scattering everything wide – map, torch, food, Kerry – and that was what frightened her above all else. Her dad's fear – and the threat of his abandonment. He spun around on his heels, eyes comically wide, and then he hauled her to him and pulled her up.

Her breath. A bird scream. A rush of something. Could it be water? Had she heard water before? *No*, the little voice said. *It's not water.* She tried to say *Dad?*, but she couldn't.

"It's coming!" Her dad's voice sounded completely alien to her: high-pitched and far too young. He'd been just as scared as her all along. He grabbed her hand and started running. She had time enough to pick up the torch – just that – and then they were sprinting through the gathering grey shadows; sliding and stumbling over bracken and buried tree roots, their breath pluming around their heads like a private fog. Something was running alongside them, snapping twigs and branches, and keeping pace as if the forest was nursery-planted instead of wild.

Kerry was sobbing – she thought she was sobbing. The path grew ever more tangled; she got the impression that they were going deeper into a spider's web instead of seeking out its wider fringes. She thought of mayflies trapped inside the butterwort's glutinous leaves.

"Dad!"

And then the call – the *Cry* – louder, deeper, closer. A hand at her neck again? She couldn't let go of the torch, and so wrenched her hand free of her dad's, patting her hair down in trembling, too cold fingers. Nothing there. She stumbled, dropping onto one knee. That rush alongside the path again. The dwindling stampede of her dad's boots. She didn't call out to him. She couldn't. Instead, she rolled off the track into the forest on the other side, clasping the torch to her chest, suffering the scratch of eager branches and thorns, breathing still white, quiet – *quiet!* – breaths.

She couldn't hear anything now, not even her dad. She didn't know what to do, but for now that was a distant consideration; one she hardly cared about.

I'll stay here until the sun comes up. I'll stay here until I can see the lake again. The cry came – both near and far. Soulless now, monotonous, it reminded her of the sound of the lighthouse in 'The Fog'. *Friday DVD nights*, while mum was salsa dancing, the little voice reminded – before her dad had decided he didn't love his daughter anymore. What if the Crier had got him? What if he didn't come back for her? What if he left her alone?

Something moved near to her. On the other side of the path. A deer? She didn't think so. It stopped. All she could hear was the beating of her heart inside her ears. In the fading light she could see little of the forest opposite; nor did she want to move her head to seek a better view.

Go away. Go away. Leave me alone.

Something scratching along the forest floor behind her. Soft, slow. The call came twice again and from two different directions. They bristled that ever sensitive hair on the back of her neck. One was near. Near enough for Kerry to hear the click of a jaw, the swallow of saliva. She screamed, rearing up from her hiding place and stumbling back onto the path. Her dad was standing less than a dozen feet away. He was facing her, his feet planted far apart, body hunched. When he saw Kerry, he pressed a finger to his lips. His other hand was tapping an unnoticed staccato against his thigh. He was looking into the forest on the other side of the path. Kerry looked too.

The Cry shivered down her spine, pulled taut her skin. It was everywhere and nowhere. She couldn't see anything in the forest. She couldn't *see* It. Though the dark had almost replaced the grey dusk, she turned back to her dad and tried to better follow his transfixed stare. His eyes looked like round, black marbles. His eyes scared her most of all.

I'm scared. I'm scared, Dad.

Quite right, the little voice said. *Because It's coming.*

And then she saw something. A shift in the gloom of the forest fringe between her and her dad. A dragged weight. A whispered sigh.

The sound rent the breathless space wide. Not a cry this time, but a scream. A furious, joyous, malignant scream. Something reared out of the forest and onto the path. A fast scuttling horror on hands and knees. Black hidden flanks and pointed hood. The trees moaned, the path trembled, and *It* went on screaming. Scuttling forward and back, forward and back. Undecided.

Kerry's neck cricked and she felt warm wetness trickle down one icy cold thigh. *Not me. Not me.*

The thing ground its teeth. It sounded like sand crushed against stone. Her dad screamed – just once, but high and long. The Crier snapped its neck around, and Kerry crammed her knuckles against her teeth to stop her own scream as it skittered away on the path – horribly clumsy, still horribly *fast* – its scuttling arms and legs working furiously beneath that long black cloak. The last she saw of her dad was a fleeing judder of neon yellow into the darkness of the trees, that terrible shadow following on behind.

Kerry ran. Spitting blood and phlegm, arms outstretched, palms scratched by closing ranks of oaks and pines and hawthorns, she ran until the way became too dark to be certain of any escape at all. She could no longer hear her dad's screams or the Crier's cries, but there was little comfort in that.

She turned on the torch. The little light did little more than champion the dark. Flailing it around her in crazy arcs, the trees loomed closer; the shadows sprang from every corner. Scuttling, teeth grinding horrors lunged for her inside them. Sobbing, she forced the torch's narrow beam onto the path with both hands. As she ran, the light's reach danced wide, but no longer *too* wide, and so she managed to keep on going.

The way became easier, broader. There were no more cries – either near or far. After more time had passed, the way became easier still: levelling out before sloping down instead of up. She was still sobbing, but now her breath came easier to her too and her terror was less unwieldy. The dance of her torch steadied, grew braver. Even as she still ran, it lingered.

The clustered white flowers of meadowsweet. The small lilac and blue wood anemone or windflower. The tiny yellow petals of wood avens, said to ward away evil. Primrose, snowdrop, bluebell. The tubular purple foxgloves swaying close to their spikes. All the profuse ferns: oak, brittle bladder and the robust bracken. Pine trees. Holly, hawthorn, blackthorn, rowan. The low hanging fingers of the silver birch: the Lady of the Woods.

Stumbling free of the forest, the torchlight flashed white across a signpost. Kerry hardly looked at it. *Public Bridleway. Ferry House 2.5mi*

Keep going, the little voice said. She kept going. She remembered a long ago summer spent in St. Andrews. Paddling in the sea, her dad lifting her high above the big waves, while her mum laughed and waved from the beach, taking photos from behind the shelter of a red-striped windbreaker.

A cry came down from the Heights behind and above her. A call that was once more as mournful as it was malign. She shuddered to her soggy, bleeding toes, but she didn't stop.

*

The ferryman found her the next day not much after dawn. Crouched down and folded into a ball against the front of her dad's Fiesta. He carried her onto the ferry and left the car behind. People stared at them both, but he didn't care and she didn't notice. He set her down on a low bench close to the wheelhouse and let her be.

The skipper asked him who she was and the ferryman shrugged.

"Gae yung to be aboot hursel."

The ferryman showed his gums. "Gae yung fer a lot o' things."

*

The sharp breeze off the lake revived her somewhat. Fresh rain stung her skin. As the boat grew closer to Ferry Nab, she turned on her bench. The far off green/brown climb of the Claife Heights dwindled into blurred distance, though she could make out the neon shouts of tourists along the lakeside paths, or climbing up towards the exposed Claife Station and its wide, unblinking eyes.

She finally dropped the torch. It rolled out past the bench and under a nearby car.

Her dad's breath on her cheek, hand on her neck. His smile dimpling his cheeks just like hers did.

I tried, Mum. I tried, but you'll never know.

You only get one dad, honey. Only one. She looked east, towards the low foothills that rose in greener steps towards the high fells in the north. *Thank God for small mercies*, the little voice said.

THE MONSTER OF RENWICK

In 1733 an incident occurred, which left the village of Renwick, near Penrith, stunned.

The old medieval church, which had served Renwick for as long as anyone could remember but which had now been abandoned because it was so severely decayed, was in the process of being demolished – when, from out of its rubble, slithered a creature that many local folk previously believed had only existed in fairy tales.

The cockatrice is one of those nightmarish bogey-beasts of ancient mythology. A horrific hybrid of lizard and cockerel, it was said to be so poisonous that its mere breath could strike a man dead, while to be caught in the full gaze of its terrible eye would be sufficient to turn you to stone. Also known as the 'basilisk', the cockatrice had been a familiar fixture in medieval folk tales. Supposedly, it could only be killed by being forced to gaze upon itself in a mirror – much like the gorgon in Greek legend – or by literally being hacked to pieces and its constituent parts burned to ashes.

Needless to say, in olden times these courageous feats had always been performed by gallant knights, usually encased in armour polished so brightly that the cockatrice's evil powers were reflected on it. Unfortunately, in the year 1733, Renwick – a poor farming community – could boast neither a gallant knight nor a suit of well polished armour.

However, the situation was swiftly resolved when a sturdy countryman named John Tallantire seized the initiative. While his fellow villagers fled in panic, he cut himself the bough of a rowan tree – rowan being famous for its effectiveness against witches, warlocks and other evil beings. By this time, the monster had taken to the wing and was swooping back and forth, eliciting screams from everyone who saw it. There are no reports of any casualties, but this went on for a considerable time before Tallantire caught it a heavy blow, which brought it to the ground, whereon he clubbed it to death.

Numerous witnesses attested to these remarkable events, as can be seen from inscriptions in the parish church at Renwick today. Remains of the animal were not preserved, but it is believed by scholars that something strange was lurking in the ruined church and that the demolition process disturbed it. The ease with which Tallantire actually killed the creature suggests that it was not a cockatrice, but some other unknown animal, maybe an abnormally *large bat. In fact, the occupants of Renwick were later referred to mockingly by their neighbours as 'Renwick Bats', though it wasn't unusual in those days for rural communities to poke fun at each other for acts of foolishness which inevitably grew more and more ridiculous with each telling.*

For years afterwards, there was alarm in the village whenever an unknown flying creature was seen swooping by overhead. Apparently, such incidents continued several times, well into the twentieth century. Even today, the cockatrice has lost none of its power to frighten. Though it is clearly one of those impossible creatures, a monster that existed in fantasy rather than nature, so baleful was its reputation that it rarely even appeared in heraldry or on church architecture, where all types of other grotesques were routinely present. The village of Renwick in Cumbria remains proud to have the only 'authenticated' sighting in the English record.

JEWELS IN THE DUST
Peter Crowther

Dear, beauteous death! the jewel of the just,
Shining nowhere but in the dark;
What mysteries do lie beyond thy dust,
Could man outlook that mark!
From *Silex Scintillans: 'They are all gone'*
Henry Vaughan (1622-1695)

Abigail Rutherford swept into the room in a blaze of maroon cotton and myriad wafts of crinoline scarves whose designs dwarfed even the ambitious creations of Jackson Pollack – comparatively pedestrian efforts as far as Abigail would have it – and whose colours would have rivalled even Joseph's fabled coat.

"Today's the day!" she announced with a bravura wave of an arm that was skinny and wattled, the fingers of the hand at the end slender enough to pick locks, pushing the sweet scent of lavender before her like a summer tide.

Tommy looked up from the comic spread out between his elbows on the floor, the gaudily-coloured pages a mystery of shape and form and secret actions in night-time cities, strangely-garbed and muscular heroes braving death – and worse! – as they swung between concrete towers and over the glittering streets far below. "Really?" he asked, pulling himself to a kneeling position.

"Really!" Abigail confirmed.

"Yay!" said Tommy.

He leapt to his feet and did a little skip and jump around the comic.

"Careful," Marianne Rutherford cautioned her son with a big smile. "You'll be wanting another copy of that magazine if you scuff the pages." She turned to her mother-in-law and tilted her head to one side as she always did when she was offering a change of mind. "Are you sure, Abby? I mean, *really* sure that today's the day? It's just Saturday – a fine August Saturday I grant you, but just another Saturday."

Abigail did a twirl and burst into a fit of coughing which soon spread into laughter. "As sure. As I'll. Ever be," she said, pausing for breaths between each point. She leaned against the wall, smiling at her grandson with thin lips that carried a swipe of lipstick, cheeks that bore the trace of hastily-applied pink-coloured powder, and eyes that carried the sky in them, complete with cotton-candy clouds. "And it's not. Just another. Saturday. It's Rush-Bearing Day."

"Rush-Bearing Day?"

"Rush-Bearing Day!" young Tommy exclaimed, his face a glade of smiles. "The festival they have down in Grasmere. When they bring the rushes into the church. In olden days people had to kneel on a hard floor, and it hurt them. So they started bringing rushes in … like a carpet."

"That's right," Abigail said, her voice not quite able to match the volume of her grandson's. "So, scoot. Young fella me lad," she added, ignoring the quizzical look on her daughter-in-law's face. She clapped her hands as though shooing errant cats busy chewing the plants in her beloved garden, the three rings – Engagement, Wedding and Eternity – giving out the faintest *clink* before settling once more.

"Make haste!" she urged.

"Bring pop. Bring crisps," she advised.

"Run and jump. And greet the day!" she instructed.

Tommy disappeared in a flash, the swinging to and fro of the room door on a steadily decreasing fulcrum the only sign that he had ever been there at all. That and the sound of small feet pounding up the stairs and a small voice calling out to the gods of childhood and eternal summer.

Marianne looked across at the window.

It was still early outside – early in big-wide-world terms, where activities among the wind-blown moors and mountains commenced long before they did inside the farmhouse cottage. Everything was new out there, as though each thing – every glimmering ray of sunlight and every tiny drop of dew – were a one-off, a never-to-be-repeated infinitesimally small theatrical performance. New and only ever *now*.

Inside the cottage, it was different.

Here, within the labyrinth of walls and windows that was the home they all shared, everything was familiar: radio news shows that forever reminded listeners of the time and what the weather was going to be like, and the sound of bacon frying and the kettle whistling on the hob, each mingling with calls for missing neckties, socks and comics, and all of them forever underpinned by the soft sussurant hum put out by the old amalgam of wooden joists and the roof of Westmorland slate stretching itself to meet the onslaught of another day. Every one of them a repeat performance. Like scenes on the video player, rewound and re-played forever without deviation.

Time stolen rather than spent.

Time waiting to die.

To Marianne Rutherford the world outside looked momentarily immense, unpredictable and somehow achingly wonderful, its sound signatures harder to place, complex rhythms and discordant refrains.

A haven.

A release.

An escape.

Marianne turned around and mentally shook off the feeling of cramp unfolding in her stomach as she took in the full creative excess of Abigail's outfit. "That's quite a combination," she said, a mischievous grin on her face as she stood up and planted a kiss on her mother-in-law's cheek. "One thing's for sure: we're not likely to lose you." She took hold of Abigail's shoulders and held her at arm's length. "My my, don't you look the bee's knees!"

Abigail shuddered, her breath coming hoarse and sounding wheezing, deep down inside her body. "The bees' knees. And the cat's pyjamas." She returned the smile and affected a small slap on Marianne's arm. "Got to. Look my. Best. On Rush-Bearing Day," she said between gulps of air. "For Jack."

Marianne fought off the frown that threatened to engulf her face. "Right," she said. "For Jack. On Rush-Bearing Day."

Marianne felt Abigail's bony shoulders stiffen as she turned her back around again, immediately cursing herself when she saw Abby wince and try to cover it up.

In truth, the dress hung awkwardly from Abigail's scrawny frame. It fell all the way to her ankles – ankles puffed up with water from the steroids. Marianne recalled those previous occasions when the dress came out – 'Red letter days,' was how Abby referred to them, by virtue of the fact that the dress was the last present from her beloved Jack – and how, in those suddenly seemingly distant days of another life, the dress extended only to just below Abigail's knees. Then the garment itself had seemed to be alive and proud, like a peacock unfurling its tail-feathers: now it looked equally as tired and spent as its owner.

"Well," she said, backing Abby gently to a chair, "I think you look wonderful and I'm sure Bill is going to think so, too."

Bill came into the room with a big grin on his face. To a degree, it managed to cover the darkness below his eyes. "You making some sandwiches, love? It's the Big Day."

Marianne gave her husband a mock salute. "Yes, Mum already told us. Rush-Bearing Day," she said, with just the slightest of upwards movements of her eyebrows. There had been so many Big Days this last ten months, as the weeks had fallen from the calendar at almost the same rate that the pounds had fallen from Abigail Rutherford's once-ample frame.

November 5th had been the first one, when Abigail had spent the full day out in the garden, taking in the autumn air as she waited to be called to join her beloved Jack. But that night, after the fireworks had finished, as they all sat down to one of Marianne's traditional Bonfire Night feasts, Lancashire hotpot with a thick crust, the table resplendent with corn cobs and red cabbage, sausages rolled in strips of bacon, bowls of peas and carrots with knobs of butter melting over them like flower-heads, and when it was all finished, Parkin cake and treacle, Abigail had announced that she didn't think today was going to be the Big Day after all. Patting her son's arm, she said, "But I expect it'll be soon," her sentences full and flowing, before the tumour eventually took away her breath.

Then Christmas Eve and Christmas Day followed, with New Year's Eve and New Year's Day itself coming on hot behind them. And January saw Plough Monday and the Epiphany . . . but still Abigail made it through to midnight, her carefully-chosen clothes returned to the wardrobe in the small room she occupied in her son's house.

Candlemas came and went and, with it, drifted St. Blaise's Day and Valentine's Day – a particularly fitting one for her and Jack to be reunited, Abigail had thought. By now, the chemo had taken a toll and she was increasingly tired.

Then St. David's Day, and St. Patrick's Day – "Good Christian men," Abigail had proclaimed to Bill, "just like your father. And I reckon that today. Will definitely be. The day he calls for me to join him."

But it hadn't been. Nor had the day the clocks went forward – "That's because. We lost an hour," Abigail had explained as Bill and Marianne had tucked her up in her bed, the shadows playing around the walls like mischievous elves. "Your dad . . . he needs. The full twenty-four hours. To get me." And snuggling down beneath the sheets, she added, "But it'll be. Soon. Easter," she said sleepily. "It was Easter when your dad met me." And she closed her eyes and smiled at the memory. "My, but he was handsome. Still is, for that matter."

By now, the cancer had spread throughout her body. It was just a matter of time.

But Easter turned out not to be the Big Day, though it was the day that the breathing apparatus was delivered to the house and, taking her first swig from the oxygen tank, Abigail winked knowingly at Bill and Marianne. "See, I told you it was going to be a big day today," she confided in them. "Just not *the* Big Day. But it'll be soon. You mark my words. Maybe it'll be the spring bank holiday."

But it wasn't the spring bank holiday, and today, August 5th, the summer bank holiday was only three weeks away. But Abigail seemed convinced. Convinced because it was Rush-bearing Day.

"Sandwiches coming right up," Marianne said, affecting a stiff-handed salute as she opened the icebox. She stared at the shelves of packages and jars, cold cuts, butter cartons and fruit juice bottles, individually wrapped cheeses from the corner shop in Eskdale, tubs of yoghurt and humous, small hillocks of salad greens, cucumber and tomatoes. "What'll it be, oh great one?"

"Everything!" Bill said. "What do you think, Mum?"

Abigail chuckled appreciatively. "Of course ... let's have everything. Let's have ..." She took a deep breath and shuddered. "Let's have sandwiches fit ... for a king and his queen," she said, her words laboured, her hand clenched but for the index finger pointing upwards and circling. "Fit for placing. Before. A visiting. Dignatory. From far-off. Alpha Centauri. Come here to spend. The afternoon." She chuckled and added, "And maybe get a little tan."

Marianne laughed appreciatively.

"Can we have peanut butter?" Tommy asked in a nasal whine as he reappeared laden with more comics. "And jelly?"

"Jelly?" Abigail said, screwing up her face. "Sounds yucky!"

"He means jam," Marianne said as she transferred more of the icebox onto the breakfast counter. "He likes jam with his peanut butter ... oh, and slices of banana."

"Ugh! Revolting!" Abigail said, rolling her eyes around and around at Tommy. "Who'd be nine years old!"

Bill loaded water into the kettle and placed it on the hob. "Let's have coffee, too. Real stuff, not the instant."

"And make it leaded," Abigail added. "None of that decaf. Not today. If I pee myself then at least it'll keep me cool."

"Mum!" Marianne said in time with Tommy's sniggers. She was slicing up a fresh-baked loaf. "I can see where we're heading with this," she said. "It's Decadent Day."

Tommy frowned as he watched his mother work. "I thought it was Rush-Bearing Day," he said to no one in particular.

"It certainly is," Bill said, and he ruffled his son's hair. "What your mum means is that it's both of them. Two days all rolled up in one."

"So what's a deck-a-dent day?"

"Dec-a-dent day." Abigail said before spelling it out and then repeating it as though it were a mantra. She slumped tiredly onto a stool and took a deep breath. "It's a day when. We don't let anything matter, Tommy. A day when. None of the normal rules. Apply."

"I'm not sure that's a good idea, Mum: we have to have ..."

Abigail nodded. "Your father's right, Tommy. We have to have. Rules. Or the world ... well. It just wouldn't. Hang together." She smiled gently at Tommy's father and then quickly looked away. "Everything would just fly off. In confusion. Like . . . *whooosh*!" She swept her arms up in the air to either side and then collapsed forward coughing.

As his father took hold of her and gently patted her back, Tommy said, "You mean like gravity?"

"That's right," Bill said softly between *shh* and *there* and *okay now* sounds as he continued to pat and rub, "like gravity." Eventually the coughing subsided.

"You okay, Gran?" Tommy had thought about it before even asking.

Maybe if she *wasn't* okay they wouldn't even leave the house. And he so wanted to go out and picnic, feel the grass springing up beneath his trainers, trying to get right inside with his toes. It had been such a long time since they'd done anything at all, what with Gran's constant coughing and that tank of air she sucked on while she was watching the soap operas on television.

As he watched her, waiting for a reply, Tommy suddenly noticed – just for the most fleeting of seconds – how thin she'd got; like she could get through doors when they were still closed. It looked to him as though Gran could do with a whole load of peanut butter, banana slices and jam sandwiches to build her up again, and maybe a couple of chocolate spread ones and a carton of vanilla yoghurt or strawberry and caramel mousse from Safeways.

"I'm as fine as wine. And as frisky. As whiskey," came the reply, though it was a little wheezy and not altogether convincing, the memory of a voice rather than the voice itself.

Tommy hoped his father hadn't noticed. He looked around at his mother and saw she was watching him as she loaded cold meats onto buttered bread and spread that gungy brown stuff that had a soppy boy's name – Hugh Muss – and looked like his poops when he was

90

poorly and they were all runny. He saw her smile at him, a strange smile, kind of sad and yet not sad.

Marianne watched her son watching her. For just a second she thought of herself back at nine years old, tried to imagine what the world looked like through those young eyes. "You ready?" she said, breaking the eye lock and placing a cheesy top on a mound of lettuce, sliced ham and pickle. "I'll be done here in a few minutes and we don't want to be waiting while you get things together."

Tommy shrugged and held out the confusion of comic. "I've got stuff to read," he said triumphantly.

"And you've brushed your teeth?"

Tommy thought for a second. What the heck did brushing his teeth matter? They were going out to eat, weren't they? He certainly didn't want all the sandwiches to taste of peppermint. Parents could be a bit daft sometimes.

He nodded. "Before," he added with a jerk of his head. "When I had a wash."

"Clean shorts?"

He looked down at his shorts, saw the dangling figure of Spiderman hanging from his belt, and then noticed the stain on his left leg just below the pocket and the bulge of his Bart Simpson handkerchief. He shifted his leg slightly and lowered the comics to cover it. It wasn't a big stain. "Can we take the frisbee?" he said, changing the subject, and he skilfully shifted the need for an answer from his mother to his father who seemed to have stopped patting and rubbing.

"Can we, dad?"

"Yeah, course. We can do anything today."

"Cos it's a deck-a-dent day, isn't it?"

Everyone seemed to find this amusing and all thoughts of clean shorts went off on the wind.

*

Abigail sat up front alongside Tommy's father, a place usually reserved for his mum. The fact was that Gran was the only one Tommy's dad would let up there, like she was the Queen visiting for the day. There was a lot of huffing and puffing as Bill and Marianne helped Abigail into the seat and fastened the belt across her. There were a couple of *Sorry Mum*s followed each time by *That's okay, son* or *That's okay, Marianne, it's just me being awkward*, and then she was in place, wheezing like Thomas the Tank Engine over at Ravenglass.

Tommy slid into the back of the Nissan, the familiar smell of creased and worn leather drifting up to meet him. He slid his comics onto the shelf behind the seat, tossed the frisbee on top and pulled his cap on tight. "We taking the roof off, dad?"

Bill Rutherford plopped into the driver's seat and looked across at Abigail. "How about it, Mum? You up for a little fresh air?"

Tommy's grandmother patted her son's knee. "Let's go. The whole way. Let's take off the sides. While we're at it ..." She glanced around at Tommy and did that spinning movement with her eyes. "And let's. Let's take off the bonnet. And the boot lid. Let's just strip ourselves. Strip ourselves down. To the bare essentials. What say you, Tommy?"

Tommy chuckled. "Sounds good to me, Gran," he said.

Marianne slid in next to Tommy and put an arm around him. "You think we should?" she said, aiming the question at Tommy's father. "Mum'll get cold."

Tommy saw his father look into the rear view mirror. It was a strange look, aimed at Tommy's mum. It said, this look, that nothing mattered today. Today, nobody was going to get cold. Today, nobody was going to get *any*thing bad.

"Okay," Tommy's mum said, responding to that wordless glance as she pulled her son close, squeezing him under his armpit sending him into paroxysms of wonderful agony. "We'll be fine and dandy back here, curled up like a couple of hibernating bears. *Woo-woo-woo!*" She squeezed him some more.

"Mum ... MUM . . . don't. *Please* don't."

She stopped and Tommy immediately wished she would do it again, but dad had started the engine and the roof was starting back on its pulley system. The summer sky revealed itself in thin slices as the canvas roof whined backward.

Clouds rolled.

Blue shone everywhere.

Birds flew and the air was thick with a million zillion microscopic bugs and midges, each of them bound for distant lands – lands such as the wheelie-bins near the back porch, or the grids beneath the down-pipes at each corner of the cottage. Those things must smell like chocolate syrup to those tiny things, Tommy thought, and just for a moment, he regretted the odd occasion when he had joined in with the other lads in the school playground, removing wings and legs from creatures that wanted nothing more than to be able to languish on a nice turd or dig deep into the potato peelings and teabags inside a bag of rubbish.

The roof reached its destination and gave out a thick grumble. Bill got out, walked to the back of the car and leaned on the canvas, first at one side and then at the other. At Tommy's mother's side, Bill leaned over and gave Marianne a kiss on the cheek. Tommy watched for a second and then looked away. He had seen something in that small affection – he had seen tears in his father's eyes. It made him feel a little anxious – the way he did when Miss Grady announced a surprise maths test and the only homework he'd done had been to catch up on what *The Avengers* were doing in this month's issue.

The comics!

He turned around to the back shelf and saw it was now securely covered by the folded roof. Oh well, he wouldn't need them until they got to where they were going. Which was –

"Where we going anyway?" he asked as his father fastened the seat belt and slipped the gear lever into reverse.

"Good point," Bill said over his shoulder as the car drifted back out of the drive and onto the road along the front of the house. "Where'd you think, love?"

Marianne didn't answer right away. Tommy turned to look up at her and he saw that she too had those same tears in her eyes. "Well, it's got to be Mum's choice," she said. "It's her day, after all."

Tommy leaned forward and stood up behind Abigail's seat. "Where we going, Gran?"

Abigail looked across at her son and, in a soft voice, she said, "All the way. We're going. All the way. Today."

Bill smiled and swallowed hard.

Tommy leaned forward. "*Where* we going, Gran?"

Abigail slapped her knees and breathed in deeply. "Well, I think we should go up to Elter Water." She shifted around so she could see Tommy's face. "It's lovely up there, and it's nice and sunny today, so you can go paddling."

"Oh, yes!"

Abigail closed her eyes and laughed. "Yes indeed!"

Tommy knelt up on the seat and leaned on the folded roof as they backed out onto the road. Then, with a slight clunk of gears meshing, they were on their way. He watched the road dovetail onto itself, cars parked at the roadside shifting by and coming together as they moved further away from the house.

*

"Love?"

"Yeah?"

"Is she asleep?"

Bill looked to his side at the crumpled-up figure. "I think so."

"So's Tommy." Marianne stroked a lick of hair from her son's forehead. "She okay d'you think?"

Bill shrugged. "Right now, all we can say is she's here."

He kept his eyes on the road as they headed down from the Wrynose Pass into Little Langdale. "You know," he said. "I started thinking this morning."

"Sounds ominous."

"No, nothing too … nothing too morbid."

"This while you were still in bed? I woke up at one point and could tell you were awake."

"How could you tell I was awake?"

"I don't know," Marianne said, suddenly wondering how it was that she *did* know but totally convinced that she did. "Your breathing changes when you're awake."

Bill was silent for a minute and then said, "No, it was while I was shaving."

"Mmm. And what were you thinking?"

He made a sound that was part laugh and part apology for what he was about to say. "I was thinking about now … the absolute now that we have right at this very instant."

"While you were shaving, you were thinking about us in the car?"

"No, I was thinking about the now that I had *then*."

Marianne glanced down at Tommy and shifted her arm. Tommy grunted and moved closer to her.

"I was thinking about *all* the nows, every single nanosecond of time that we close our eyes to because we're thinking about what's coming along, either looking forward to it or …" His voice trailed off.

Marianne reached out a hand and rubbed her husband's neck.

"I was thinking about how, when we have everything we could possibly want in the world and we're with the people we so dearly want to be with, about how … oh, it sounds daft."

"No, it doesn't. Go on. Tell me what you were thinking."

"Well, I was thinking wouldn't it be great if we could just freeze that frame. If we could just stop everything from moving on and changing."

94

"You mean ..." Marianne glanced at the back of Abigail's head and heard a soft snore. "You mean Mum?"

"Yes, but more than that. Everything."

"What else is there? What else is bothering you, love?"

"That's just it. Nothing was bothering me. And then ..." He nodded sideways at Abigail, " ... we had the visit to the doctor, then to the hospital, and then the operation, and the radiotherapy, and then – now – the shortness of breath, another visit to the doctor, the x-ray ... and here we are. Waiting."

They had been told that Abigail had three to six months, though the likelihood was that it would be closer to three. Then, as the breathing worsened, even that prognosis seemed to be a little overly optimistic. They were looking at weeks, the doctor had told them, Abigail nodding, a small smile of acceptance on her lips.

"I'm not sure I'm foll ..."

"Well, it was all that – *all* that – that kind of started me thinking about how brief it all is. The time we have, you know? But how, if we added every single fraction of time together and truly appreciated it, life would be almost endless." He slowed to negotiate the busy streets of Elterwater village.

"But it still wouldn't *be* endless," Marianne said. "Mum, and *my* mum and dad ... they wouldn't always be with us. And Tommy would still grow older and he'd still find his own life and his own adventures."

"Yes, I suppose that's it."

"What's it?"

"What you said . . . about adventures. That's what life is, just one big adventure."

"Oh, love," Marianne said, her voice soft and low. "It'll all work out okay."

Tommy sat up quickly, his head narrowly missing Marianne's chin, and said, "We here yet?"

Bill turned the wheel and moved through a gap in the traffic, the car juddering as it moved onto the rough track leading down to the lakeside. "Almost," he said. "Couple more minutes."

*

She could feel him in the car right next to her, smell his cologne and the grease he used to put on his hair. But she knew that if she opened her eyes he wouldn't be there. There would only be the car, and her

95

son and Marianne and Tommy, and outside the window it would be a world where her husband no longer existed.

Oh, Jack, she thought, squeezing her eyes tight, *I'm causing them such sadness.*

They love you, Abby. The wind whispering through her hearing aid sounded just like his voice. Sounded just the way he always spoke to her. *Be happy with that. Your time will come. And it won't be ...*

She felt small hands on her shoulder, rubbing it gently. "Gran? You awake?"

She lifted her head to make out she'd just woken up and hadn't heard the conversation her son and Marianne had been having but the truth of the matter was she didn't sleep too well now, and her dreams – such as they were – were filled with images of the cancer turning itself over and over inside of her.

"I definitely am awake," she said. She turned to look across the lakeside meadows and, just for a second, she thought she could see a party of young girls clad in green and white gowns, their hair filled with summer blooms, carrying a white sheet between them. But it must have been the sunlight through the trees and refracting through the window glass, because there were no girls and there was no sheet.

"We parking down by the lake, love?" Marianne asked.

Bill didn't speak.

"Love?"

"Oh, yes, sorry. I was just thinking how deserted it is."

"And on Rush-Bearing Day, too!" Tommy added. "Maybe everyone's gone somewhere else."

It was true. Since they had pulled onto the dirt track leading down to the lakeside parking area, they had not seen another car nor even walkers out in their boots and backpacks.

"It's nice. It's not – " Abigail ventured stiltedly, " – too crowded."

But there *were* people there, weren't there? She could see them . . . there behind the trees and just around back of the bushes . . . could see their smart jackets and ties, the occasional flash of a flower-patterned dress, the tall outline of a church banner dangling with ribbons. She squinted her eyes and concentrated but the lake shores were empty.

Bill pulled the Nissan up onto the grass a few yards up from the lake. The air was filled with the sounds of summer, of sunshine and of water lapping on the ancient stones of the lakebed. Bill got out and pulled the seat forward for Marianne before going around to let Abigail out. Tommy ran his feet on the carpet like a train, his hand clasped on the bright yellow frisbee and his lungs greedily gulping in the outside air.

"Just hold your horses there a minute, pal, while we get your Gran out," Bill chided.

Marianne went around to the trunk and got out the hamper, setting it down beside her on the grass. Then she lifted a pile of old sheets and rugs.

Tommy pushed the now vacant seat forward and made to slide out but the sight of his father holding onto his Gran stopped him in his tracks.

Bill held onto Abigail tightly and Tommy could see her thin arms dithering from side to side, like a butterfly not sure of whether it wanted to settle on this flower or maybe this one, and her hair blowing in thin wisps in the gentle breeze.

"You okay, Mum?"

"I'm fine, love," came the reply. "Just as fine as wine."

"Not too cold?"

Now with a firm hold on the Nissan's door, Abigail straightened up and smoothed out Tommy's dad's collar. The smile she gave him was a secret smile, knowing and sad. Tommy frowned and though he hadn't made so much as even the tiniest noise, both of them turned to look at him. "We're just fine," she answered, with that big grin and a hunch-up of her shoulders that suggested being a part – along with her grandson – of some great and exciting plan. "Aren't we, Tommy?"

"We sure are," Tommy agreed, and just to prove it, he lofted the frisbee high into the sky, tracing its path with his hand over his eyes as though he were saluting it.

"Tommy," Marianne shouted, "will you come and take some things, please? Let's get this picnic sorted!"

*

Jack came to see his wife after they had eaten.

Bill had gone down to the lake's edge with Tommy, and Marianne – who had started out with such fine intentions to read the daily newspaper – had succumbed to the after-effects of the food and the sunshine, her eyelids drooping slowly until they had closed completely.

Abigail watched her son and grandson while she listened to their distant voices, mingled in with the sound of her own breathing and Marianne's soft snores. It was as though they were in a different world, the two men – a world that Abigail was able to look into and hear but one which she could not actually visit.

He's a fine boy, Jack said hunkering down beside her.

"Heaven's sake!" Abigail said, the words coming out as a hiss, her hand up to the collar on her sweater, fingers trembling over the chain he had bought her those many long years ago.

Shh! he whispered, glancing at Marianne.

"You gave. Me a start," Abigail said.

He shifted around so that he was in front of her and smiled. *You look as handsome as ever, Abby . . . very handsome, if you don't mind my saying.* His eyes travelled up and down her form and Abby felt a blush starting in her cheeks. *You're wearing my dress*, he said.

"Of course!"

You look . . . beautiful.

Abigail shook her head and made to reach out to him. But Jack pulled away. *Ah ah*, he said, *that's not in the rules.*

"Can't I. Touch you?"

He made a tight-lipped mouth and shook his head, his eyes mischievous as ever. *Not yet, anyways.*

"But I thought – " She lowered her voice when Marianne shuffled onto her side. "I thought. You'd come. For me. I thought. Today. Was the day. The special day."

All days are special, Abby. What's so different about this one?

"Well, I thought you'd come for me today." She hung her head down and said, "I'm ill, Jack. Terribly ill."

I know that, Abby.

"I'm going. To die."

Yes, you are.

"And soon."

Right again. Soon. But not today.

Abigail looked up at her husband and just for a second, he looked seventeen years old again and then he was thirty-something. Then in his fifties. Then he was a young chap of two. Seemed like he couldn't stay put for more than a minute at a time.

"So when – " she asked, " – exactly?"

Jack shrugged. The sound of laughter drifted over from the lake and Jack and Abigail turned to look. Tommy was doubled up in hysterics pointing at his father. Bill was standing pulling up his trousers – even from here they could see that Bill had somehow finished up in the water.

They're going to come back, Jack said, turning back to face her. *I have to go.*

"But you didn't. You didn't. Answer me, Jack. When?"

I don't rightly know, Abby. But someday soon. Maybe tomorrow; maybe next week . . . He shrugged again. *Like I say, soon. But it might not be a day that has anything written beneath it on the calendar. There'll be nothing special about it.* He looked back at Bill and Tommy, slowly making their way up the embankment towards them. *And certainly nothing special about it for them.*

With Jack's attention momentarily distracted from her, Abigail wondered whether she could shoot out her hand and take a hold of her husband's wrist . . . whether doing so – her living skin joining up with the her husband's ghost's – might mean she would die right there and then.

But the laughter drifted up to her and into her head like the fizzy bubbles from a bottle of lemonade, and she turned, her hand halfway out in front of her but stopped short of its target. Bill waved to her and she raised her hand and waved back, feeling suddenly weak but somehow strong as well.

"They can't see you," she said as she looked back at him.

Jack nodded. *But I'm going to have to go anyway.*

"Do you. Do you have to?"

He nodded again, this time with a deep sadness etched into his face – his seventy eight-year-old face, the one she had watched those years ago, lying so still on her pillow as he drifted away from her, his hand locked in hers as he fought to stay another few minutes.

Like I said, Abby, all days are special. And, right now, these last days you're spending with Bill and his lovely wife and that fine boy . . . these days are special to them. These days are like small gems . . . like jewels in the dust. Make them count. Every single one of them.

And then he reached out and touched her cheek.

Fire and ice.

Soft and hard.

Dark and light.

A thousand sensations shot through Abigail Rutherford's face and coursed up and down her body, setting her fingers to tingle and her toes to curl.

I was never real good with rules, he said.

"I love you so much, Jack," she said, her words coming out in a stream without any pauses for breath.

I love you, too Abby. I always will. And then he was gone.

Tommy was the first one to appear, the sound of his pounding feet waking Marianne in a fluster.

"What's the matter? What's happened?"

"Dad – " Tommy could hardly speak from a mixture of exertion and laughter. "Dad fell in the lake!"

"I didn't fall in the-"

Marianne got to her feet. "Bill? Are you okay, darling?"

"I'm fine." He flapped his trousers at her and gave a weak smile. "Paddled out a little too deep, that's all."

"You should've seen him, Mum! Gran, you should have – "

Abigail nodded and made a mock-scowl. "He was never. Very good. On his feet. Your father," she said. She pulled the blanket from around her shoulders and threw it over towards her son. "You make sure. They're dry. You'll catch. Rheumatics."

Tommy frowned. "Room attics?"

"Quiet now, Tommy. Let's get your father dried and back home."

Drying his feet while Marianne and Tommy loaded the picnic things into the boot, Bill sensed he was being watched. He shook his head. "Could've happened to anyone, Mum," he said.

"I know. But it was. Always you. It happened to."

He wiped out his shoes and, pulling a face, slipped them onto his feet.

"You had a nice time?"

She nodded emphatically. "I've had a wonderful time."

"How you feeling?"

She lifted a hand to her cheek and rubbed the spot where Jack had touched it. It felt warm. Special.

"I'm feeling. Just fine," she said. "It's been. A great day."

Bill nodded and, just for a second, he frowned.

She reached out then and took her son's hand. "A special day."

For the rest of her life – a rich, happy and fulfilled life . . . and one which turned out to be a little longer than she had once hoped – Abigail Rutherford treated *every* day as a special day, savouring every minute and every hour as though it truly was her last.

Which, of course, is what we all should do.

THE DEVIL'S HOLE

n the 1840s, a desperate convict escaped from a prison work-farm on the moors north of Swaledale. For three days he headed west across country, finally hiding on the forested shores of the River Eden, near Kirkby Stephen. He was a very dangerous man who had originally been imprisoned for breaking into houses to steal valuables and beating their owners within an inch of their lives, so there was great urgency to recapture him. Armed and mounted prison officers, with packs of bloodhounds and even the support of local militia units, came in pursuit.

The escaped criminal was cunning and resourceful, but he was soon tired and hungry. It was February and bitterly cold. It rained incessantly and there was almost nothing to live on from the land. At last, feeling cornered by his pursuers and knowing that, after leading them such a merry dance, it would go hard for him if he was caught, he clambered down into a deep gorge, and insinuated himself into the abyss known as Coop Kernel Hole, into which powerful cataracts poured from the overflowing river.

The manhunt was now foundering in the worsening weather. Winter storms were howling across the land; raindrops fell like pellets of ice. With no reports that any of the villages or remote cottages in this region had been attacked, the decision was reached that the villain had either made good his escape or had died from exposure to the elements. A few of the prison officers made a last search of the river shore before heading for home, whereupon they were astonished to find the man they had been chasing tottering along a path towards them, a bedraggled and gibbering wreck. He fell on his knees when he saw them, begging to be taken back into custody but first to a parson or minister, as he had a great weight of sins to clear from his soul.

The prison officers were bemused that such a hardy individual could be reduced to this wretched state. The weather was foul, but this man was known to be tough and incorrigible. They refused to do as he asked until he told them what had happened, to which he readily agreed. They took him to some shelter, where they provided him with fire and warm brandy. With shaking voice, he told them that he had worked his way down to the very bottom of Coop Kernel Hole. He didn't know how deep it was, but he was sure he was in the very bowels of the Earth. At which point he was assailed by the most frightful sounds: a thunderous grinding as of colossal machinery, accompanied by screams, cries and wails. He listened to it for several minutes, his blood running cold, before it struck him that these were the lamentations of the damned.

He had climbed down to the very cusp of Hell itself.

The prison officers assumed the fellow had lost his mind through hunger and deprivation, and he was sent back to prison in a police-ambulance. Before they departed, two curious officers climbed down into Coop Kernel Hole themselves. In the very depths of that terrible cavern, they too heard eerie sounds – an immense crashing and grinding of rocks. But no shrieks, screams or voices begging for relief. They soon put this down to the echoing roars of the cataract, as it spilled from one hollowed out level to the next.

On re-ascending to the surface, they congratulated themselves on having a good tale to tell their work-mates, only to be confronted by a shepherd, who was startled to see where they had emerged from. They explained what had happened. The shepherd did not laugh as they'd expected, but told them Coop Kernel Hole had long been known in these parts as the Devil's Grinding Mill because of the strange and frightening sounds that often issued from it.

ABOVE THE WORLD
Ramsey Campbell

Nobody was at Reception when Knox came downstairs. The dinner-gong hung mute in its frame; napkin pyramids guarded dining-tables; in the lounge, chairs sat emptily. Nothing moved except fish in the aquarium, fluorescent gleams amid water that bubbled like lemonade. The visitors' book lay open on the counter. He riffled the pages idly, seeking his previous visit. A Manchester address caught his attention: but the name wasn't his – not any longer. The names were those of his wife and the man.

It took him a moment to realise. They must have been married by then. So the man's name had been Tooley, had it? Knox hadn't cared to know. He was pleased to find that he felt nothing but curiosity. Why had she returned here – for a kind of second honeymoon, to exorcise her memories of him?

When he emerged, it was raining. That ought to wash the fells clean of all but the dedicated walkers; he might be alone up there – no perambulatory radios, no families marking their path with trailing children. Above the hotel mist wandered among the pines, which grew pale and blurred, a spiky frieze of grey, then solidified, regaining their green. High on the scree slope, the Bishop of Barf protruded like a single deformed tooth.

The sight seemed to halt time, to turn it back. He had never left the Swan Hotel. In a moment Wendy would run out, having had to go back for her camera or her rucksack or something. "I wasn't long, was I? The bus hasn't gone, has it? Oh dear, I'm sorry." Of course these impressions were nonsense: he'd moved on, developed since his marriage, defined himself more clearly – but it cheered him that his memories were cool, disinterested. Life advanced relentlessly, powered by change. The Bishop shone white only because climbers painted the pinnacle each year, climbing the steep scree with buckets of whitewash from the Swan.

Here came the bus. It would be stuffed with wet campers slow as turtles, their backs burdened with tubular scaffolding and enormous rucksacks. Only once had he suffered such a ride. Had nothing changed? Not the Swan, the local food, the unobtrusive service, the long white seventeenth-century building which had so charmed Wendy. He had a table to himself; if you wanted to be left alone, nobody would bother you. Tonight there would be venison, which he hadn't tasted since his honeymoon. He'd returned determined to enjoy the Swan and the walks, determined not to let memories deny him those pleasures – and he'd found his qualms were groundless.

He strode down the Keswick road. Rain rushed over Bassenthwaite Lake and tapped on the hood of his cagoule. Why did the stone wall ahead seem significant? Had Wendy halted there once, because the wall was singing? "Oh look, aren't they beautiful." As he stooped towards the crevice, a cluster of hungry beaks had sprung out of the darkness, gaping. The glimpse had unnerved him: the inexorable growth of life, sprouting everywhere, even in stone. Moss choked the silent crevice now.

Somehow that image set him wondering where Wendy and the man had died. Mist had caught them, high on one or other of the fells; they'd died of exposure. That much he had heard from a friend of Wendy's, who had grown aloof from him and who had seemed to blame him for entrusting Wendy to an inexperienced climber – as if Knox should have taken care of her even after the marriage! He hadn't asked for details. He'd felt relieved when Wendy had announced that she'd found someone else. Habit, familiarity and introversion had screened them from each other well before they'd separated.

He was passing a camp in a field. He hadn't slept in a tent since early in his marriage, and then only under protest. Rain slithered down bright canvas. The muffled voices of a man and a woman paced him from tent to tent. Irrationally, he peered between the tents to glimpse them – but it must be a radio programme. Though the voices sounded intensely engrossed in discussion, he could distinguish not a word. The camp looked deserted. Everyone must be under canvas, or walking.

By the time he reached Braithwaite village, the rain had stopped. Clouds paraded the sky; infrequent gaps let out June sunlight, which touched the heights of the surrounding fells. He made for the cafe at the foot of the Whinlatter Pass – not because Wendy had loved the little house, its homemade cakes and its shelves of books, but for something to read: he would let chance choose his reading. But the shop was closed. Beside it Coledale Beck pursued its wordless watery monologue.

Should he climb Grisedale Pike? He remembered the view from the summit, of Braithwaite and Keswick the colours of pigeons, white and grey amid the palette of fields. But climbers were toiling upwards towards the intermittent sun. Sometimes the spectacle of plodding walkers, fell boots creaking, sticks shoving at the ground, red faces puffing like trains in distress, made his climb seem a mechanical compulsion, absurd and mindless. Suppose the height was occupied by a class of children, heading like lemmings for the edge?

He'd go back to Barf: that would be lonely – unless one had Mr Wainwright's guidebook, Barf appeared unclimbable. Returning through the village, he passed Braithwaite post office. That had delighted Wendy – a house just like the other small white houses in the row, except for the counter and grille in the front hall, beside the stairs. A postcard came fluttering down the garden path. Was that a stamp on its corner, or a patch of moss? Momentarily he thought he recognised the handwriting – but whose did it resemble? A breeze turned the card like a page. Where a picture might have been there was a covering of moss, which looked vaguely like a blurred view of two figures huddled together. The card slid by him, into the gutter, and lodged trembling in a grid, brandishing its message. Impulsively he made a grab for it – but before he could read the writing, the card fell between the bars.

He returned to the road to Thornthwaite. A sheen of sunlight clung to the macadam brows; hedges dripped dazzling silver. The voices still wandered about the deserted campsite, though now they sounded distant and echoing. Though their words remained inaudible, they seemed to be calling a name through the tents.

At Thornthwaite, only the hotel outshone the Bishop. As Knox glanced towards the coaching inn, Wendy appeared in his bedroom window. Of course it was a chambermaid – but the shock reverberated through him, for all at once he realised that he was staying in the room which he had shared with Wendy. Surely the proprietress of the Swan couldn't have intended this; it must be coincidence. Memories surged, disconcertingly vivid – collapsing happily on the bed after a day's walking, making love, not having to wake alone in the early hours. Just now, trudging along the road, he'd thought of going upstairs to rest. Abruptly he decided to spend the afternoon in walking.

Neither the hard road nor the soggy margin of Bassenthwaite Lake tempted him. He'd climb Barf, as he had intended. He didn't need Mr Wainwright's book; he knew the way. Wendy had loved those handwritten guidebooks; she'd loved searching through them for the self-portrait of Mr Wainwright which was always hidden among the hand-drawn views – there he was, in Harris tweed, overlooking Lanthwaite Wood. No, Knox didn't need those books today.

The beginning of the path through Beckstones larch plantation was easy. Soon he was climbing beside Beckstones Gill, his ears full of its intricate liquid clamour as the stream tumbled helplessly downhill, confined in its rocky groove. But the path grew steep. Surely it must have been elsewhere that Wendy had run ahead, mocking his slowness, while he puffed and cursed. By now most of his memories resembled anecdotes he'd overheard or had been told – blurred, lacking important details, sometimes contradictory.

He rested. Around him larches swayed numerous limbs, engrossed in their tethered dance. His breath eased; he ceased to be uncomfortably aware of his pulse. He stumped upwards, over the path of scattered slate. On both sides of him, ferns protruded from decay. Their highest leaves were bound into a ball, like green caterpillars on stalks.

A small rock-face blocked the path. He had to scramble across to the continuation. Lichen made the roots of trees indistinguishable from the rock. His foot slipped; he slithered, banging his elbow, clutching for handholds. Good Lord, the slope was short, at worst he would turn his ankle, he could still grab hold of rock, in any case someone was coming, he could hear voices vague as the stream's rush that obscured them. At last he was sure he was safe, though at the cost of a bruised hip. He sat and cursed his pounding heart. He didn't care who heard him – but perhaps nobody did, for the owners of the voices never appeared.

He struggled upwards. The larches gave way to spruce firs. Fallen trunks splintered like bone hindered his progress. How far had he still to climb? He must have laboured half a mile by now; it felt like more. The forest had grown oppressive. Elaborate lichens swelled brittle branches; everywhere he looked, life burgeoned parasitically, consuming the earth and the forest, a constant and ruthless renewal. He was sweating, and the clammy chill of the place failed to cool him.

Silence seized him. He could hear only the restless creaking of trees. For a long time he had been unable to glimpse the Swan; the sky was invisible too, except in fragments caged by branches. All at once, as he climbed between close banks of mossy earth and rock, he yearned to reach the open. He felt suffocated, as though the omnipresent lichen were thick fog. He forced himself onward, panting harshly.

Pain halted him – pain that transfixed his heart and paralysed his limbs with shock. His head felt swollen, burning, deafened by blood.

Beyond that uproar, were there voices? Could he cry for help? But he felt that he might never draw another breath.

As suddenly as it had attacked him, the pain was gone, though he felt as if it had burned a hollow where his heart had been. He slumped against rock. His ears rang as though metal had been clapped over them. Oh God, the doctor had been right; he must take things easy. But if he had to forgo rambling, he would have nothing left that was worthwhile. At last he groped upwards out of the dank trough of earth, though he was still light-headed and unsure of his footing. The path felt distant and vague.

He reached the edge of the forest without further mishap. Beyond it, Beckstones Gill rushed over broken stones. The sky was layered with grey clouds. Across the stream, on the rise to the summit, bracken shone amid heather.

He crossed the stream and climbed the path. Below him the heathery slope plunged towards the small valley. A few crumbs of boats floated on Bassenthwaite. A constant quivering ran downhill through the heather; the wind dragged at his cagoule, whose fluttering deafened him. He felt unnervingly vulnerable, at the mercy of the gusts. He face had turned cold as bone. Sheep dodged away from him. Their swiftness made his battle with the air seem ridiculous, frustrating. He had lost all sense of time before he reached the summit – where he halted, entranced. At last his toil had meaning.

The world seemed laid out for him. Light and shadow drifted stately over the fells, which reached towards clouds no vaster than they. Across Bassenthwaite, fells higher than his own were steps on the ascent to Skiddaw, on whose deceptively gentle outline gleamed patches of snow. A few dots, too distant to have limbs, crept along that ridge. The fells glowed with all the colours of foliage, grass, heather, bracken, except where vast tracts of rock broke through. Drifts of shadow half absorbed the colours; occasional sunlight renewed them.

The landscape was melting; he had to blink. Was he weeping, or had the wind stung his eyes? He couldn't tell; the vastness had charmed away his sense of himself. He felt calm, absolutely unselfconscious. He watched light advancing through Beckstones Plantation, possessing each successive rank of foliage. When he gazed across the lake again, that sight had transfigured the landscape.

Which lake was that on the horizon? He had never before noticed it. It lay like a fragment of slate, framed by two fells dark as storms –

but above it, clouds were opening. Blue sky shone through the tangle of grey; veils of light descended from the ragged gap. The lake began to glow from within, intensely calm. Beyond it fields and trees grew clear, minute and luminous. Yes, he was weeping.

After a while he sat on a rock. Its coldness was indistinguishable from his own stony chill. He must go down shortly. He gazed out for a last view. The fells looked smooth, alluringly gentle; valleys were trickles of rock. He held up his finger for a red bus to crawl along. Closer to him, red dots were scurrying; ladybirds, condemned to explore the maze of grass-blades, to change course at each intersection. Their mindless urgency dismayed him.

They drew his gaze to the heather. He gazed deep into a tangled clump, at the breathtaking variety of colours, the intricacies of growth. As many must be hidden in each patch of heather: depths empty of meaning, and intended for no eye. All around him plants reproduced shapes endlessly: striving for perfection, or compelled to repeat themselves without end? If his gaze had been microscopic, he would have seen the repetitions of atomic particles, mindlessly clinging and building, possessed by the compulsion of matter to form patterns.

Suddenly it frightened him – he couldn't tell why. He felt unsafe. Perhaps it was the mass of cloud which had closed overhead like a stone lid. The colours of the summit had turned lurid, threatening. He headed back towards the wood. The faces of sheep gleamed like bone – he had never noticed before how they resembled munching skulls. A group of heads, chewing mechanically, glared white against the sky and kept their gaze on him.

He was glad to cross the stream, though he couldn't feel the water. He must hurry down before he grew colder. The hush of the woods embraced him. Had a sheep followed him? No, it was only the cry of a decaying trunk. He slipped quickly down the path, which his feet hardly seemed to touch.

The movement of silver-green lattices caged him. Branches and shadows swayed everywhere, entangled. The tips of some of the firs were luminously new. Winds stalked the depths of the forest, great vague forms on creaking stilts. Scents of growth and decay accompanied him. When he grabbed a branch to make sure of his footing, it broke, scattering flakes of lichen.

Again the forest grew too vivid; the trees seemed victims of the processes of growth, sucked dry by the lichen which at the same time lent them an elaborate patina of life. Wherever he looked, the forest seemed unbearably intricate. How, among all that, could he glimpse initials? Somehow they had seized his attention before he knew what they were. They were carved on a cracked and wrinkled tree: Wendy's initials and the man's.

Or were they? Perhaps they were only cracks in the bark. Of course she and the man might well have climbed up here – but the more Knox squinted, the less clear the letters seemed. He couldn't recapture the angle of vision at which they had looked unmistakable.

He was still pacing back and forth before the trunk, as though trapped in a ritual, when stealthy movement made him turn. Was it the shifting of grey trees beneath the lowering largely unseen sky? No – it was a cloud or mist, descending swiftly from the summit, through the woods.

He glanced ahead for the path – and, with a shock that seemed to leave him hollow, realised that it was not there. Nor was it visible behind him as far back as the wall of mist. His reluctant fascination with the forest had lured him astray. He strode back towards the mist, hushing his doubts. Surely the path couldn't be far. But the mist felt thick as icy water, and blinded him. He found himself slithering on decay towards a fall which, though invisible, threatened to be steep. A grab at a crumbling trunk saved him; but when he'd struggled onto safer ground, he could only retreat towards the tree which he had thought was inscribed.

He must press on, outdistancing the mist, and try to head downwards. Wasn't there a forest road below, quite close? But whenever he found an easy slope, it would become abruptly dangerous, often blocked by treacherous splintered logs. He was approaching panic. As much as anything, the hollow at the centre of himself dismayed him. He had intended to welcome it when it had grown there, in his marriage and afterwards; it had seemed safe, invulnerable. Now he found he had few inner resources with which to sustain himself.

The mist was only yards away. It had swallowed all the faint sounds of the wood. If he could only hear the stream, or better still a human voice, a vehicle on the forest road – if only he had gone back to the hotel for his whistle and compass – But there was a sound. Something was blundering towards him. Why was he indefinably distressed, rather than heartened?

Perhaps because the mist obscured it as it scuttled down the slope towards him; perhaps because it sounded too small for an adult human being, too swift, too lopsided. He thought of a child stumbling blindly down the decayed slope. But what child would be so voiceless? As it tumbled limping through the mist, Knox suppressed an urge to flee. He saw the object stagger against a misty root, and collapse there. Before he had ventured forward he saw that it was only a rucksack.

Yet he couldn't quite feel relieved. The rucksack was old, discoloured and patched with decay; mist drained it of colour. Where had it come from? Who had abandoned it, and why? It still moved feebly, as though inhabited. Of course there was a wind: the mist was billowing. Nevertheless he preferred not to go closer. The blurred tentative movements of the overgrown sack were unpleasant, somehow.

Still, perhaps the incident was opportune. It had made him glance upwards for an explanation. He found none – but he caught sight of a summit against the clouds. It wasn't Barf, for between the confusion of trees he could just distinguish two cairns, set close together. If he could reach them, he ought to be able to see his way more clearly. Was he hearing muffled voices up there? He hoped so, but hadn't time to listen.

He wasn't safe yet. The mist had slowed, but was still pursuing him. The slope above him was too steep to climb. He retreated between the trees, avoiding slippery roots which glistened dull silver, glancing upwards constantly for signs of the path. For a while he lost sight of the unknown summit. Only a glimpse of the cairns against the darkening sky mitigated his panic. Were they cairns, or figures sitting together? No, they were the wrong colour for people.

Above him the slope grew steeper. Worse, twilight was settling like mist into the woods. He glared downhill, but the fall was dim and precipitous; there was no sign of a road, only the grey web of innumerable branches. He groped onward, careless of his footing, desperate to glimpse a way. Surely a path must lead to the cairns. But would he reach it before dark? Could he heave himself up the slope now, using trees for handholds? Wait: wasn't that a path ahead, trailing down between the firs? He stumbled forward, afraid to run in case he slipped. He reached out to grab a tree, to lever himself past its trap of roots. But his fingers recoiled – the encrusted glimmering bark looked unnervingly like a face.

He refused to be reminded of anyone. He clung to the hollow within himself and fought off memories. Yet, as he passed close to the next tree, he seemed to glimpse the hint of a face composed of cracks in the bark, and of twilight. His imagination was conspiring with the dimness, that was all – but why, as he grasped a trunk to thrust himself onward, did each patch of lichen seem to suggest a face? The more closely he peered, enraged by his fears, the smaller

110

and more numerous the swarming faces seemed. Were there many different faces, or many versions of a couple? Their expressions, though vague, seemed numerous and disturbing.

For a moment he was sure that he couldn't back away – that he must watch until the light was entirely gone, must glimpse faces yet smaller and clearer and more numerous. Panic hurled him away from the lichen and sent him scrabbling upwards. His fingers dug into decay; ferns writhed and snapped when he grabbed them; the surrounding dimness teemed with faces. He kicked himself footholds, gouged the earth with his heels. He clutched at roots, which flaked, moist and chill. More than once he slithered back into the massing darkness. But his panic refused to be defeated. At last, as twilight merged the forest into an indistinguishable crowd of dimness, he scrambled up a slope that had commenced to be gentle, to the edge of the trees.

As soon as he had done so, his triumph collapsed beneath dismay. Even if he glimpsed a path from the summit, night would engulf it before he could make his way down. The sky was blackening. Against it loomed two hunched forms, heads turned to him. Suddenly joy seized him. He could hear voices – surely the sound was more than the muttering of wind. The two forms were human. They must know their way down, and he could join them.

He scrambled upwards. Beyond the trees, the slope grew steep again; but the heather provided easy holds, though his clambering felt almost vertical. The voices had ceased; perhaps they had heard him. But when he glanced up, the figures hadn't moved. A foot higher, and he saw that the faces turned to him were patches of moss; the figures were cairns, after all. It didn't matter: companionship waited at the summit; he'd heard voices, he was sure that he'd heard them, please let him have done so. And indeed, as he struggled up the last yards of the slope, the two grey figures rose with a squeaking and rattling of slate, and advanced heavily towards him.

NIGHTMARES OF BURNMOOR

During the time of the Napoleonic wars, a young farm worker who lived in a small village on Burnmoor, close to Wast Water, was fatally injured in an accident.

His mother, who had lost her husband in a similar accident only a couple of years earlier, was driven half-mad with grief. She was taken so ill that it was decided she could not attend the funeral, which would be held at a chapel in the town of Boot, several miles away in Eskdale. When people died in these remote fell-side communities, it was common practice for their coffins to be carried on horseback to the nearest church or chapel along 'lychways', or 'corpse paths' – isolated moorland routes. One such – a very notorious one – lay across Burnmoor, and at all other times apart from funerals, it was shunned by the local people.

On this particular occasion Burnmoor was shrouded with fog. The cortege proceeded with difficulty, the horse and many of the mourners stumbling along, tripping on stones and slipping in the dewy grass. At length, they passed a thicket of leafless, twisted trees, which for some time had been a source of superstition in the area. The horse carrying the coffin became particularly skittish at this point, and, when an odd, scornful chuckle was heard from inside the thicket, it bolted, carrying the coffin away.

Chaos followed, as the funeral party sought to recapture the animal. But though they searched for hours, there was no trace of it. The following day, the fog had lifted, but still neither the horse nor the coffin of the young man could be found.

When the grieving mother received this news – that her son had been denied a Christian burial by forces unknown – her horror was compounded and she fell dead on the spot. With a great sense of foreboding, the villagers now prepared for a second funeral in the same week.

When the sad day came, the mother's coffin was carried on a different horse, but along the same route. However, at the same point, close to that twisted thicket of trees, another eerie chuckle was heard. The horse became hysterical and raced across the moor with such strength and speed that nobody was able to catch it.

Like the first horse, it was never seen again.

No explanation was ever provided about the noises from the thicket, and it is unknown what became of the two horses and their grim cargoes. But rumour still holds that, on black, moonless nights, *two phantom beasts with oblong boxes loaded onto their backs can be seen chasing each other wildly around the desolate moor, a shrill voice sounding from the box at the rear, bemoaning her loss and wailing for the return of her son.*

THE JILTED BRIDE OF
WINDERMERE
Gary Fry

Nobody could ever have described Trish and Martin as love's young dream.

I'd known them both a long time and had endured all the wild swings of their on-off relationship. A quiet, relatively stable companion, I'd rarely taken sides, often talking either of them down from a high moral position after one violent row or another. Or another. Or another.

Yes, they'd always been *that* kind of couple, one who couldn't live together and struggled to get by apart. But then suddenly – approaching their thirties, with biological clocks ticking inexorably towards oblivion – they'd decided to get married.

When I first heard the news – Martin had called me at home while I was reading – I was put in mind of a comment once made about the great historian Thomas Carlyle and his wife: that as long as they were still together, they were unable to make two other people unhappy. In truth, however, the moment hadn't lent itself readily to wit; the news had actually come as a shock to me.

Still, I stood dutifully by as they went about preparing their wedding, which would be a lavish affair in the glorious Lake District, hosted by a classy hotel with sweeping views of majestic Windermere.

I was asked to be best man of course, and was also tasked with the role of organising Martin's stag do. On the morning of this grand hoolie, Trish called me on my mobile – her lovely voice was like fresh water breaking on some ancient rock – and told me, with all the directness I'd come to expect from her, not to let her lummox of a fiancé get arrested or into any other trouble. I assured her that nothing like this would occur – I'd always been willing to do so much for her – and then went about my elected duties with a policeman's seriousness of purpose.

The good thing about being a bachelor was that you never had to be home at a pre-specified time. The bad thing about being teetotal was that even if you did stagger in at some unthinkable hour, you had nobody to answer to anyway. And that was pretty much what happened that night.

I'd been tired from another long shift at work, and so at two a.m. I left the partying guys to debauched tomfoolery. By this stage Martin had decided to balance bottles of beer on his forehead, and as his other mates had encouraged him to do the same with pint glasses, then litre jugs and finally larger vessels of Lord knew what quantity, I quietly made my exit. They surely couldn't get into much trouble if they just kept on playing silly games like this.

My walk home that evening was tainted by vague feelings of regret. I spotted many lovers walking hand-in-hand down side streets, climbing into taxis, huddled against walls. The city could be a cruel place for a man essentially alone in life.

However, there was the beautiful Lake District to look forward to at the weekend. As soon as I got back into my squat terraced house, I sent Trish a text – *all ok x your man safe x sleep well, my dear* – and then went to bed with a sensible mug of malted milk to chase the chill from my bones.

The bad news – no, scratch that: the *terrible* news – came the following morning.

It was one of Martin's work colleagues, another guest at the stag do, who called me. Apparently he and the other guys had moved on from the pub and found a sordid nightclub, all thumping sound and dazzling light. Here they'd "bumped into" a bunch of girls, including "some lass who knew Trish quite well, like." And that was the last the blokes had seen of either her or Martin, "cos they'd both gone off, innit, to the lavs or summat and, well, you don't need an imagination, do you?"

Once I'd managed to translate this tradesman's speak into coherent English (Martin ran a builder's yard and this fella was, I believed, one of his skivvies) the truth hit me hard. Only a few nights before getting married to the delectable Trish, the groom had scored a cheap moment of ecstasy with some strumpet. Worse, this woman *knew* the bride-to-be.

Hey look, I'm no prude. Despite a somewhat chaste reputation among peers, I believe I understand human passion, insurmountable desires and the thorny perils of temptation. But just then I was angry. For only one night, I'd been tasked with keeping my roguish mate Martin free from petty corruption – and I'd failed, hadn't I? I'd basically let my old friend down (Trish, I mean: the delectable Trish).

Some copper that makes me, huh?

Once I'd come to terms with the problem, however, I decided I needed a plan. In anticipation of the late night out, I'd booked a day's Leave from work, and my first job that morning was to drive round to Martin's gaff and extract some pretty fast answers.

I don't conduct many interrogations as a policeman, and certainly none at the station in those sense-depriving rooms. That's not my role. Still, when the moment beckons I can often rise to the occasion.

In the event, however, getting information out of my seriously hungover friend was like stealing snuff from some incapacitated fool. I asked him, "Okay, Martin, you have to tell me: who *was* she?"

And he replied without a moment's hesitation.

Christ, I thought, suddenly observing his bejewelled grin: at some primal level, he might even feel proud about having bedded *Alice Simmons*.

Which was not to say the girl wasn't quite a catch. The age-old proverb reminds us that there are plenty of fish in the sea, but girls like Alice render such wisdom meaningless. She was *the* fish, the one great anglers use their best rods to catch, who sometimes falls into eager hands and yet who always wriggles free, ever wild and alluring …

Needless to say, at the nightclub last night, Martin had bonked her in the blokes' bogs.

So yes, here was a problem, all right. In just two days, one of my best friends was marrying another of my best friends, and suddenly Alice Simmons threatened to jeopardise the whole event. There was surely only one thing I could do: go see the girl.

Alice lived in the north of Leeds, and I had to skillfully manoeuvre my hatchback along several litter-strewn streets before finding her pad. She worked as a P.A. somewhere in the city, yet lived like a penniless student. After answering my terse knock at her front door, she looked as good as could be expected, given that it was now nearly noon and she'd clearly just got out of bed. Her thick hair was gypsy-dark, her eyes sparkling like small stones at the bottom of some freshwater pool. She obviously knew what I'd come for, because before I could speak, she said, "Oh look, it's Mr Uptight. Come to slap the cuffs on me, have you? Come to arrest me on a charge of … moral indecency?"

I managed to rise above all this, like a scuba diver coming back to the surface of some oily, stagnant pond. "I think you know what I've come for, Alice," I said, striving to remain calm and neutral. "Martin and … Trish are good friends of mine. We all go way back. So don't spoil their big day. You've had your bit of fun. Now what say you leave it there, eh?"

"Move along, please? Nothing more to see here?" She laughed horribly. "Is that what you're saying to me, mate?"

Something about the way she lampooned my profession got under my skin, though I managed to control myself and reply, "If that's the way you want to think about it, yes."

And without waiting for a response, I turned to head back for my car, hoping this impish girl wouldn't add more.

But of course she *did*. Folk like her *always* did.

"I would have thought *you'd* have been pleased, Mr Creep," Alice called, stepping back from the doorway with another cruel laugh. "If Martin was a free man, it would clear the way for *you*, wouldn't it?"

Whatever she'd been implying by this comment, I tried not dwell upon until the words had ceased rolling around my skull. And soon, believing my job was done, I set about preparing for the Lake District.

I'd booked a single room at a B&B in the charming town of Bowness, on the lip of Windermere. I'm very fond of reading, and on this trip – between attending to my duties as best man and taking in a few touristy activities – I thought I might get round to a couple of books I'd been hoarding lately. Eventually I chose a collection of M.R. James ghost stories and a non-fiction guide to Cumbria. I looked forward to a few creepy sessions with the Master's spooks, as well as learning something from the other book about the region, which I'd visited several times in the past.

Trish and Martin gave me a lift there in their bright new BMW. Martin's business had been doing well lately, and with Trish's steady income from mobile hairdressing, they were hardly short of cash. That was how they'd managed to hire such a desirable hotel. Once we'd parked up in the place's forecourt, the sight and sounds of lapping Windermere brought back memories for me – of day trips during my youth, of my parents' tense coexistence. I remember swimming regularly, and how once, after re-emerging from the lake, it was clear that my mum and dad had been arguing again. They'd always kept these squabbles private, fearful perhaps of corrupting their only child. I sometimes wonder, however, whether such an effort to hide such rancor had actually resulted in *more* damage than the blazing alternative …

These unwelcome ruminations were cut short by the sight of something breaking the water's surface. A fish, had it been? Certainly something dark and slippery, which promptly plunged back into the depths of the lake.

I glanced away and turned my attention back to all my responsibilities this weekend.

Alice Simmons had of course been invited to the wedding – after all, it wouldn't have been possible to *un*invite her without arousing the curiosity of Trish. Therefore I imagined part of my role would involve keeping this vampish predator from both bride and groom, at least until the day after the wedding when they would flee in a hired limousine for the airport and then Barbados. This honeymoon location was a surprise Martin had in store for Trish, and I just hoped she wouldn't experience any others on what should be the happiest few days of her life …

Look, I need to be honest here. I've always had a *thing* for Trish. We go way back, she and I – even further back than Martin goes with the two of us. Trish and I had grown up as nippers in the same street, bonded by a lack of any other children to play with in such a bland neighbourhood. For many years, before the inevitable turmoil of puberty, the issue of a sexual liaison wasn't part of our friendship. We were simply pals, playmates, sometimes rival soldiers, often fellow nurses – whichever game took our fancy, we could improvise with almost intuitive familiarity. We were, in short, like brother and sister – or at least that was what Trish once told me, when we were fourteen or fifteen, that oh-so-difficult age, with hormones zinging around like sprats in a deep blue sea. For me, however, our relationship had grown into something rather more than platonic affection. But by that time Martin had blundered onto the scene, and I'd lost Trish for good.

But I don't want any sympathy. I truly believe I'm better off alone in life. I've seen what love can do to people, and it rarely involves only champagne and roses …

That afternoon I strolled through Bowness with my travel case, admiring the snaking high street and all its shops, pubs and restaurants. I had a coffee in a small tearoom, while soaking up the atmosphere and watching boats cut across the lake. Later, I checked into the B&B I'd sourced online. It was a small, poky building, sandwiched between a confectioner's and a quaint row of handicraft stores. Once its buxom landlady had shown me upstairs, I noticed that my room was quite cramped, but after being left alone, I decided that I'd enjoy my stay. The place was cosy and rather charming. An old-fashioned sash window looked out onto Lake Windermere, and if there was a little evidence of rot in the room – a fetid smell of damp – this only added to the place's aged ambience.

After all the week's tensions, I napped almost as soon as I lay down on the single bed. My dreams were of squelchy things, flopping forth from water, multi-limbed and slimy ... When I awoke I could smell that rank odour again, forceful and acrid. Over a cup of tea, I read a few M R James stories, followed by a chapter about the town in which I was staying. The Cumbrian guide was very interesting; before the weekend was over, I hoped to get through much more of it.

That evening, the last before the couple's big day, I met Martin and Trish and a group of their guests at a restaurant in town (these were mainly family members, but the company of such folk on a weekend like this was unavoidable). The meal was very enjoyable, three belly-rupturing courses. An early spring sunset bestowed its brightest wishes on the forthcoming nuptials, and the waiters – swarthy Italians with darkly brooding postures – served us dutifully with knowing glints in their eyes.

I was just beginning to relax from feeling tense (apparently a splinter group of guests was also out in the town, headed up by the indefatigable Alice Simmons) when something went terribly wrong – for me, at least. After dessert and coffee, we'd all ordered nightcaps, though, sensible to the last, I'd asked for only a mineral water. I didn't want to have to deliver my best man's speech the following day with a headache; I was nervous enough as it was.

When the glass of still, transparent liquid arrived, I didn't suspect anything untoward, even though I'd seen Martin follow one of the waiters to the bar a few minutes earlier. I'd assumed he'd been going to the toilet, but the cloying heat in the restaurant had been affecting me and I hadn't been able to watch him properly. So then I knocked back a mouthful from the glass – and discovered at once that I'd been given *vodka*.

For a dreadful moment, as the spirit burnt my gullet, I was torn between swallowing the lot and spitting it out at several of the well-dressed guests at our table. In the event, I managed to work half back into the glass, yet habitual decorum – the kind drilled into me by my fiercely proud parents – prevented me from getting rid of the rest in any other way. So I was forced to swallow it, almost choking in the process. Seconds later, I saw Martin approaching the table, chuckling furtively.

He'd angered me greatly. For a minute or so, I even found myself hoping that Alice Simmons would arrive and tell the bride-to-be her sordid little secret. This wasn't because I wanted to hurt poor Trish; rather, to get back at Martin, and not simply on account of the nasty trick he'd just pulled on me. In fact, I wanted to make him suffer for having stolen my ... my ...

But no, I prevented my mind from running that way. Instead, I merely laughed as the alcohol started feeling for my thoughts, like some sea monster's tentacles reaching for prey. And a moment later I made my excuses, offered Trish an awkward kiss on one cheek, scrabbled out a few notes to contribute to the evening's bill, promised everyone I'd see them tomorrow, and finally swayed for the exit.

The stroll back to my accommodation – was it really a *stroll?*; maybe *stagger* covered it better – involved many reminders about why I never touch booze. When I reached the lakeside, I thought I could hear things far too unsightly to show themselves, fumbling at the frothing fringe, eager to wriggle ashore ... I looked away and simply kept on walking, stumbling, righting myself, and then walking again. After reaching my B&B, my mind churned like an ancient geezer, like the earth opening up to let in something terrible which simply didn't belong here.

Then I glanced up at my room's window – to see a face glaring back, its features half-consumed, as if by ragged-toothed sea-life.

But of course this was just fanciful, just a consequence of the many nebulous thoughts I'd been suppressing all day. After blinking rapidly, I looked again at the uncurtained window and saw nothing other than the moon's reflection, half-concealed by an unstable shadow.

I went quickly inside, somehow using the stairwell to defy gravity and reach my room upstairs.

There were damp footprints on the carpet. This was the first thing I noticed after sitting on the bed and kicking off my shoes. I stood back up at once and switched on the light I'd failed to activate upon entry. And yes, faint yet inarguably present, a number of wet patches now moved from one side of the room to the other, halting just in front of the solitary window. My first thought was that I'd surely brought in this water from outside – it had been raining a little this evening – but then my attention was switched elsewhere.

I'd heard a splash of something in action to my right – from the tiny en suite bathroom. Its door was presently closed, though now emboldened by vodka sloshing around my brain, I quickly turned the handle to make its hinges scream.

Inside there was nothing other than a neurotic spider in the bathtub, whose angular legs pumped as it fled my shadow. Looking around and seeing nothing else of any note, I ascribed the noise I'd heard to the toilet's cistern filling up, before returning to the main room and falling upon the bed.

I decided that some light reading would sober me up before sleep. I reached for the book I'd been browsing earlier, the detailed guide to this fascinating county. The chapter I'd begun was all about the Lake District, and there was a whole section devoted to local legends, community traditions, infamous tragedies and even ghostly sightings in the area – the usual sensationalised regional fare.

Nevertheless, I read on eagerly, desperate now to rid myself of spirits of a more pernicious nature.

In 1834, a man had drowned his family in Lake Ullswater after discovering that a foreign business venture in which he'd invested his life savings had resulted in his bankruptcy. By all accounts – or rather, by decidedly questionable accounts – the family members' restless lost souls were supposed to roam the lanes alongside the lake, each seeking warmth and shelter.

In 1902 a pair of young lovers had been murdered in Grasmere. Their bodies had been dumped in the nearby lake from the boat of their killer, a well-respected resident of the town who'd gone on to murder six other people, before being captured by the police. And yes, the victims' spirits still roamed the lanes where blah de blah blah de blah.

I was now struggling to remain awake. However, I knew that if I drifted off with so much booze inside me, I'd feel dreadful in the morning. *Damn you, Martin*, I thought, and then suddenly felt even angrier about what he'd done to me. I pitied Trish all over again, but keenly aware of the dangers of thinking this way, I quickly turned my attention back to the book's squirming text.

In 1934 a young woman had drowned herself in the depths of Windermere. The reason for this had been desperate and tragic: she'd been jilted at the altar by her rotten fiancé. A sad and familiar story. The spirit of this girl, however, wasn't reputed to roam the lanes of her native town, which had of course been quaint Bowness. In fact, she was said to haunt a bedroom in the house she'd once occupied with her parents. There was an old photograph of the property in which this blighted room was located.

And of course I was dismayed to realise that it was *this* B&B – the one in which I was now staying.

Jerking up from my prostrate position, I glanced down at those damp patches on the carpet. Then I panicked, feeling horribly sick. My head swam, as if gallons of water were coursing through it.

However, after a minute or so, I'd managed to calm myself. Even though the photo in the book displayed my room's window, I reasoned in a slightly inebriated way, it wasn't necessarily true that I was now staying in the girl's former bedroom – was it?

There was another thing, too – perhaps one I should have considered first: the tale of the jilted bride of Windermere was just a ghost story, surely no more real in substance than any of M R James's sheeted ghouls. The wet on the room floor might be seepage from a leaky ceiling. And surely the sounds I'd heard from the bathroom earlier could be ascribed to faulty plumbing, no more or no less.

I should therefore try and suppress any irrational conclusions. Tomorrow was a big day and I desperately needed rest. I would just have to take a chance on not waking up with a hangover.

Very soon, before I could even remove my daytime clothing, sleep claimed me with a lover's embrace – and held me there all night.

When I woke the following morning I was soaking wet. This always happened to me after drinking: terrible night-sweats. The stuff saturating my sheets smelled bad, too. I've always tried to keep my body free from toxins, but on this occasion there must have been some pretty nasty ones in my blood. When I rolled over to climb off the mattress, I noticed how the damp had formed a shape like another person in the bed, as if someone had moulded him or herself into the contours of my frame. I tried hard to ignore the impression that the scent of my perspiration was pungent – like impure lake water.

I took a shower, willing the pounding liquid to slice all the fretfulness from my mind. However, whenever I opened my eyes to glance around the bathroom, I thought I saw fluid figures lurking in my vicinity, sometimes even stealing my way. Or perhaps there was only *one* – a shortish entity with streaks of wet hair, its face filthy and rotten … But of course I knew that nobody else was here and that these vague images were just residue of dreams induced by the book I'd read the previous evening.

I dressed in my best suit and spent an hour or so rehearsing my speech. As ready as I'd ever be, I checked about eighteen times to make sure I had the wedding ring Martin had entrusted to me. It was a big diamond number that had cost more than one of my monthly pay packets. Finally, satisfied all was well, I left my room. The sound of water dripping from behind once I'd closed the door was surely just patters of the light rainfall against that old window.

Bad weather looked set to befall Martin and Trish's wedding. Their relationship had been so stormy, and I could almost believe that some supernatural force was now commenting on their impending nuptials with cosmic disdain. I wasn't feeling too clear-headed as I walked towards the big hotel in which the betrothed couple and all their family and friends had been staying. In the past, such a delicate state of mind had often led me to entertain bizarre notions. Indeed, as I skirted choppy Windermere, I struggled hard to eliminate any foolish connection between its restless waters and the moisture I'd found in my bed that morning ...

I don't have much to say about the ceremony, except to point out how divine Trish looked. One of her friends was a dress designer and had managed to create a stunning outfit "on the cheap" (Martin's all too typical description to me recently). I'm not ashamed to admit that I almost cried as, accompanied by her ageing father, Trish came to stand beside her intended and me. However, I was surprised by how angry I also felt. I suddenly imagined that the jilted woman I'd read about last night must have suffered something similar after realising that her fiancé had abandoned her. If only that could happen today, I found myself thinking, and soon pictured myself filling the position vacated by another no-good man. Trish and I would go on to live happily after, just the two of us at first, but then maybe, a few years down the line, a couple of kids and ... and ...

As I've already said, I wasn't in my right mind that day.

It happened – the thing which finally tipped me over the brink – later that afternoon, during the champagne reception. All the guests were getting drunk as I stumbled through my best man's speech. I've never been much of a public speaker – I've never been much of anything, in truth. But I'm steady and reliable, two good-enough qualities. However, what Martin did just after I'd begun speaking to the gathering was enough to override even my patience.

I'd opened my speech with a few select anecdotes based on our childhoods together, Trish and me. I'd told the giddy assembly about epic bike rides, a few pranks we'd played on neighbours, and even the time we'd stolen a fishing rod from the banks of a river before spending the rest of that hot summer's day trying to earn our lunch with limp, bobbing bait; we'd caught only colds.

There was laughter from the crowd – polite, alcohol-induced laughter. Still, this was pleasing to me ... until Martin said what he said.

I wanted to tell myself that my old friend was simply drunk, though I knew this wouldn't legitimise his behaviour. I understood as well as anyone that Martin often acted in the same way when he was sober. On this occasion, the offending article had been a comment, uttered *sotto voce*, yet audible all the same – at least to me standing right beside him.

"*Oh, do get it over with, you boring sod,*" he'd hissed between teeth as tight as the strap on his wallet was reputed to be.

I knew this rumour was also true. Poor Trish practically had to go begging before he'd let her have any of his money. Why else had it taken them so long to get married? The reason was simple: Martin hadn't wanted to pay for such an "expensive gig." As long as he had Trish in his bed, what did he care about "a bit of pointless paper"? These had been the very words he'd used. It was how he saw his marriage to my oldest friend – the woman, if I'm honest, I secretly loved.

A bit of pointless paper.

I nearly lost my temper and was about to denounce the man as unworthy of Trish when I suddenly glanced up – and spotted my means of salvation, of cold and telling revenge.

There was a woman in the room's doorway. She stood alone, backlit by faded light, and the sparkly sequins on her dress gave her a look of something wet and slimy, as if her flesh was made of scales. But then I adjusted my focus and immediately recognised her.

It was Alice Simmons. And she was smiling from ear to ear.

I think she could tell, in that knowing way she seemed to summon at will, that I'd just been offended by Martin. Once I'd stumbled through my toasts (and after Trish's ageing father had received similar short shrift in the speaker's corner), I went to the bar and confronted Alice, who'd already sunk her hooks into another poor sap of a man.

Before I could speak, she turned, looked at the bride and groom across the room, and said, "They make such a lovely couple, don't they? It's a shame, really. *Such* a shame."

Despite the way I was feeling – full of retributive rage – I didn't reply. I knew I ought to remain mindful of the reputation Alice had of twisting everything to her own devices. But then she pushed a little harder, and I'm afraid this was just too far.

"Trish isn't a bad sort, really. I mean, Martin'll never want for a clean pair of socks, will he? But . . . well, at the end of the day, that isn't what guys are truly after, is it?" After a lengthy pause, during which the DJ kicked off a tacky disco, Alice added with a feigned sigh, "Yes, I don't think it will be long before Martin is knocking on *my* door again."

The thoughts this comment incited in me were almost savage enough to prompt violence. That this tipsy strumpet (by her slightly slurred tone, it was obvious she'd been drinking all day) had belittled the only woman I'd ever been attracted to was one thing. But to suggest that Trish was second-best to the vulgarity Alice and Martin represented was just too much. However, the worse thing was that she might be right about one thing: Martin probably would soon commit adultery with Alice.

Retaliating with a deviousness to match hers, I snapped back, "Oh, you think so, do you?" By this time raucous music was rolling around the dance floor. "Well, that's not the impression *I* got," I added, deliberately vague.

Maybe if Alice had been sober, she wouldn't have risen to my bait. But she wasn't sober. She was *saturated* by booze. Her voice now slightly self-conscious, she asked, "What … what do you mean?"

And I was more than happy to elaborate. "Oh, it's really quite simple, love. Martin told me you were *crap* that night. In fact, this convinced him that … that Trish was the one for him. So it's because of *you* that he went through with the wedding." These lies had come effortlessly, and I was now well in the flow. "Sometimes it takes a *disappointing* last fling to realise that all the other fish in the sea – yes, even the exotic ones, which actually taste of poison – are not worth worrying about."

I'm reluctant to reveal in detail just what happened next. It's not something I'm proud of, to be honest. What I will say is that before I'd even managed to down even one glass of lemonade, the whole room erupted – in warring relatives, friends of the bride and groom, and even previously impartial observers. Alice had of course gone directly across to Trish to tell her all about her new hubbie's stag night exploits. To lend her frequent spitefulness veracity, Alice's sexual *modus operandi* involved raking manicured fingernails down her victims' backs. And only after a few minutes of incredulous protest did Trish admit that Martin *did* presently have such minor cuts on his back. He'd apparently told Trish that he'd caught himself on a lintel at work. He'd even got her to kiss the scars better, from one end to the other and then back again.

To say the evening ended prematurely would do it a grave disservice. The termination of merriment was authentically nuclear. There would be no first night of passion for the bride and groom. Trish immediately vowed to never have anything to do with her "lying, cheating sod of a husband". The final scene involved me,

Martin's dutiful best man, stepping in to try and tend to so many open wounds.

"Trish, my love," I said to my oldest friend, who'd now been reduced to a pitiable wash of tears. "Let me take him away with me, just for tonight. We can all get together tomorrow and talk this through. Yes?"

Huddled close in my arms, Trish protested, though I managed to hold her as tightly as I could. This was a lover's embrace, the most secure kind in such an unforgiving world. Trish had always known this, even when we'd been kids together. We understood each other well, and at our best were as one.

After she'd calmed down, she nodded and then wafted a hand, as if to be free of the loathsome man she'd just married. As I stepped back to drag the shell-shocked Martin towards the hotel's exit, I noticed Alice Simmons smirking broadly, one hand holding the latest in a long line of ruined anglers who'd toiled at her toxic lake. Then Martin and I went out.

We'd got as far as moonlit Windermere before he finally spoke. "I've really done it now, haven't I?" he asked, hoisting a huge bottle of beer he'd managed to retrieve from the hotel bar. He supped from its neck, flinching as the yeasty liquid combined with all the champers he'd also sunk. But then he offered me a leery smile and added, "Mind you ... even having just one crack at Alice wasn't half worth it."

I felt like hitting him and I'm convinced I would have done so if I hadn't suddenly heard a gurgling sound from the lake. I glanced that way and saw only ripples on the water, as if something had just broken the calm surface, before ducking back to familiar depths.

Whatever this had been – an errant fish, maybe – it had tripped a fuse in my mind, summoning reason. Martin was just drunk, I reminded myself. He was *very* drunk and didn't know what he was saying. Of course he hadn't meant to hurt Trish *deliberately*, no way at all.

Like the drowning man clutching at proverbial straws, I tried to convince myself this was true as I directed the groom back to my accommodation – the small B&B which had once been home to a family whose daughter had suffered similar wedding day distress ... I attempted to suppress *these* thoughts too, especially after beginning to suspect I could hear damp, unsteady footsteps pursuing us along all the back streets I'd chosen in order to avoid any other pedestrians.

Just my imagination, I told myself. Just auditory hallucinations induced by emotional arousal. Indeed, when I looked up at the building to which we were heading, there was nothing at my room's window but a scattering of reflected stars.

Once I'd got Martin inside the building – he was now singing a troubled song about tainted love, which had seemed to prompt a swift escalation of those wet footfalls in our wake – the landlady came to greet us and I was able to shut the front door and anything else out. Then I said, "I'm afraid there's been a bit of trouble at the wedding I was telling you about yesterday. This is the groom."

"He's very … *drunk*, isn't he?" the landlady replied, and we both watched as Martin took mighty gulp from that large bottle of beer.

"He'll be okay after some sleep," I explained, and wondered whether this was true. *Once a sod, always a sod* – that was a motto by which I'd oriented my life. Maybe all bobbies find it difficult to avoid drawing such sour conclusions about humanity.

The landlady said, "Well, he won't be able to stay in your room, I'm afraid. It's not that I'm unwilling to help you out, my dear. It's to do with health and safety regulations. Imagine if there was a … well, an *accident*." Her voice had grown vague, as if she'd experienced trouble in this property, perhaps even in the room in which I'd been staying … But then she added quickly, "I'm afraid one of you will have to pay for another room. However, you're in luck. The one directly next door is free. He can have that."

My next response was intuitive – the kind of action whose origins are unknown until long after the event, with only the benefit of hindsight. I said, "I want to get him settled down soon, if I can. He's in a hell of a state. I'll take him up now." I paused, thought for a moment while listening carefully for any more noises from outside, and finally added, "He can have my room."

And ten minutes later, Martin was tucked up in my bed. Those wet sheets had been changed, so I knew I should be grateful to the landlady for not offering me a disapproving look downstairs. The damp spots on the carpet had dwindled to a faint row of shadowy stains. I took up the book I'd been reading the previous night, vaguely aware that I'd left a chapter unfinished. What with the upheaval of the last few hours, I was unable to recall what this had been about. Then I stooped to Martin and said, "You get some sleep, mate. We'll try patch things up tomorrow. But for now you need to rest."

At that moment, something seemed to stir in the bathroom, but this latest noise had surely just been the shower-head dripping a bullet of water into the bath.

127

"Yeah," Martin mumbled, his mouth still suckling that beer bottle. Despite being laid flat on his back, he was somehow able to work at its contents. There was a large quantity of liquid left inside. "Yeah, she'll forgive me, won't she? She's as good as gold, really. She doesn't hold grudges. She'll be fine, fine, fiii ..."

I wasn't sure who he was referring to and was quite unable to dwell on the issue. Another watery sound had just come from the bathroom. However, I dismissed this, and then, a taut feeling energising my limbs, I stood up, stepped out of the room and shut the door. I had the key to the room and once I'd locked it, I told myself I'd done so in my friend's best interests. In his present condition, he might stray from the bed, stagger onto the landing and even tumble down the main staircase. Accidents just like this – simple, foolish and eminently avoidable – happen all the time. I'd learned that from my job.

After again handing my credit card to the landlady, I retired to the room situated beside my previous one. It was getting on for ten p.m. and the moon through the window was a pale, bloated object in a pitch-dark sky. Last night, when I'd seen its reflection in the window next door, the face surely hadn't been so complete ... However, this thought didn't trouble me for long. After all the day's exertions, I was exhausted and I knew that a quiet spell of reading would settle me for sleep.

There was a message from Trish on my mobile. It read: *I cant believe hed do that, the sod, but do make sure hes ok x thanks mate, I luv u.* She was obviously very drunk; this was the only time she'd ever revealed any intimate feelings towards me. Still, I knew she wasn't thinking clearly for another reason: she'd just asked me to take care of her husband, despite him ruining everything they'd ever had together. Once she sobered up, she'd surely see that. There was nothing left of their relationship; I was now convinced of it.

Feeling rather uncomfortable with my own role in what had happened today, I sought distraction in the book I'd brought from my previous room. This wasn't the collection of M R James stories, even though that was, at some subconscious level, the book I'd been expecting. It was the guide to Cumbrian history. And then I *did* remember what I'd been reading about last night.

The jilted bride of Windermere.

Perhaps I'd abandoned this story through sudden fearfulness. Over the page was more about this unfortunate woman. I read on, and was soon back in the grip of the tale. The author had already suggested that the bride who'd drowned herself in Windermere still occupied her former home. She was waiting, claimed the next part, for her treacherous lover to return and spend a first night with her. However, it was clear that this ghostly girl – who'd been dead for over eighty years, and might now be half-rotten and eaten away – had rather less than pleasure to bestow upon her once dishonest spouse.

This was all nonsense, of course, and in any case my attention was soon snatched from the book by the sound of something stirring in the next room.

I sat up in my new bed, listening carefully. Then the silence of the rest of the building dramatised the noises now growing louder behind the wall which separated my present location from my previous one.

Had Martin, with so much drink in his system, just got up to use the toilet? Certainly the footsteps I now heard were unsteady, as if the walker was incapacitated in some discomforting way. I placed my ear to the wall and heard a low, snaffling sound of snoring. But surely that couldn't be right: if Martin was asleep – just who was pacing the room?

There followed a quick splash and a gurgle. Was the cheating man now washing his hands in the sink? However, these liquid sounds seemed much closer to me than that. The bathroom was located on the far side of the room, beyond the bed. But the noises I could hear were surely undiminished by distance. It was as if whatever occurred in that room was happening only inches from me.

All the same, I pressed my ear closer to the wall, listening eagerly.

There was a sound like gargling, full of smothering wetness – the world's stickiest goodnight kiss. Then a moment later, as the snoring I'd detected earlier seemed to die away, there was a noise like demented, girlish laughter, though such a loose example, it was impossible to believe it had come from a mouth which possessed a coherent structure. And when this sound had ceased, just as abruptly as it had begun, those footsteps struck up again – slow, muted, sloshing.

It was then that I jerked away from the wall, every part of me shaking as if some frightful fever was taking maximum grip.

I decided at once that Martin had just being using the bathroom. I tossed aside the book, flicked out the room's light with a strand dangling above the headboard, and finally forced myself down into the bed for some merciful sleep.

I didn't wake again until morning, until stark sunlight had chased countless demons from my mind. I'd dreamt of terrible, garish events, and the worst thing was that *I'd* been their architect; *I'd* been the one triggering them all into action. As I dressed for the day, I tried to suppress these dark recollections. I had much work to do, not least an attempt to repair whatever hurt Martin had caused Trish yesterday.

When I went to rouse my friend from slumber, he was dead of course.

What must have happened was this: after visiting the bathroom last night, he'd returned to bed, took up that beer bottle again, and lay on his back while swigging from its neck. This would account for the gleeful, slack-jawed laughter I'd heard, and that sudden silence afterwards. With his mouth full of beer, Martin had surely then lost consciousness, his muscles relaxing to allow the unforgiving liquid into his lungs. And he'd drowned, simple as that.

It's important to forgive the offhand way I'm announcing all this. I'm a policeman. I see this stuff all the time. As I've already said, it happens all too easily – tragic but true.

Once I'd feigned a cry of horror and after the landlady had come running upstairs, we both stepped close to the corpse and pushed back his neck. It was true that the liquid which poured out of his mouth didn't resemble beer. It was silty and impure, and stank like a rancid pond. However, this was surely just an effect of stomach acids, the natural reflux of a body threatened with extinction. In any case, the man was still clutching that bottle, and I had a solid witness for that. Yes, it was booze which had done for Martin, no question about it.

An hour later, after the local police had arrived (my job in another county's force led the officers to trust me without hesitation), I headed across the town for the hotel in which two major pledges had been made the previous day. In this tawdry age, however, such vows were easily broken, just as Martin had proved. It was different from the nobler past, when a man would tend to act in less vulgar ways. Indeed, for *jilted* in 1934 read *adultery* now. But the hurt caused by each act was much the same … and demanded similar retributive action.

I genuinely believed – even back at that stage, in such a nebulous state of mind – that I and my new assistant had served our finest dishes cold. As cold as a huge lake.

As I again skirted the fringe of beautiful, mysterious Windermere, I'm sure I saw something briefly break its surface, wriggle momentarily with a slimy darkness, before returning – perhaps satisfied at last – to the water's heaving belly.

I offered a little wave of gratitude, and then headed off to see my beloved Trish, to offer her bad news, and to support her through this difficult time.

Maybe I could now show enough compassion to make her feel the same way about me.

THE HORROR AT CARLISLE CASTLE

The Jacobite rising of 1745 is a story tinged with all kinds of romantic melodrama. Even now the names of those involved stir the blood: Bonnie Prince Charlie, Lord George Murray, Flora MacDonald. The very name given to the rebellion – 'the Forty-Five' – and the names of so many places where the Jacobite banner unfurled in the highland wind – Glenfinnan, Prestonpans – evoke colourful images of a tartan-clad army charging through the heather with swords and shields, while British redcoats flee in terror.

Sadly, this owes more to patriotic fantasy than historical reality.

Bonnie Prince Charlie's attempt to overthrow the house of Hanover and return the Stuarts to the British throne was ill-conceived from the start. To begin with, he himself was Italian and his family's claim to the crown was some fifty-six years out of date. Not all of Scotland's Catholic highland clans, from whom he recruited the bulk of his soldiers, even wanted the return of the Stuarts much less were ready to fight for it. In the end, of course, the 'Young Pretender' did put a brave and sizeable army together, and invaded England with troupes of bagpipers leading his vanguard. But in April 1746 it ended in gruesome disaster at the battle of Culloden, when basket-hilted broadswords and hook-handed pistols proved no match for muskets, bayonets and heavy guns manned by expert crews.

The highland army was annihilated. Some 2,000 were slain, among them many illustrious names – Mackintosh of Farr, MacGillivray of Dunmaglass, Fraser of Inverallochie. Countless others were horrifically wounded, and left untended while the redcoats – many drawn from Scottish lowland regiments but driven by a xenophobic hatred of their northern cousins – prowled the bloody field, finishing them off with cold steel. The survivors met an even worse fate.

In the mid-18th century, there were few rules governing the treatment of prisoners of war. But even if there had been, the victor at Culloden, the bluff William Augustus, Duke of Cumberland, regarded the Jacobites in no such terms. As far as he and his men were concerned, they were rebels and lucky they'd been spared at all. Over 150 of them were thus chained together, and marched south from Scotland, a homeland which, though they didn't know it at the time, they would never see again.

At Carlisle Castle, the English bastion on the north Cumbrian border, which had only recently been recaptured from the Jacobites, the prisoners joined those survivors of the Jacobite garrison, and were crammed into two or three subterranean dungeons. The door was locked and for the next few weeks they were forgotten. Nearly 400 men were packed together in the most hellish conditions, with no light, no air, no sanitation, no food and no water, during the course of which absence from the world they were tried and sentenced to death. Even before these penalties could be carried out, they died in droves, either from the pain of untreated wounds, from gangrene, or from tortured, claustrophobic madness. In due course, those remaining were made to draw lots from a hat, and the losers taken outside in small groups. Many were instantly blinded by the sunlight they'd been denied for so many days, but at least this meant they could not see the gallows on Harraby Hill, where they were to be hanged, drawn and quartered.

The traditional punishment in England for treason, hanging, drawing and quartering was in force from 1351 until 1814. By the 19th century it merely meant hanging until death and then beheading, but in earlier days it was a far more grisly spectacle. The miscreant was bound hand and foot, and lynched to the gallows crossbar, where he was suspended for several minutes in order to appreciate the full agony of asphyxiation. At the point of death, he was cut down, laid on a table and disemboweled. Executioners of the time so perfected their skill that the miscreant usually lingered through this ordeal for minutes, and even had enough life left in him to watch his own entrails be burned. After this, his head was hacked from his shoulders, and his body cut into quarters, which would be displayed at the gates of strongholds associated with his crime. Portions of the Jacobite victims would remain on spikes over Carlisle's city gate for the next thirty years.

At least twenty of these unfortunate prisoners were dispatched in this way, until a court order commuted the harsh sentences to exile for life.

Carlisle Castle survives as a grim relic of a turbulent past. The only remaining evidence of the 1746 atrocity are the so-called 'licking stones' in its dungeon, sections of brickwork which were licked smooth by the tongues of the parched Jacobites as they sought to relieve their thirst with moisture from their prison walls.

WALK THE LAST MILE
Steven Savile

I'll always remember holding her hand.

I'm a tactile person. I can't remember what she was wearing – not the specifics. It was a summer dress, blue I think, with white lace trim and yellow flowers. Or they could have been white flowers. Daisies instead of Buttercups. Maybe. But I can remember exactly how it felt to hold her hand and run together through the barley fields. We had a picnic. I remember that, too. She made these wraps that were really just cheese and ham sandwiches rolled in flatbreads. There was white wine. A small half-bottle. Good stuff. Not that I knew much about wine. Back then I couldn't tell you if the grapes were trodden by barefoot virgins at the foot of Mount Olive or if they were crushed by wee Jimmy Krankie. She'd stolen it from the pub.

Her dad owned the pub. Big Dave.

I haven't thought about him in years. It's funny how these things creep up on you when you let your guard down, isn't it?

I remember so much of that day, but not any of the important stuff. I don't remember what her skin smelled like, or what colour her eyes were. Blue or green? I want to say that they were green, because that would make her more interesting, wouldn't it? But they were probably blue. Or one of each, like David Bowie?

I do remember that she had something wrong with her thumb. It wasn't webbed or anything weird like that, but the knuckle was messed up. She used to pop it out of joint and let it dangle because she knew it grossed me out.

You're supposed to remember your first, aren't you?

God help me, I don't.

Not properly.

Lick and touch and smell – those things I remember.

Not her name.

I remember she had a cute little mole on the side of her left breast. If she'd ever grown old I am sure it would have sprouted hairs and looked like a witch's tit.

'If'.

That's a powerful word.

Like 'yet', that's another one.

I like both of those words. A lot. I like the fact that I can say, "I haven't been to the moon yet," and it implies that I still could, if I really wanted to, and that somehow it's within my control. Or "I'm not sure I am ready to confess yet," suggests I might be, one day. I could say, "If you ask me nicely," and it sounds you actually have some say in the outcome. Funny things words. I'm sure there must be a phobia where people are frightened of them. If not there really ought to be.

Where was I? Oh, right, if wishes were fishes and all that jazz. I can't remember her name, but hand-on-heart, I wish I could. I think about her a lot. I think about holding her hand, still slightly buzzed from the white wine and feeling very grown up. Summer love. Happens so fast. Seventeen years old, 1988, mercifully grown out of the Howard Jones haircuts and the fluorescent Nik Kershaw gloves and into a slightly more dangerous – at least I liked to think so – obsession with The Killing Joke's *Love Like Blood,* Jesus and Mary Chain's *Darklands* and The Teardrop Explodes' *Reward.* It was all about being 'indie' back then. I was a rebel without a clue. I went for dark and brooding mistaking it for interesting. But it was hard to be all dark and brooding in the bright summer sunshine of Beetham with all the tourists, the wind surfers and the clotted cream scones. But I tried valiantly until she smiled at me.

My first summer love. Killed with a smile. Killed with a kiss.

What was her name?

Rachel? Robin? Rebecca? Something beginning with an R. Rowena? Maybe. It feels right. I've just remembered the lyrics of one of the songs I was obsessed with back then: *I want you to burn like I burn.* I can't remember what the song was called. I remember what the album cover looked like. It was a family portrait, one of these old ones, like something out of *Bonanza*, with Hoss and Little Joe at the dining table, but it looked vaguely sinister. I loved the song. It was smoky and powerful and full of love, but laced with a darkness I was just beginning to understand. It seemed to speak to me in a way that other songs hadn't. The underlying message, if I am right, was that you lost your identity when you fell in love. How that other person suddenly becomes the centre of everything and it's all consuming, like a black hole pulling you in. *In your light I crumble.* That was it. That was it exactly. She smiled at me and in that smile I crumbled. But more than that. I wanted her to burn like I burned. Inside. I was on fire.

She spoke to me first. *That* I do remember. None of it would have happened if she had just ignored me like everyone else did back

135

then. But fate is written, right? That's why it's fate. She could no more have *not* talked to me back then than I could have not suggested we go for a walk to the waterfall – the most romantic place I could think of within walking distance of Beetham, and remote enough for us to be alone and maybe fool around some, whilst managing to sound like this big sweet sensitive guy. I remember trying to explain that love and death were my twin religions as we walked to the picnic spot. It was meant to sound deep in that earnest way of teenage boys struggling to be men. It probably came over a little bit creepy given the inverted silver crucifix around my throat and the studded dog collar strapped around my wrist.

I had a crumpled second hand copy of Jean-Paul Satre's letters to Simone de Beauvoir. It had been my 'Bible' ever since I'd first heard about it in the Lloyd Cole song. Not that I'd ever let on to having listened to *Rattlesnakes*. It didn't fit with my carefully cultivated image.

We lay back in the long grass and I read to her.

Words are the way to a woman's heart, don't let anyone tell you any different.

She had a delicate china-doll body. My index fingers almost touched when I held her waist and her small ripe nipples pressed up against the cotton of her summer dress as she leaned in to me for that first kiss. She wasn't wearing a bra. I can remember that, too. I can vividly recall the first touch, the first time my skin touched her skin, and the electricity that passed between us. It was as though her life-force used me as a conduit, racing down into the earth – to dust returned. The contrast of the softness of her breast, the curve of it as I cupped it in my palm, and the rough edge of her nipple as it hardened beneath my hand. I'd never felt anything like it before. It was like ice melting in my hand, the way it changed state, becoming something different. But completely unlike it at the same time. Both more and less alive, if that makes sense?

And, as crazy as it sounds, I can remember the slight hitch of her breathing and the way her lips parted, like she was breathing out her soul, when my fingers found her and slipped inside.

I'd never touched a girl before. Not like that. I didn't know what to expect. What it would feel like. I didn't expect it to change, too. Not from the coarse wiry brush of tight black pubic hair to the dryness of skin, and then, as it parted beneath my touch, to the suddenly slick wetness between. It should have been Heaven but it felt like Hell.

No, that's wrong.

Not Hell. But it was hot. I'd expected it to be cool, cold even, but why would it have been cold in the crux of her being, her core? I pushed, probably a little too roughly, forcing a finger inside. I remember thinking that I'd just opened the way into her, like I'd forced a hand through her chest into her heart. Her secret self, if you like. Not that I place any great stock in flesh and blood. I mean it's not as though her cunt was conscious. It didn't breath and think, it only fucked. And as glorious as that act was, it still wasn't powerful enough for me to remember her name, was it?

But be that as it may, I became a man that day. Just not the sort of man I'd dreamed of being when I still wore those fluorescent gloves and day-glo socks. I became the sort of man your soul can't legislate for. They called me a monster, but that's so banal. Small minds use small words. I was a man in the most glorious sense of the word. Potent. Powerful. A life giver and a life taker.

But I'm getting ahead of myself. The fucking didn't come 'til well after the touching. The two aren't mutually inclusive – or is that exclusive – at least not in my world. I reserve the touching for when I want to be filled up. And for when I want to consume.

So we ate. I read to her. We laughed. She talked. And then we walked to the waterfall. I told her that the route we were taking was one of Lakeland's corpse trails. Years ago, back before there were roads everywhere and everyone had cars this place was really remote, but people still lived out here in these outlying villages. Lived and died here. And when they did people would have to gather together and carry the dead back to the nearest churchyard. That's what the corpse trails were. Paths of the dead. We walked in their footsteps, ghosts of the ghosts. I impressed her by pointing out the iron rings in the limestone rocks, explaining that pallbearers would thread ropes through the rings and use them as anchor-points to haul the coffins up the cliff. I made crazy faces and bounced scary echoes off the rocks.

The waterfall itself was a powerful thing to behold, but slightly disappointing in many ways, too. It wasn't this huge thing like Niagara. It was smaller. Less elemental.

It fell maybe one hundred feet, just dropping away. We stood right on the edge, looking down at the white spume frothing away at the bottom. The river splashed around the flat stones we used like a causeway to cross from one side to the other. It wasn't as risky as it sounds. It was no more than ankle deep and we could have waded across if we'd wanted to, there was barely any undertow, but instead we decided to play a game of 'step on a crack, break your mother's back' only this time it wasn't cracks in the pavement, it was if we got splashed.

Young love.

We scrambled down the muddy bank to the foot of the waterfall. I remember standing knee-deep in the foam spouting – in my most serious and sonorous voice – the last stanza of *Death* by William Butler Yeats. It was the only poem I remembered by heart, and I loved the notion that man had created death. Like the words 'if' and 'yet' there was a power to the notion that men had some control over things like that, even if it was just an illusion. She applauded and then giggled.

I didn't like being laughed at.

The next hour or so are less vivid when I think back on them. I asked her to walk the last mile with me to the fairy steps. I'd heard about them, obviously. They were Beetham's only tourist attraction so it was hard to spend any time in the village and not hear about them. It was such a long time ago. Details blur with distance. The clarity of it all fades with the filter time. Life's treacherous like that. You think 'Ah, this, this I will remember forever' but you don't. You can't. You forget. That's the secret of memory. You forget. So you need to do it again. At least I do.

There was a newfound intimacy to it all, though. I do remember that.

She nestled her head on my shoulder when we sat, and played with my hair as we walked, and she talked. Incessantly. She talked about everything and nothing and I have no idea about any of it. She might as well have been reading the telephone directory.

I didn't like this change in things.

I liked it when there was distance. Space. I felt comfortable then. Without it I felt – ugly. It was as though, suddenly, I was stripped not only naked of the black clothes I'd made my uniform and she wanted to see the man like he was something worth seeing. I wanted to hide. To disappear back beneath the clothes and be anyone but me, but she wouldn't let me. She linked arms as we walked side by side and asked me to tell her about the fairy steps like I was the font of all fucking wisdom.

So I told her the legend because it gave me a chance to become someone else. And for a few minutes as we walked that last mile to the stone steps carved in the limestone cliffs I became the storyteller. We walked to Underlaid Wood, following the dry-stone walls and the bridal path to skirt the farms on the way to Carr Bank and the tower farm – at least that's what I called it, because it had a square stone tower like a castle beside the main fourteenth century farmhouse. There were peacocks in the yard, strutting with their plumage out. I'd never seen a peacock in real life before. And then we followed the limestone pavement into the woods. It was only visible in patches. Sunlight filtered through the leafy canopy of the trees, transformed into gold coins scattered across the ground at our feet like Leprechaun's treasure. That was when I started to tell her about the Fae King and the binding promise he'd made to the Grail Knight. How the knight had been gifted with second sight, and when searching for his love, who had disappeared, spirited away from her bed by one of the fae, he had found this trail and followed it to the steps, where his gift of second sight had revealed the secret entrance into Underhill, beneath Arnside Knott, their hidden kingdom.

I was weaving my own spell. I made it sound magical. Turning it into a fairy tale. I told her how the knight had cornered the Fae King, tricking him into his promise – a challenge, in fact. – if he ever wanted to see his beloved again he would have to navigate the descent of the fairy steps to Underhill without so much as brushing the limestone walls on either side of the crevice. If he could do that, he could ask any boon of the king, including the return of his woman. The knight was a huge powerfully built man, fully armoured in plates of steel. The gully at its narrowest was no more than a foot or so meaning surely it was an impossible challenge.

She was desperate to know if the knight saved his beloved. I didn't have the heart to tell her there was no such thing as a happy ending. Not for the knight, not for his beloved, and not for her.

I don't remember when it changed. When it stopped being sweet and romantic and became something darker, but it was somewhere along that last mile through the woods. You see, I wasn't just talking about the knight, I was talking about me. Believe me, second sight isn't a gift. It's a curse. To walk into a room and see the echoes left behind by everything, by all of those vast powerful emotions that etch themselves into the wood and stone like ghosts, is a curse. I can't turn it off. I can't stop seeing these things, and the temptation is to stop living here, now, and surrender to them and start living amongst them, all of the *thens* that these places cling to. To become a ghost inside your own life. That's no gift.

Maybe she laughed at me again. Maybe that was the trigger. Or maybe it was when I pushed her down into the tall grass scattering the gold coins of sunlight beneath us and she tried to push me away. Or maybe it was when I tore at the buttercups on her dress. Or the daisies. I really don't remember.

She didn't laugh though.

Not after I pushed her. She'd stumbled back, the look on her face so close to that same look of shock, the parted lips, the heavy breathing, as when I did things with my fingers. I sung to her then, straddling her, my knees pinning her arms down, and for the longest time she seemed to think it was a game. The shock in her face was replaced by something else. I want to call it love. It's the closest I've ever been to seeing love, I think, as something real, tangible. Adoration. The adoration of man. It could have been the name of painting by one of the great pre-Raphaelite masters. It *should* have been. I hit her then, for the first time, knocking the smile from her face. She cried out, but she didn't cry. She was strong. That made it better. More exciting. I hit her again, this time she bled where her gum tore against her teeth. Her teeth! I remember now she had this gap between her two front teeth that was supposed to be beautiful, like Marilyn Monroe's beauty spot, but which was nothing more than an imperfection. Flawed beauty is less beautiful. It just is.

I wiped the blood away from her lip. It smeared across her teeth. It's the little things you remember. I don't remember the fucking. I don't remember what I was thinking as I tore away at her panties, or what I was feeling – apart from hard – as I forced myself into her. I don't remember any sweet words of love. There's only one thing I can remember saying, actually. It wasn't vulgar or beautiful. It wasn't about seduction or ownership. It was about death. I told her that I was giving her a gift unlike any other, that she would live forever, here, because of me. That anyone cursed with second sight would be able to see her here forever.

And then, while she bled from the brutality of my cock I reached down for a jagged piece of rock lying between the sunlight coins and hammered it against her face over and over again, not stopping even as the bones cracked and I stole her face so that no-one, not even her own mother, would ever recognise her again. And even after the light in her eyes – what colour were they? They were red. I can remember now. They were red, filled with blood – had gone and they'd glazed over.

Then my appetite became voracious.

Nothing could sate it.

Not her neck.

Not her breast with its mole or her hard nipples.

Not the soft meat of her thighs or the strings of sinew and fat beneath her flat stomach. I fed – gorged – on her. Consuming her flesh in the same way that I had consumed her innocence. And all because she smiled at me.

But I could not eat her all.

Funny that, the first time I was down between a woman's legs to eat her out I tore away the folds of her labia lips with my teeth. I'm not sure that's what they had in mind when they coined the term. But she tasted good. I wiped my lips with the back of my hands, smearing her blood across my face, then stood up. She was a mess, my first. I got better at it the more I practiced, but that first time I was nothing more than an enthusiastic amateur fumbling and fucking my way through the whole thing and just wanting it to be over because I couldn't enjoy it.

But it wasn't about enjoyment. Not ever. It was about survival, and it survived it. Isn't that what it's like for all of us that first time? Aren't we all terrified our inexperience will disappoint our partners? Don't we want to make it memorable? To give all of ourselves to them in ways we've never given ourselves before? That was one of the things she'd babbled as we walked that last mile. I can remember it now that I think about it, her voice soft, serious, as she told me she wanted her first time to be special. That she wasn't that kind of girl. That she didn't sleep around, and that when she found the right guy, when she knew it was right, she wanted to give herself body and soul to her lover.

I took her at her word.

Body and soul.

She was mine.

I gathered her into my arms tenderly. After all she was part of me now. We were joined forever. Lovers. I stood up. She was lighter than I'd expected, or maybe I was stronger for the adrenaline pumping through my system? I carried her towards the fairy steps just over the rise, knowing exactly what I was going to wish for if I made it all the way to the bottom without touching the sides.

Like those pallbearers years before me, I stepped into the narrow gully. The limestone sides were inches away from my shoulder as I took the first and second steps down. I had to stop before the third, adjusting her weight in my arms and angling her body slightly so her bloody face wouldn't leave a tell tale red smear on the rock. The fourth and fifth steps were easy but then the walls narrowed impossibly. The was no way I could make it with her in my arms, so I pushed her in front of me, letting her fall. She twisted and tumbled and hit both sides of the gully on the way down to the bottom. She wasn't going to be making any wishes. Unencumbered, I wriggled

141

through the narrowest gap, not daring to breathe for fear my bloodstained shirt would brush up against the limestone and damn me, and then I was on the other side and looking out over Arnside Knott and the Fae Kingdom of Underhill. I could see them all. Waiting for me. Hunger. Expectancy in their eyes. I was one of them. A fae creature. Their nostrils flared at the scent of blood. I walked towards them, holding her in my arms again as an offering to set before the king.

He knew what I was going to ask for in return for the dead girl. I had done the impossible. I had negotiated the narrows and made it to the bottom without touching the sides, and in return I was going to demand my wish.

I had earned it.

What did I wish for?

I wished that I'd get away with it.

THE POLTERGEIST OF WALLA CRAG

Walla Crag, a high rock overlooking Derwent Water in Borrowdale, is reputedly the haunt of a malignant spirit that was banished here after a Catholic exorcism.

The story dates back to the days of Lowther Hall, a medieval manor house which stood on the site of Lowther Castle. In the 1760s, it was occupied by Sir James Lowther, 'Bad Lord Lonsdale', who was an MP and Lord Lieutenant for both Cumberland and Westmorland. An influential politician and wealthy landowner, he was much feared by the local peasantry, who he is said to have oppressed and terrorised in various ways. Such was the menace he instilled in his tenants that reputedly the streets of towns and villages would fall completely silent when he rode through them.

Under such circumstances, it might be thought that his eventual death would have been a cause for celebration, but when he died the torment didn't end, for James Lowther's troublesome spirit would not rest. According to tradition, Lowther Hall became the scene of astonishingly violent poltergeist activity. There was frequent tumult throughout the building and its stable blocks, and blows were stuck against staff and visitors. Even on the day of Lowther's funeral, or so the story goes, the attending clergyman was viciously attacked by an unseen entity and almost thrown from his desk. The Hall, so shunned by common folk during Lowther's lifetime, now, during his death, became regarded as an edifice of evil. Travellers would go to great lengths to avoid even passing close to it, especially at night.

The haunting allegedly persisted until the end of the eighteenth century, when a Catholic priest was eventually asked to drive away the unclean spirit. By all accounts, the Latin rite of exorcism was performed but only with great difficulty. According to beliefs of the time, evil spirits would resist with every inch of their power if attempts were made to banish them to Hell. Other, more earthly destinations were thus favoured instead. As a result, the fearsome soul of James Lowther was finally – though only after many torturous hours – dispatched to distant Walla Crag.

For a time, the crag, which stands 1,234 feet above sea-level and can now be reached by climbers, was said to have become a perilous place. Anyone who ventured up there was likely to be attacked and maybe even cast into the abyss. A second ceremony was thus held at a later date, and the spirit interred inside the crag itself, from which it has never escaped. Unsubstantiated rumours tell how, even in *modern times, those who have ascended to Walla Crag have placed their ears against the rock and heard muffled shrieks of anger from deep inside.*

FRAMED
Peter Bell

Fret not thyself because of evil-doers,
Neither be thou envious against the workers of iniquity
Psalms 37

The palest hint of a cold October dawn was emerging from behind Wakebarrow as the Banks brothers eased the battered Land Rover along the track into the woods. The stars were still prominent and a bright full moon picked out the white boles of the birches, offering sufficient illumination for them to carry their unwanted burden down the twisting footpath to the graveyard of the ancient church of St Bede at Oxen Fell. They had eschewed the more convenient parking place on the neatly cropped grass outside the lych-gate, it being imperative that their vehicle, and its illicit load, were not seen in the area at such an unholy hour. Some of the local farmers were known to be abroad well before daybreak, workaholics, primed like birds to a lifetime of arising at first light. Jake and Joe Banks were running late, and night's dubious cloak of security was, sooner than expected this cloudless morn, becoming distinctly threadbare. For the night's job, so cleanly executed, had thrown up an unexpected problem.

In a way it was their own fault – or at least Jake's, for it was he who had cased the joint. The framed Turner sketches, mounted on the tall walls of the spacious dining room at Helton Hall, the 17th century mansion near Grange-over-Sands, had appeared to the untrained eye to be considerably smaller and more manageable than in reality they were. It was not the drawings themselves – Jake had made short shrift of cutting them from the frame, rolling the priceless treasures into one of the circular tubes used to protect saplings from the depredations of deer, and slinging them in the back of the truck amidst sundry other legitimate forestry gear. Nor was it their surprising weight, for they were strong lads; rather it was the awkward size of the two elaborately-gilt frames – crazy, Joe thought, for such trashy little scribbles. They were not going to be easy to hide or dispose of, at least until the affair had blown over.

It had been Jake's idea to conceal them in the churchyard.

"There ain't nobody comes rootin' round that graveyard," he jeered, when Joe raised objections, "apart, that is, from Dolly and

dotty Doreen when they come to tidy graves and do church out – an'
that's not 'til Saturday." He gave a knowing laugh. "Not scared of
the old tales are yer?"

Joe grunted noncommittally; he didn't want to lose face before
his twenty-five year old brother, eight years his senior. As a matter
of fact, Joe had never liked the place. He had a more vivid
imagination than Jake, and as a boy had listened, petrified, to
Granddad Banks' yarns. There was the black dog of Wakebarrow,
said to be seen shortly before a death in the family; old Mrs Grayson
at the Manor had died of a stroke the day after her daughter was
frightened off the fell by such an animal – though the local farmers
insisted it was a sheepdog gone feral. It was said, with regard to St
Bede's, that Aloysius Slee, an indefatigable verger of a hundred
years or so back, who rested somewhere in the churchyard, assumed
grisly guard against would-be violators. Certainly, when they were
children, there had been an inexplicable death – and, by all
whispered accounts, an appalling one – befalling a thief who had
broken into the church and rifled the vestry. Well, Joe reassured
himself, a couple of stashed picture frames from Helton Hall were
unlikely to stir the vengeful wrath of Mr Slee.

*

The burglary of the Hall had been arranged by an insider. Don
Wilkes, a local wide-boy, had somehow inveigled his way into the
service of Helton's owners, the de la Poles, whose residence in the
district went back to Tudor times, currently away in France. Don,
who worked as a groundsman, had ensured that windows were
unlocked and alarms disconnected. The security, indeed, was
laughable for such a property – though tutelage during the summer
opening season if the masses strayed onto prohibited lawns or
touched forbidden furnishings, spoke if anything of a surfeit of zeal.
The family was not well-liked, and this had allowed the never-too-
robust consciences of the Banks boys to be easily appeased.

It had been a moment's work to seize the pictures, conveniently
stacked in advance by Wilkes beside the window, and put them into
the waiting vehicle, their access to the spacious grounds having
likewise been arranged by their capable co-conspirator. Don was a
good bloke, but, they more than suspected, would reap a more ample
reward from the theft than they, he being the contact for the fence
who would purvey the goods – the respectable Roger Dunn, of
Dunn, Son and Nephew, who operated under the cover of an

146

antiquarian book shop in Sedbergh – to a Japanese client who had 'ordered' the two sketches of Lake Coniston for his private collection. There were few pies in which Don Wilkes did not have his finger; he had gone a long way since the old days when Jake and he poached game on the Holker Hall estate. Still, Joe reflected, he had been promised more cash for the job than a month's wages with the Forestry Commission.

Jake had insisted they did not return direct along the main Windermere road, but take the tortuous route via Oxen Fell, along by Ellers Fell and the Myreground plantations, thence to Birks. Here, where Joe lived alone with their semi-invalid mother, Amy Banks, in a run-down former farmhouse, they would separate; and Jake would go on to Kendal, staying as usual with his girlfriend, Jean. It was best, they agreed, that they be not seen together until the scene had settled. Jean – who imagined it was a poaching expedition – had already guaranteed an alibi, and Joe thought he could rely on Mother to do the same. Whenever there was mischief in the area the Grange-over-Sands constabulary paid the Banks a routine visit; and Mrs Banks tended to resent what she saw as persecution of a rough but ready pair of young lads.

"Can't see why we're comin' this way," Joe complained. "If police are out after poachers, they'll be up 'ere, not down on main road."

Recent years – since the advent of the wealthy Sir Hilary Grainger at the Manor, who had paid canny farmers many times over the odds to acquire extra shooting land – had seen a proliferation of pheasants, which, respecting no territorial boundaries, provided abundant temptation to the more enterprising locals.

"Police won't be out this way t'night," Jake replied dismissively. "Dan was sayin'. They're short staffed on account of that murder in Preston. There's CCTV cameras an' all along main road. We don't want car picked up on 'em … First thing's t' get shut of them frames."

Joe was feeling increasingly uneasy. It was one thing to be fined for pinching a few dead birds, but works of art – this was a new departure, and he wished he'd kept out of the whole thing. But it was certainly a load of cash.

"Why can't we just get on 'ome, Jake?" he whined. "I'll burn 'em back of barn later. Don't fancy messin' round down at church this time of night."

"Nope!" Jake said firmly. "Too risky. They may be out lookin' before yer get round to lightin' a fire. Nope, only thing to do is 'ide

147

'em. Then when coast's clear, like – weeks, months, whatever – I know a feller down in Morecambe, exports stuff like this to the States, asks no questions. For time bein' they're 'ot stuff, DNA an' all!'

"We used gloves!"

"Aye, that we did, but there's ways, the wood rubbin' on clothes an' that, specially 'ow we've 'ad to' eft the buggers. No, mate, only way's to get rid!"

Taking one frame apiece, the brothers stumbled their way down through the moonlit trees, tripping on roots, snagging their unwieldy load against low branches. Had they blown a trumpet it could scarcely have announced their presence more loudly. Joe felt jittery, his heart leaping to his mouth as a brace of pheasants, roosting in the trees, flew up in squawking terror. The wood gave way to a patch of bracken-tangled fell, little more than a hundred yards, yet precipitous and knotted with last summer's still dense, resilient growth. The dark silhouette of the church, hidden from moon and dawn alike by a stand of black yews, crouched ominously; the graveyard was a hole of blackness.

Once amidst the graves, whether because the dawn was growing or their eyes had adjusted to the gloom, they could make out detail well enough. Jake had remained mysterious as to where the frames would be stashed. Joe had imagined they would be buried. There was a three week old grave – John Jones from Hollows Fell if he remembered aright – maybe here the loose earth would provide an easy excavation; but Jake was making towards the church itself, by the older stones and slabs.

"Come on, lad, it'll be bloody sunshine soon, an' Jenks'll be about, lookin' for 'is lost sheep."

"Yer not diggin'? ... Then where ..?

"Don't be soft, Joe, we'd be 'ere all day diggin' ... 'elp me pull back one of these 'ere slabs."

Joe's stomach churned. "Openin' a grave ... Jake, are yer mad?' His voice reached a squeak.

"Shush! Yer'll be wakin' dead y'self! ... Look, these buggers 'ave been restin' 'ere 'undreds of years. They won't be bothered now. An' there ain't no-one remembrin' 'em either. Come on, it'll take two bodies to get this shifted."

The low slate slab was inset by time into the encroaching bank, festooned with briar. With no leverage other than their hands, their fingers sliding repeatedly away from the mossy surface, wrists lacerated by the thorns, the task proved impossible. They debated going back to the car for a tool, but Jake had a better idea: down at the east end, where a footpath entered the graveyard from nearby Kirk Farm, were three very old raised tombs, each one topped by a heavy granite canopy, evidently for privileged members of the community, their names long weathered to anonymity.

"This'll do," said Jake, dumping his burden on the middle slab, more substantial than its neighbours. "Alls we needs do is push top over, an' slide 'em in. There'll be room enough. Come on, 'eave!"

Even so, it was an effort to slide the slab, despite two men's strength. Deep in the shadow of the yews, which seemed actually to suck the light, it was hard to see. The slab moved sluggishly – probably for the first time since its incumbent took up residence – making their hands chafe; then suddenly of its own accord, almost as if assisted from within, it shot across and tilted, propelled by gravity. It was only with considerable vigour, making them sweat even in the chilly dawn, that they recovered its balance, wedging it with an effort upon the top of its lower neighbour. There was just enough space to insert their irksome load, though the larger frame required main force, only slipping into position following a dismaying sound of wood splintering beneath.

Breathless, they paused, before attempting the relocation of the canopy. While Jake went aside to relieve himself, Joe peered apprehensively into the tomb, hoping not to confirm what he thought they'd broken inside. As he did, the moon cleared the yews, its pale light shining within, and Joe caught a glint of gold. Jake's back was still turned. Greed displacing fear, he reached down and retrieved a ring that could only have burst from the coffin underneath. As he did, a terrible screech seared the twilight. An eldritch white shape flitted above his head from the church's eaves towards the yews.

He cringed in terror.

It even gave Jake a shock.

"What in bloody 'ell's name's that?"

Then they laughed: the barn owl perched superciliously atop the tallest yew, hissing at them, angry at the invasion of its dawn solitude.

"Come on,' said Jake. "Let's get this back. I need a drink, an' it's waitin' in flask at car!"

It proved not so easy to return the slab. Even when it was more or less in position it gently rocked where previously it had lain as firm as the stone from which it had been hewed. It was the best they could do.

149

They stumbled back up the fell into the wood. A holly branch tore off Joe's cap as they passed into the trees, causing him to turn. The rising moon made of the gravestones grim silhouettes and shadows, except for a triangle of blackness in the lee of the church, where a tall straggling juniper for a moment looked like a man with outstretched arms. His nerves were in tatters; all the way he worried about what he had purloined. That night, to poaching he had added into his portfolio art theft and grave robbing. It was quite a learning curve.

Back at the vehicle they rolled cigarettes and quaffed generously from a bottle of Johnny Walker.

*

Over the next few days Joe lived in endless trepidation, the worse for being unable to rely on his elder bother's devil-may-care bluster. Despite the latter's dire instructions against, he tried calling his mobile, but it was permanently off. News about the break-in at the Hall, a visit from the police, an untoward discovery in the graveyard – all these contingencies haunted him. Every knock on the door, every voice of a visitor, every car sidling up the lane, he expected to see the police.

And there was the matter of the ring.

It was a gold ring set with a pale lilac stone. The Victorians, he had heard, often buried loved ones with precious trinkets, secure in a more God-fearing age against the risk of desecration. It would certainly fetch a fair penny – he'd seen things like it on the *Antiques Road Show* – a nice bonus on top of the proceeds from the Hall. On the other hand, there were Granddad's yarns – and it wasn't only Granddad, quite a few of his mother's elderly friends could tell a fine tale. And there was something – despite his youthful atheism – blasphemous, something especially heinous, about stealing from a grave, violating holy ground.

He pondered returning it, but apart from the practical difficulty of moving the slab on his own, there were obvious reasons to stay clear of a scene of stolen goods. It would be reckless to go in daytime, when he risked being seen by Jenks if no-one else; whilst the idea of returning alone at night would call for a hardier soul than Joe Banks. There was also the worry that if the police searched the house (which they could easily do, on the pretext of looking for illicit game), they might very well look askance at his ownership of so exotic an item. Mother kept a jewel box underneath the bed in the spare room filled with worthless items belonging to her own mother, of mere sentimental value; he hid the ring inside it until such time as he could decide its future.

The slightest noise at night – and they were numerous in the creaking wood-beamed house with its mouse population undeterred by the idle cat that sunned itself all day in the window or slept before the fire – made his heart race. He was forever surveying the garden, glimpsing dark shapes in the shrubbery that clustered uncomfortably around the dwelling, or lurking in the encroaching pinewood. The braying of a donkey up in top pasture (sold by Jenks for a small fortune to Grainger) in the middle of the night quite upset him; and never had he noticed so many owls—or was it one and the same?—swooping beneath his window.

His mother remarked on his brooding, setting him worrying that his behaviour did not seem normal – a classic sign the police looked out for when investigating suspects in a crime. It was from her he first heard news of the burglary.

"Been a break-in down at 'elton 'all," she announced over breakfast. "You know – the posh place where Jenny got given sack for givin' a bit of lip. Serves the buggers right!"

Joe's stomach churned. It was difficult to avoid sounding too interested, and yet insufficient interest might look suspicious too.

"It was on local TV news," she went on. "They were talking to Don. You remember Don? Don Wilkes? Went to school with Jake? Well, sounds like 'e's got a nice number down there, 'e were always one as lands on 'is feet. Found the place broken into, early hours t'other night. Some paintings gone, worth a fortune, they say. It's in paper too. Here ..."

She handed him the *Westmorland Gazette*.

Joe yawned, affecting desultory interest. It was on the front page, banished to second story by the headlines: a developer's threat to Forestry Commission woods at Grizedale. Well, they could burn them all down for all he cared; they'd worked him like a slave in that place. Butterflies in his stomach, he turned to the account of the burglary.

Priceless Turners Stolen from Insecure Mansion

Don had certainly cooked up a plausible story, though how far it would stand intense scrutiny was anyone's guess. The insurance company didn't like the lack of security, but would probably have to pay up; they, at least, could be expected to pursue the case with zeal,

151

even if the police cared little for the negligently rich. An old green Land Rover had been seen in the area at three in the morning, and the police would welcome any information pertaining to such a vehicle. The owners had not yet returned from France, but Mr Wilkes was putting things in order.

The reference to the Land Rover was worrying. What especially irked Joe was the estimated value of the sketches, a seven figure sum, "perhaps even more on the black market". It put their own share in perspective. Yet they would carry the can if it all came out. He wouldn't mind knowing what Don's cut was.

*

Dolly Higgins entered St Bede's churchyard as usual on Saturday at 10am sharp, accompanied by Tracy, her ill-tempered Yorkshire terrier, and Doreen Grimshaw, her fifteen-year old assistant.

"Now you be checkin' for dead flowers on graves, Doreen, and clear 'em up. An' I'll go in and 'oover church … Oh, an' make sure Mr Jones is alright, there's no foxes been at 'is grave."

The ritual was so well entrenched, it scarcely needed articulating. Doreen waddled her slow, lazy way amongst the graves, humming.

Dolly Higgins, ten years a widow, was a fit woman for seventy-eight. She had been performing this task now for forty-seven years, and had never once left the valley, except for her sister-in-law's funeral in Settle. Her husband had farmed a smallholding until rheumatism and arthritis put an end to working. Dolly enjoyed her job. There was hardly a detail in church and churchyard alike that escaped her eagle eye. Glancing round as she approached the porch, she noticed that the lilies on Millie Rutt's grave would soon need replacing, that Jenks had still not attended to the leaning stone by the lych-gate, that a lager can had been thrown on the pathway and that moles had been at work again.

Inside the church, Dolly paused and imbibed its gently sacred atmosphere, enhanced today by the sparkling November sun glinting through the east window, with its stained-glass saints and crucifixion. She was polishing the carvings on the Lishman pew when she heard Doreen's dull tones.

"Dolly, there's a man."

"A man, Doreen?" she replied without looking up, in a kindly voice. "Is it Jenks, dear?"

"No, Dolly," the girl said. "It's a great big man an' e's lookin' at me … e's got a funny smile, I don't like 'im."

Doreen, as they put it, was 'not one hundred percent'. It was rumoured she was like that because her mother had tried to make away with her before she was born, and it had gone wrong.

Sighing, Dolly arose. The girl could be trying. But, these days, the things you heard, she'd better make sure.

"Alright, love, jus' show me where 'e is."

"It's 'ere, where we come in, Dolly."

The girl led Dolly to the east wall, where the three raised tombs were. Of course, there was no-one.

"E's gone," Doreen said, wide-eyed.

"Okay," Dolly said sharply, "now let's forget this nonsense, Doreen, and get down to some work. Look at the weeds on that grave there …"

Dolly paused.

She turned back towards the tombs – the slab on the middle one was an inch or so askew. It had never been shifted in her time. It was most odd.

It was Old Aloysius Slee's tomb – not that anyone would know that now, apart from herself and one or two of the older villagers; the inscriptions had long been illegible. It was bigger than its neighbours, and longer; he was said to have been a giant of a man. So favoured had the zealous verger been in his day that the Lishmans, squires of the Manor, had honoured him with a resting place next to their own, Ebenezer on the right and Hannah Lavenia on the left.

Dolly inspected the slab; there could be no question of her moving it on her own.

"Doreen," she called. "Go and see if Jenks is down in paddock, and tell 'im to bring tractor."

Jenks backed up to the gate, complaining, and with a contraption of chains harnessed to the slab, gently eased the tractor forward until the heavy stone slid away, resting once again on the tomb of Ebenezer Lishman.

"What's this?" exclaimed Dolly, peering within, as Jenks returned from the tractor.

"Is it a man?" asked Doreen asked.

"No, love, no! Don't be silly! … It's wood … Picture frames, by look of it."

She met Jenks's eye.

"It were in *Gazette*," she exclaimed, aghast. "Them pictures from 'elton 'all! Worth a million, they said!"

Jenks was rummaging within, lifting out the frames.

"More like fifty quid," he laughed lugubriously. "Ain't no pictures 'ere, only frames. Must've dumped 'em. Better tell police, though."

The two young constables who arrived several hours later appeared to Dolly Higgins little impressed at this significant event in the annals of Oxen Fell. One of them even yawned while he listened to her account.

"Someone local, do you think?" asked Jenks.

"No, not very likely, sir," said the taller one, smiling patronisingly. "It's a professional job. They'll strip out the drawing, then dump the frames – they just found somewhere remote, that's all. No-one would know this place existed."

"Aye, no-one 'cept locals," insisted Jenks.

"Not the first time stolen goods have been concealed in a cemetery, sir," said the other shortly, "but of course we'll ask around."

They took statements, photographed the scene, removed the frames to the police car, and departed, promising to "keep them informed".

*

When the police called at Birks it was not about the Helton job.

Joe quailed when he heard the rap on the door – the rap he had long been expecting – a nd saw the dark uniforms upon the threshold. They were not the usual lads, either; there was a senior officer in his fifties with greying hair, an inspector by the look of it, and a young female constable.

Their faces were grim as they asked to come in. The policewoman broke the news to Mrs Banks.

"It's about your son, Mrs Banks."

Jake had been found dead in peculiar circumstances. The Land Rover he was driving had crashed into the woods and plunged to the bottom of the disused slate quarry near Wood Farm, less than a mile away; his body was still at the wheel, severely maimed. Evidently he had lain there for several days; it was surprising no-one had found the wreck before or heard the accident. They presumed it had occurred at night.

"We'll have to thoroughly inspect the vehicle, of course," added the policeman, "and there will need to be an inquest … but it seems clear enough, Mrs Banks …"

He looked towards his young companion.

"We're sorry, Mrs Banks," the woman interjected, smiling solicitously, "you see, there was an opened bottle of whiskey in the car."

"Your son, madam, was nearly three times over the legal alcohol limit," the man added.

The inspector then asked a series of roundabout questions, seemingly irrelevant to the accident, concerning Jake's movements and people he knew, including whether he had been at home this week at nights, and whether he had recently spoken of visiting the Grange-over-Sands area in the crashed vehicle.

It was Joe's grisly task, in lieu of his distraught mother, to accompany the officers to Barrow-in-Furness to identify the corpse; which, as they cautioned, had ghastly mutilations, even though he had not apparently gone through the shattered windscreen. Their surmise was that a bird of some kind, or even a fox, had entered the twisted vehicle and begun to feed; that would explain the missing eyes, and the lesions. He may, at first, have been still alive; there had been strange contortions of the arms and legs, indicative of struggle, when they found him. The wreck, they told Joe when he casually asked, was still where it had been found; a contractor with a winch would be retrieving it in the morning.

*

Joe had to make his own way back in a taxi, and during the journey he tried hard to persuade himself that the officers had not eyed him suspiciously when he enquired about the vehicle. Already he had heard about Dolly Higgins's discovery: trust the old cow to notice something like that! Yet, despite their evident suspicions, the police had apparently pulled no threads together yet; though, of course, they might be lying low, watching him, awaiting their moment to pounce.

Joe alighted at the *Fox and Hounds*. Once it had sped off he hurried in the direction of Wood Farm. Surreptitiously surveying the scene, he scrambled down to the quarry. It was high risk, but if the police found the drawings, who knew where it would end?

Miraculously, the police appeared not to have searched the vehicle: the sapling tubes were untouched, the priceless drawings still coiled safely within. Any relief, however, quickly gave way to anxiety about disposal. He had no idea what arrangements Jake had made to pass on the goods. He didn't fancy confronting the slippery Wilkes, and had no idea at all what he would say if he entered the premises of Dunn, Son & Nephew and presented two stolen works by Turner. Extracting them from the tubes, he stuffed the sketches beneath his jacket. Within half an hour, before the wood-burning stove in the kitchen, he watched as a million pounds went up in flames.

There was one more thing he had to do before he could sleep soundly in his bed. It was already twilight. He retrieved the ring, got a crowbar from the garage and took a deep swig of Johnny Walker.

Outside, it was a cold starless night, the darkness deepened by the overarching canopy of trees.

The tall, burly figure draped in black that waylaid Joe in the lane and escorted him to the graveyard was not a policeman.

*

Saturday again – the weeks went by so fast! – Dolly Higgins and her entourage found themselves once more at St Bede's. Doreen, humming behind, carried fresh lilies for Millie Rutt, while bad-tempered Tracy scurried ahead, growling as she scampered through the gate, in particularly irascible mood today. The dog was grunting and snuffling by old Slee's tomb, yapping furiously.

Dolly paused in her tracks. She had been most meticulous last week with a grumbling Jenks, making sure the slab was repositioned with mathematical exactitude, four square upon its base. It had been moved – again – and this time it was out by far more than an inch: there was a narrow gap. It was a grey, frosty morning, leaden clouds dulling what little light there was. She could not quite make out within whatever it was that was driving Tracy into a frenzy.

"Doreen, love," she called calmly. "Get Jenks. Down in paddock."

Doreen plodded away.

Soon Jenks was back on the scene. Cursing, he repeated his manoeuvre with the tractor, while Doreen gawped and Dolly stood over the tomb. The slab moved slowly, then tilted violently, this time crashing to the floor, cracking in two.

Dolly peered inside, then recoiled.

"Good God Almighty!"

"Is it a man?" asked Doreen.

Dolly shooed her away. "Doreen, love, go home … go on, quick, quick! Leave them lilies."

It was, indeed, a man, or at least a youth …

Joe Banks was on his back, torn and bloody, legs and arms all cringing before him as if he were fending something away. And the state of his face! ... What was left of it! No fox would do that!

"Those Banks boys," she declared, as Jenks joined her. "I knew they'd come to a bad end. Wrong-uns, the pair of 'em!"

She sighed and shook her head.

"I knew it," added Jenks grimly. "Mixed up in that robbery, young beggars! Gang murder, likely! To keep 'em quiet – I've read about them things in paper."

Dolly kept her own counsel. Her mind was running back ten year or so ago, to what happened to that poor lad from Liverpool, the one who stole the collection money from the vestry.

The dark day was growing colder, gloom gathering though it was not yet noon. She drew her shawl more closely round her, shivering, and swept her eyes about the graveyard, back towards Aloysius Slee's desecrated tomb. Could that be the laughter of a woodpecker, so late in the year?

Millie Rutt's fresh lilies lay scattered in the weeds where Doreen had cast them, and Tracy continued to growl.

FIEND'S FELL

Look on a map of northwest England now, and you won't find any such place as Fiend's Fell. But look on a map predating 1608, and you'll find 'Fendsfell' just north of Penrith. Compare the two and the mystery will be explained, for you'll observe that this vast, mysterious massif at the extreme north end of the Pennine Mountains has now been renamed 'Cross Fell'. At 2,930 feet, it is the tallest peak in the entire Pennine range, and is frequently to be seen covered in cloud or mist.

The sinister stories that surround Fiend's Fell are legion. It was long said to be the home of Peg Sneddle. She was an evil enchantress, who would ride the Helm Wind, a shrill blast of very cold air – a meteorological oddity unique to this part of the country – casting curses on all who saw her. Its lower slopes, which were just as trackless and desolate as its fog-shrouded summit, were the hunting grounds of the barguests, or 'hill-ghosts', ferocious demonic dogs, who would seek unclean souls, tear them from the flesh of their owners and carry them off to Hell. The eviscerated victims would then become barguests too, and run for eternity with the blood-soaked pack.

If all of this sounds like fable and fairy tale, it did not in times past, when the dangers of Fiend's Fell were taken very seriously indeed. Its name was changed to Cross Fell in 1608, when a tall stone crucifix was erected on its summit to try and ward off the evil that plagued it. Of the crucifix there is no longer a trace, not even a stump. But this is perhaps understandable, because according to superstition there has been no let-up in the frightening events occurring up there. Incidents have been reported right into modern times: chilling cries have been heard, phantom figures seen capering in the mist.

Religious groups of various denominations were once regularly called on to perform services on Cross Fell, in order to cleanse it. But they no longer participate. As far as they are concerned, the whole thing is country nonsense, though cynical observers feel that the real reason they avoid the fell may be because none of those attempted exorcisms in the past – including one performed by St. Augustine in the Dark Ages – were successful before, so why should they succeed now?

Why a place should have such an evil reputation for no obvious reason – either mythical or real – only asks more unanswerable *questions. Even today, no roads lead up to Fiend's Fell. Perhaps with good reason.*

NIGHT OF THE CRONE
Anna Taborska

A weight of Awe not easy to be borne
Fell suddenly upon my spirit – cast
From the dread bosom of the unknown past,
When first I saw that family forlorn.
Speak Thou, whose massy strength and stature scorn
The power of years – pre-eminent, and placed
Apart, to overlook the circle vast –
Speak, Giant-mother! tell it to the Morn,
While she dispels the cumbrous shades of Night;

Let the Moon hear, emerging from a cloud;
At whose behest up rose on British ground
That Sisterhood in hieroglyphic round
Forth-shadowing, some have deemed, the infinite
The inviolable God, that tames the proud.

William Wordsworth

TEK CARE
LAMBS
INT ROAD

The home-made sign toppled to the ground as the SUV swerved into it, then ran it over. The three youths in the back of the Range Rover tumbled from one side of the vehicle to the other, cursing profusely.

"Ten points if you hit a lamb!" Zed grinned at the driver from his prime position in the passenger seat, then ran his hand through the thick dark blonde hair that covered his ears and almost reached his chin in a kind of matted, over-grown bob. Had his nose been a bit smaller, and his eyes a bit bigger, he might almost have passed as attractive. There was no doubt he had a certain charisma and menacing charm, which probably contributed to the unquestioning loyalty he inspired in his friends. None of them had the slightest idea that Zed (christened 'Brian' by his doting mother) only kept them around for his own amusement and to help him get what he wanted from life.

160

"No problem!" responded Johnny. At twenty he was the eldest, but also the smallest of the youths, and the only one to have once held a driving licence. What Johnny lacked in size and wit he made up for in unpredictability and violence. He'd gotten by in school by being a total psycho and he got by with girls by forcing them. His drug of choice – which he indulged in at every given opportunity – was speed, which no doubt contributed to his regular bouts of mania and over-excitement. A casual observer might have described him as something of a killer-dweeb.

"Unfortunately, it might actually *be* a problem," Zed grinned. Johnny glanced at him quizzically. "You only get lambs here in spring," Zed explained.

"Oh yeah ... But you said ... oh, it was a joke!" Johnny finally got it. Anybody else would have had their nuts ripped off and shoved down their throat for making a joke at his expense, but as far as Johnny was concerned, Zed was God.

"Don't worry about it, man," Zed told him. "It's twenty points for a granny."

*

The short drive from Langwathby, through Little Salkeld, was uneventful. The yuppie couple they'd stolen the SUV from must have alerted the police by now, but Zed figured that they could safely drive as far as the stone circle without getting caught. Once there, they'd ditch the vehicle under the tree in the small parking space to the side of the path. It would be dark soon and nobody would think to look for the vehicle at a heritage monument off the beaten track. Besides, if anybody asked, they would deny all knowledge of the theft.

They followed the signs for *The Druid's Circle* and were soon turning left off the road onto the narrow track. As they drove through a small copse of trees, the first stones came into view, but so did a pink Mini Metro tucked neatly under the tree where they'd planned to park.

"Stop here," Zed told Johnny.

"Where?"

"Pull in behind that pussywagon."

Johnny obliged and the five of them got out.

"Looks like we have company," said Zed, moving swiftly in search of the intruders, followed closely by Johnny and Franko – Zed's friend since primary school, as intelligent as Zed but the least secure in the group due to his ill-disguised distaste for vandalism, theft, cruelty to animals, and the odd attempted rape or mugging. A plain-looking, quiet boy of eighteen, Franko was grateful for the sense of belonging he got from the group, and still retained something of his schoolboy crush on Zed. Although the recent escalation in the group's violence made him feel increasingly uneasy, he enjoyed all the drink and drugs, and these got him through the worst of it. Besides, he had the distinct feeling that leaving was not an option. At least tonight they weren't going after anything that had a pulse, so Franko felt relatively relaxed as he hurried after Zed and Johnny.

Spike – an overweight and singularly unpleasant-looking skinhead – was the last to scramble out of the car. He came to a halt beside Rizla, a swarthy youth with long black hair, who had produced a penknife from his jacket pocket and was busy carving away at the front of the SUV.

"What yer doing?" asked Spike.

"Wait and see." Rizla skilfully cut out the top of the first 'R', the first 'E' and the second 'R' from the 'RANGE ROVER' sign above the grille. He finished his handiwork and stood back, then cast Spike an expectant glance, but Spike didn't get it.

"What?"

"Hangover, man," explained Rizla. "Look, it says 'HANG--OVER'."

Spike peered at the vandalised sign. "Oh, yeah. I see it now."

"Spike! Rizla!" Zed's voice reached them from the field beside the track. "Come and meet our new friends!"

Spike and Rizla hurried over, hardly noticing the spectacular stone circle they were entering in their hurry to do Zed's bidding. Cornered by Zed, Johnny and a despondent-looking Franko, next to an enormous pale grey, crystal-streaked stone, were two teenage girls: a skinny little blonde and a girl with dyed red hair. The redhead was probably not much older than her girlish friend, but her shape was already impressively curvaceous. Zed figured that at least one of them had to be seventeen, as the pink Mini couldn't have belonged to anyone else.

"This is Spike," Zed nodded in the direction of the panting skinhead, "and this is Rizla – so known for his unparalleled ability to roll a Camberwell Carrot in under ten seconds." The red-haired girl giggled self-consciously, and her friend tried to smile, but both looked distinctly frightened. "This is Trish," Zed introduced the redhead to Rizla and Spike, "and this ..." Zed smiled at the little blonde, who blushed and lowered her eyes, "is Amy."

There was something about frightened little girls that rocked Zed's world, and his jeans were already starting to get a little too tight around the crotch. Judging by the unsavoury glint in Spike's eye, he evidently felt the same, while Rizla couldn't take his eyes off Trish's chest, and extended his hand to the girl, who shook it reluctantly.

"I've just been persuading the ladies to join us for the evening," Zed explained to the latecomers.

"Cool," Rizla commented, his eyes still glued to Trish's boobs; the outline of her nipples visible through the tightly stretched pink fabric of her top as a cold breeze stirred around the stones. Trish pulled her jacket around herself self-consciously.

"We've got to go," she said.

"You're very brave to be camping this time of year." Zed ignored Trish, focussing his attention on the petite blonde. "So where exactly are you ladies staying?"

"North Dy..."

"Amy!" Trish quickly silenced her friend. Amy blushed, upset at herself for falling into Zed's charm-trap and almost giving away their location for the night. "We've got to go," repeated Trish, trying to push her way past Zed.

"Not so fast!" In a split second Johnny had Trish firmly by the arm and was leering at her in a way that made her nauseous with fear. She could feel Johnny's stale cigarette breath on her face, and for a moment she froze. Amy made a move towards her friend, but the huge skinhead barred her way, grinning lecherously.

"It's okay, Johnny," Zed surprised his friends, much to the girls' – and Franko's – relief. "We have business to attend to, but I'm sure we'll catch up with the ladies later." Sick with disappointment, Johnny let go of Trish; Zed was right – they had a plan to stick to, but surely a half-hour digression couldn't hurt?

"Catch you later, ladies," Zed crooned after the pair as they fled for their car.

"Yeah, catch you later," echoed Spike.

"What's the matter, Johnny?" teased Zed, sensing his pal's growing tension.

"Man, how could you let a chance like that get away?" whined Johnny, looking increasingly as if he were about to re-enact the head explosion scene from *Scanners*.

"Relax man, you heard what the blonde bitch said," soothed Zed.

"What?"

163

"They're at North Dyke Farm."

"What? How d'yer know?" demanded Johnny, the angry scarlet already draining from his face.

"She said."

"She started to say something, but she never finished coz the other bitch stopped her."

"She said 'North'," Zed continued patiently. "Well, they said they were camping, and there's only one campsite around here that's open in October, and that's North Dyke Farm. It's just past Great Salkeld, and it's a piece of piss to get to. Once we're done here it will be night, everyone will be in bed. We'll drive round and surprise them."

Rizla and Spike stared at Zed in admiration, Franko eyed him with trepidation and awe, while Johnny's shoulders slumped with relief.

"Don't worry, man!" Zed patted Johnny on the back, "You'll get to have your little party. We all will."

"Zed, man," Johnny's mood – ever volatile – went from barely suppressed rage to deep affection in under a second. "You're the best!"

"I know," grinned Zed. "Now let's get the stuff out the car."

As they followed Zed back to the Range Rover, Franko paused for a moment and took in the eerie beauty of the desolate place. The track the youths had driven in on cut through one side of the Bronze Age stone circle known as Long Meg and Her Daughters, and carried on past a nearby farm, now dark and deserted. The Daughters were vast rhyolite boulders placed in a flattened oval almost 360 feet in diameter at its widest point. Twenty-seven of the stones still stood; thirty-two had toppled over or sunk into the ground, leaving only flat, lichen-covered grey slabs in the grass; the others that had once made up the original number of about seventy had vanished – below the earth perhaps. Sixty feet southwest of the circle stood Long Meg herself – an imposing twelve foot high megalith of brooding red sandstone, watching over the smaller stones and the fields beyond. Its four corners faced the points of the compass, and three clearly visible spiral, ring and concentric circle patterns had been cut into its northwest face thousands of years ago. The sun had just set and a bloody glow still lingered above the horizon, enhancing Long Meg's ruddy hue.

"Trippy, huh?" Rizla paused for a moment by Franko and followed his gaze.

"There's a story about the stones," Franko told him. "A landowner once tried to blow them up, but a massive storm broke out and his workmen refused to carry on with the demolition."

"Just as well we're only here for the treasure then, isn't it?"

"I think that's what the landowner was after too," said Franko, but Rizla was already halfway to the Range Rover. Something about the hunched, human-like form of the towering sandstone unnerved Franko, and when the cold breeze started to whisper among the stones he hurried after his friends.

They pulled their supplies – spades, pick-axes, torches and beer – out of the car, and prepared to return to the circle.

"Let me torch it," Johnny got out his Zippo and turned back to the vehicle with a look of unhealthy excitement.

"Yeah, man, let's torch it!" Spike joined in. He looked round at Zed, like a dog waiting for its owner to throw it a stick.

"Not yet," responded Zed. "A fire here would be visible for miles. Besides, we'll need it to pay the bitches a visit. When we're done, you can torch it."

"Oh, OK." Zed's genius never ceased to impress Johnny. He put his lighter away, and he and Spike followed Zed, Franko and Rizla back to Long Meg.

*

Life in Langwathby did not suit Zed and his friends. The tranquil beauty of the village with its stone and slate cottages, and eighteenth century church, all surrounded by rolling green fields, did nothing for them. They were frustrated and skint. After all, what can you do when you've been banned from the only pub, and the main attraction on offer is *Eden Ostrich World* (at which you also happen to be less than welcome after throwing stones at the llamas and traumatising a chipmunk)? Zed had long thought about raiding St. Peter's, but they'd probably have gotten away with no more than the contents of the collection box, and besides, the church was too visible and they were notorious in the village already. The only options open to the youths were preying on unsuspecting tourists – of whom there were not that many, particularly in autumn and winter – and the occasional raid on nearby Penrith, but even that wasn't easy without a car.

Zed often wondered why on Earth his parents had left London; certainly the move had not done them any good. Zed's mother had taken to her bed soon after, rapidly developing an affinity for prescription painkillers and tranquilisers. Zed's father tried to bring up his son to be a decent human being, but any attempts at discipline inevitably led to recriminations and attacks from his wife, and ultimately failed, at which point he upped and left while Zed was still at school. Zed blamed his useless bitch mother for his father's departure, and their subsequent lack of money. He never expressed his true feelings to her, and always addressed his mother in a warm, if somewhat calculated and patronising manner, but nevertheless he saw her money and her drugs as fair game, and regularly stole them from the top drawer in her bedroom. But the pittance that she had stashed was not enough for a decent life – and certainly not one away from Langwathby – so when he read something on the internet about treasure buried under Long Meg, he latched onto the idea a bit too fast and a bit too uncritically, immediately hatching a cunning plan, which his friends would put into practice for him.

*

"Don't piss on them!" Rizla snapped at Johnny who'd wandered a little way off and was urinating on one of the fallen boulders. The others looked at Rizla like he'd just gone mad.

"What did you say?" Johnny had that *Scanners* look again.

"Don't piss on them, man. It's unlucky."

"What the fuck are you on about?"

"It upsets the dead."

"What the fuck have you been smoking, you fucking hippie fuck?" Johnny zipped up his jeans and strode over to Rizla with clenched fists. The long-haired youth stood his ground.

"I've been smoking the same stuff as you. I'm not a hippie. And it upsets the dead."

"Rizla!" Amused by the entire situation, Zed nevertheless decided to break things up before they got out of hand. "They're not gravestones," he said, leaning on the spade he'd been using to dig under Long Meg. Franko and Spike had also paused in their work and were observing events with some interest.

"They're not?"

"No, man."

"Oh, okay." Rizla turned away from Johnny and directed his attention back to Long Meg. Johnny started after him but Zed held him back.

"Let it go; we've got work to do."

166

Johnny took a deep breath and nodded at Zed. They rejoined the others at the megalith, and resumed digging – all except Rizla, who took out his penknife, chose a prime spot to the right of Meg's circular 'cup and ring' pattern, and began carving his name. He twisted the point of his knife into the sandstone. A faint rumble of thunder growled somewhere nearby. Rizla stopped short; a thick viscous substance had seeped out onto his knife.

"What the fuck?" Rizla inspected the tip of his blade.

"What is it, man?" Zed stopped digging.

"Blood... I think." Rizla smelled the muck on the blade, then tasted it and winced.

"Be more careful," Zed told him.

"It's not mine."

"Whose then?" Zed put down his spade and walked over to Rizla. Soon all of them were gaping and dabbing at the oozing spot.

"It's bleeding." Franko shone his torch onto the stone as a thick globule of what undeniably looked like blood trickled from the tiny hole that was Rizla's attempt at the letter 'R', and started to pool in the dips and grooves of the spiral pattern.

"It's a mineral deposit of some sort," said Zed. "You must have exposed it to the air and it's reacted with the oxygen or something."

"It tastes of blood," Rizla protested.

"It's probably made of the same stuff as blood," Zed told him. "Probably iron oxide or something. Now leave it and help us dig."

They carried on digging at the base of the stone. Spike was strong, but his weight and general lack of fitness were starting to take their toll. He swung his pick-axe increasingly wildly, almost hitting Rizla.

"Watch it!"

"Fuck off!" Spike swung the pick-axe once more, but, instead of breaking the earth, it connected hard with Long Meg's side. Spike winced from the unexpected contact with the rock.

"Jesus!" Johnny covered his ears against the jarring thud. Blood-coloured dust rose in the air from where the pick-axe had struck, and a small fracture appeared in the stone. Just then a flash of lightning lit up the sky, accompanied by a deafening crack of thunder. A second lightning bolt followed almost immediately, striking and splitting a tree at the edge of the field with a loud bang, and sending half of it toppling to the ground in flames.

"What the fuck?!" Rizla dropped the spade he was holding, and Spike stared at his pick-axe in disbelief. A peel of thunder cracked directly above the stone circle, a violent wind arose out of nowhere

167

and rain started to pour from a sky that had suddenly turned pitch black.

"What's going on?" shouted Johnny.

"I don't know," Zed struggled to be heard over the howling wind. "But we need to take a break."

"Whadda we do?" yelled Spike.

"We go to plan B."

"What's plan B?" shouted Johnny.

"Bitches!" Zed managed to grin despite the hail stones that had started pelting the ground all around him. "Grab the tools and meet at the car!"

"Shit!" Franko's house keys fell out of his pocket as he grappled with a spade and torch, while trying to do up his jacket at the same time. "Wait up!" he shouted as he fumbled around on the ground. He switched on the torch and swept the beam over the grass. A mist had crept over the ground, and bounced Franko's torchlight back at him. Finally his fingers connected with metal. He stuffed the keys into his jeans pocket and got up to follow his friends. But the mist had become a thick, drifting fog, and even with the torch on he could see nothing. "Hey, wait up!" he yelled, but his words were devoured by the wailing wind.

Franko headed in the direction where he thought they'd left the car. As he moved the torch's beam around in front of him, his heart suddenly skipped a beat. Directly ahead of him in the eddying fog, Franko thought he saw two malevolent red eyes staring at him. The torch fell from his hand and went out. He cried out in alarm, then cursed himself for having smoked too much weed earlier. He picked up the torch and set off for the car, then realised that he'd lost all sense of direction in the shifting fog and had no idea which way to go.

"Hey, guys!" Franko shouted into the night, but his voice was carried away by the storm. There was no way his friends could hear him. His only option was to go back to Long Meg; if he fixed the location of the huge stone in his mind, he should be able to navigate the short distance to the dirt track and the car without too much trouble. But when he looked back to where he'd just come from, all he could see were wind-driven banks of milky fog, punctuated by bouts of rain and hail, and occasional glimpses of the profound darkness beyond. Confused, he staggered the few paces to where Long Meg should have been, but there was nothing there. The fog must be playing tricks on his sense of distance. He kept going until he almost fell over a boulder – but it wasn't Meg; it was one of the smaller stones that made up the circle some sixty feet from Meg. He must have walked right past the megalith in the miasma.

The lashing rain was beginning to soak through his jacket, and a hailstone the size of a grape hit him on the arm, causing Franco to cry out in pain. Desperate and cold, he moved away from the circle again, in another attempt to locate Long Meg. As he staggered first one way and then the other, he became aware of another sound over the howling of the wind and the pounding of the hail. It was like the flapping of giant wings, as if a colossal bird were flying overhead. Then a shadow fell over him.

Franko looked up and saw a hovering shape – black against the pale fog.

"Shit!" Terrified now, he started to run, falling a couple of times, smearing himself in mud and cow dung. He fled through the stone circle, the creature in pursuit – once above him, once behind him, then beside him – gliding effortlessly on the storm. As Franko dodged past one of the tumbled stones, the thing was suddenly in front of him. As the youth came to an abrupt halt, he saw the creature clearly for the first time. It was humanoid in form; hunched over, unnaturally twisted, and smaller than Franko had originally thought. It wore a tattered black cloak that swirled around it in the gale, giving it the impression of being larger than it actually was. Its gaunt face was scarred and craggy – like ancient rock. Its bloodshot eyes glowed with an age-old malevolence that spoke of torment and rage, of knowledge of the lowest depths of Hell, and of a need for vengeance that would never be satiated.

Despite the corrupt hideousness of the visage before him, Franko somehow knew that whatever it was, it had once been female.

The crone extended her arms to the youth, as if inviting a lover to share an embrace. Her skeletal fingers ended in long, curved talons, like those of a bird of prey. She reached out for Franko, and he staggered back, tripped on the edge of a toppled stone, flailed around wildly in an attempt to regain his balance, then fell over backward, hitting his head on another boulder. As he lost consciousness, the last thing he was aware of was the crone gliding towards him, and then a familiar voice shouting over the wailing wind.

"Franko!"

The crone turned her attention from the unconscious youth, and headed for the second desecrator.

"Where the fuck are you?" Rizla moved the feeble beam of his torch around the stone circle. How typical that Zed should pick on him to go looking for that moron in the middle of a storm. "Franko!"

And then a lighting flash lit up the sky, and Rizla saw it – a monster from Hell bearing down on him from above, framed by whirling fog and blinding rain. Rizla didn't even have time to yell 'What the fuck?' as the thing swept down and clasped him in its bony but inhumanly strong arms. His lungs filled with the stench of sulphur and putrefaction, then emptied of breath entirely as the crone's embrace squeezed all the life out of him and shattered every bone in his body.

*

"You might as well turn off the engine."

Johnny did as Zed told him. "Can't we just leave those hippie fucks behind?" he asked.

"You never know, we might need them," said Zed, without really meaning it.

"We can handle two bitches between the three of us," urged Johnny. Spike grinned in the back seat.

"Spike?" Zed turned at once to the oversized thug. "Would you mind ... ?"

"Sure Zed. I should've gone in the first place. No point sending a boy to do a man's job."

"Thanks ... man," replied Zed, smiling at his own wit. Spike pulled his hood over his head, took a torch, and clambered out into the storm. He didn't mind doing things for Zed; if it wasn't for Zed he'd have ended up in prison a long time ago. Thanks to how smart Zed was, he could indulge in his two great passions – hurting people and damaging property – with little risk to himself. And Zed's inventiveness when it came to aberrant and criminal behaviour was truly admirable. Spike would never forget how Zed helped to get him off arson charges when he'd burnt his grandmother's house down – with his grandmother in it – by some very quick thinking, careful planning and framing the ginger-haired kid they'd hated at school. Yes, Spike would do anything for Zed, and retrieving some hippie fucks from the stone circle was the least of it.

With all these loyal thoughts milling around in his head, Spike found himself in the middle of the circle. A little surprised, he looked around for the massive red boulder they'd been digging under, but Long Meg was nowhere to be seen. Spike shrugged his shoulders.

"Rizla! Franko!" he yelled, and took a step forward. His foot connected with something soft, but offering enough resistance to send him sprawling. He fell heavily, landing on the offending object. It was wet and sticky, lumpy and broken.

"Shit!" Spike scrambled up with difficulty, and stared at the crumpled form at his feet. It had jeans, a black leather jacket, and long black hair. "Fuck!"

Spike started to back away in horror from what was left of Rizla, then thought better of it and, after casting a quick look around, turned the body over and went through the corpse's pockets until he found Rizla's wallet and drug stash. He took the drugs, pulled all the money out of the wallet, which wasn't much, then discarded the wallet and turned to go – and came face to face with a wizened old hag dressed in a ragged cloak and stinking of decay, mustiness and a choking, cloying odour like rotten eggs.

"What the fuck?" The monstrosity reached for Spike, and he swung his torch at her, connecting with her head. A trail of what looked like blood-coloured dust rose from where she'd been hit, but the crone hardly winced.

"Shit!" Spike hit her again, the impact sending the torch flying from his hand. This time she let out a snarl and a low, creaking moan – like the sound of shifting, breaking rock. He turned and ran, making sure to avoid tripping over Rizla's corpse again.

Spike panted through the fog, rain and hail; his sweat hot, then cold; steam rising off him as though from an over-taxed cart-horse. Within seconds he was wheezing with exertion, his lungs felt like they were on fire, and his heart seemed to be thumping somewhere in his throat, ready to explode. As he turned around to see if the obscenity was gaining, the crone was upon him, her talons clawing his face. Then she had him in her arms, and Spike managed a feeble squeal as her grip tightened, and all the fat surrounding his organs was mashed into a reddish-white jelly, and his stomach, his spleen, his liver, lungs and all his other organs were compressed and ruptured like blood-filled sacks. A gurgling sound emanated from the youth's pain-distorted mouth, then his bulging eyes popped right out of their sockets as the crone crushed his insides into a steaming, gelatinous mass.

*

"Man, this sucks!" Johnny was getting angry again, and Zed was starting to worry about the others.

"Something's up," he told Johnny.

171

"They're just pissing around. Let's just go." Johnny didn't share Zed's concerns. "You can have the blonde bitch and I'll take the redhead." But even as he said it, he knew that Zed wouldn't leave Spike. Besides, Rizla had all the drugs; Rizla always had drugs. If it wasn't for the fact that Rizla's cousin was an acid chemist, and Rizla was always generous with his cousin's handouts, Johnny would have had the hippie fuck's balls before you could say 'lysergic acid diethylamide'.

"Something's wrong. Let's tool up and sort things out." Zed climbed out of the car and grabbed a pick-axe from the trunk. Johnny produced a chain from an inside pocket of his jacket. It was his regular weapon of choice – not strictly illegal, and in the right hands it could inflict a hell of a lot of damage. And his were definitely the right hands.

Johnny turned up his collar against the raging storm, and he and Zed strode side by side to the circle.

"Where's Long Meg?" Zed looked around, bemused, and figured the thick fog must be impairing visibility and sense of space.

"Huh?"

"The stone we were digging under!" Zed raised his voice over the wind. "I don't see it!"

*

Meg had stood for thousands of years, rooted to the desolate spot by a man of magic more powerful than her own. She'd tried to break free; she had used all of her will and power and spirit to tear herself from her craggy prison. She'd writhed desperately, and her determination was so great that she'd even managed to lift herself in the air so that when the stone jail finally set around her, it was several times the size of her slim body. Trapped within the jagged prison, her youthful skin, her beautiful face, her bones and hair, and even her soul had turned to cold, unfeeling rock. And yet she'd been aware of every year that passed, of all the elements battering her overblown, twisted form; doomed forever to gaze upon the members of her coven, entrapped too because they had followed her.

It was said that if someone counted the same number of rocks twice, the spell would be broken, and Meg and all her 'Daughters' would be released. While she waited to be set free, the torment she suffered and the passing centuries caused Meg's youth and beauty to fade. Within the rock, Meg's skin withered, her body became wizened, her face weather-beaten and eyes rheumy. But the magician

172

had made sure that the stones changed and shifted, and no one could count the same number twice. Meg and her sisters would never regain their rightful lives, but Meg's blood had been spilt, and that granted her freedom for just one night. She could not avenge herself and her sisters by taking the magician's life, for he was long dead. But at least she could have a small revenge – on the men who'd cut her and made her bleed.

And there they were – grasping their pathetic weapons, as if they thought they could break her. Meg raised her arms in anger, her rage lifting her high off the ground and into the storm. With a shriek like the wind blowing through a hollow cave, she swooped down on the pair.

Zed and Johnny saw her at the same time. Zed froze, but Johnny raised his right hand and, chain held firmly, threw himself forward to meet the atrocity that lunged at them from above. With his own yell of rage, Johnny swung his chain, connecting heavily with the hardened lump that was the thing's left breast. Dust rose from the wound and the creature hissed, wrapping itself around the youth, clinging and squeezing with all four limbs and shrivelled, craggy body. Johnny fell to his knees, screaming to Zed for help. Zed took one look at the obscene tableau before him, and fled for the Range Rover.

As the crone crushed Johnny's body to a pulp, Zed started the engine and put his foot down. The tyres spewed up mud as he tried frantically to turn the car around on the narrow track. His customary composure had evaporated – much at the same time as the unfortunate Johnny's last breath – and his desperate manoeuvrings to get the car to do what he wanted were becoming increasingly frenzied. Finally he got the vehicle to point in the right direction and then he floored it … straight into a tree.

Before he could recover from the whiplash, the windscreen imploded – spraying him with thousands of tiny glass fragments – and the monster had a hold of him, and was pulling him out and up. Then Zed was flying through the air, bleeding from where the creature's talons pierced his skin; flying, screaming, through the night sky, the icy fog, and the biting wind and rain. Beneath him he could just make out the grey-white forms of Long Meg's Daughters – paler than the fog that pooled around them. Then he was falling – not from a great height, but far enough to dislocate his shoulder as he made contact with the ground. When he looked up, the crone's rheumy, bloodshot eyes stared into his own, and then she pounced. As she crushed the life out of the violator, she realised that breaking his bones would not satisfy her. She ripped into his flesh, gulping down the blood that spurted from his face and neck. When she was satiated, she sensed something stir in the darkness behind her.

*

Franko regained consciousness to find the crone crouched nearby, watching him closely. She bared her teeth at him, and he saw that they were small and razor-sharp, like those of a lamprey he'd seen on a wildlife documentary. Some of them had rotted away and the spaces that were left oozed putrescence, but those remaining looked lethal enough, and were stained with blood.

Franko scrambled backward, twisted round and with a single deft movement – with which he rather surprised himself, as he was no great athlete – leapt up and ran. The back of his head felt cold and clammy from where he'd cut it open during his fall, but he didn't feel pain as adrenaline coursed through his body. The crone too was taken by surprise at the unexpected flight of the last desecrator – her bloodlust and killer sense dulled after feasting on the one before – but she threw herself after him in pursuit.

Franko ran blindly, not caring which way he went. He broke clear of the stone circle and ran across the open fields, heading for trees and shelter. Once he ran straight into a barbed wire fence, but managed to disentangle himself, and kept going despite bleeding from his hands and head. The crone seemed less sure of herself away from the circle, but still pursued him. She almost caught up with him in the open, but then he was under trees and running, stumbling, through the woods that stretched to the old gypsum mine and the River Eden beyond. The gold and russet splendour of the beech and oak trees was obscured by the darkness and fog, and Franko had to be careful not to trip on a root or knock himself out on a protruding branch. The trees also slowed down his pursuer, but never stopped her, as glided silently, eyes fixed on her fast-tiring quarry.

Exhausted and breathing heavily, Franko half ran, half slid down a steep embankment, managing to stop just in time to avoid plunging down a precipitous set of slippery steps. He realised where he was: just above the sealed entrance to the abandoned gypsum mine – a creepy place at the best of times. He wanted to turn back rather than risk falling on the steps in the pouring rain. But as he looked back, he saw the crone behind him, gaining. He ran, stumbling and sliding down the steps. Remarkably he survived the descent, turning right and heading past one of the eerie boarded-up mine entrances, along the path that led to Lacy's Caves.

As he hobbled along, Franko prayed not to fall into the river, which – fed by the staggering amount of rain that was pouring down – now raged to his left. If he could only get far enough ahead for the creature to lose sight of him for a few moments, he could hide in the caves until morning, and then try to make his way back home, or to the nearest farm.

Franko cast a desperate glance over his shoulder and saw that the crone had indeed fallen behind – he knew that she was following, but she was far enough away for him not to see her in the dense fog. Mustering the remains of his strength, he climbed the short steep path up to Lacy's Caves, and crept inside. Feeling his way carefully along the walls in the pitch blackness, he moved to the farthermost chamber and slumped against a wall, close to one of the other entrances, which opened directly out of the embankment onto the wild, rainwater-swollen river below. There he half crouched, half lay in the darkness, trying to still his racing heart and quieten his breathing.

Franko knew Lacy's Caves well, but not the details of their inception. Had he been familiar with their history, the irony of his choice of hiding-place would have been lost on him in any case, given his current predicament.

Lacy's Caves had been made on the orders of the same man who'd tried to blow up Long Meg and Her Daughters. Colonel Samuel Lacy, the eighteenth century dandy who seemed hell-bent on perfecting nature (and the work of anyone who'd gone before him) had – presumably after his failure to destroy the several thousand year old stone circle that stood on his land – ordered five chambers to be hacked out of the living rock overlooking the River Eden, for the amusement of himself and his fashionable friends. Samuel Lacy was long gone now, but his caves remained; making a lasting mark on the local landscape was perhaps what the Colonel had wanted all along.

Franko listened closely, but couldn't hear anything apart from the hissing river. As his breathing slowed, and the adrenaline in his body gradually dissipated, he realised how cold and tired he was, and not a little faint from the blow to his head and the dizzying chase through the woods. He started to wonder whether, in fact, getting hit on the head had caused him to imagine the whole insane episode with the monster – either that, or maybe Rizla's cousin hadn't been able to resist adding a little something extra to the SuperSkunk that Rizla had scrounged off him. Just as Franko started to let his guard down, a shuffling noise in the darkness startled him. He pressed himself against the wall of the cave and tried to be as quiet as possible. But it was no use – a triumphant, rattling shriek pierced the silence, and the crone came leaping out of the shadows, straight for the terrified youth.

Franko stumbled back and, as he did, his head span; he lost his balance, and fell – right through the chamber opening, his body plunging into the wind and rain, and the raging river below. Had he held out a moment longer, Franko would have seen the first light of dawn fall into the cave, and the hideous crone writhe and transform into a young woman of delicate, unsurpassed beauty, then fade away to nothing and disperse in the early morning light.

*

Franko's body wasn't found, and will probably wash up in the Solway Firth one day. His friends, on the other hand, were discovered by shocked tourists visiting the third largest stone circle in Britain. The police pathologist had no explanation as to why every bone in the young men's bodies was broken; he only commented that it was as though they'd been pulverised by the weight of a huge boulder. But the fact that the twelve foot sandstone megalith commonly known as Long Meg was dripping with blood and other human tissue led officers to conclude that a Satanic cult was most likely involved. The site of Long Meg and Her Daughters was closed to the public, but further investigation revealed – nothing.

THE TORTURED SOULS OF
LORD'S RAKE

C *limbing folk will be familiar with Lord's Rake, once one of the most popular routes to the summit of England's second highest mountain, Sca Fell Crag (though recent landslides have now made it far more treacherous than it used to be). In essence, it is a high-walled, scree-filled gully, very steep, running laterally across the Crag from an equally perilous but in this case very exposed ridge called 'the Mickledore'.*

This is not a particularly difficult climb by Lake District standards. It is arduous in that it involves a lot of hard walking, and at certain times of year, winter in particular, when 'the Rake' is packed with snow, it can be more demanding than usual. But the most daunting feature of Lord's Rake is its eerie atmosphere. Even hardened 'fell-bashers' with many years' experience have spoken of the 'watching silence' when up there alone, and sometimes strange visual and auditory effects – especially when the cloud is low, because, at 3,000 feet above sea level, it doesn't require extreme weather conditions for Lord's Rake to suddenly be filled with swirling, murky vapour. Those chancing its cold, rocky embrace on these occasions often find themselves completely blinded.

The Mickledore itself has an unearthly feel.

Bridging the gap between Sca Fell Pike and Sca Fell Crag, it is often blasted by high energy winds – even on days when there doesn't seem to be much of a wind anywhere else. On still days, the Mickledore too can be veiled with dense, rolling mist, which has variously been described as "white", "grey", "black" and sometimes even "green". At times like this, people have spoken of meeting long-dead relatives on the Mickledore, or of sighting phantom figures approaching them through the murk – but from a great distance, which could only mean they were standing or walking on thin air. But it is up in the Rake itself where these manifestations take a turn for the genuinely disturbing. Several times in the fog, while scrambling up the chute alone, climbers have reported being followed by heavy feet – "elephantine feet", as one veteran of the hills described them – clumping through the scree in angry pursuit.

Legends of gigantic grey figures haunting Britain's mountaintops are not unusual, but generally they are confined to the Scottish

177

highlands. In England, they are unique to this particular peak. But it isn't just footsteps that have supposedly been heard. Roaring voices or shrill cries have sounded from on high, and sometimes cackling laughter. Of course there are numerous explanations for these events. The acoustics of Lord's Rake are a law unto themselves. Voices carry and echo unnaturally. The crack of a falling stone can sound like thunder on the lower slopes. The wind itself may wail and moan with the intense anguish of a Hell-bound soul.

In the Dark Ages, much of what we now call the Lake District was settled by Norsemen. Their myths spoke of trolls – evil spirits of the Earth who during daylight were composed of rock and mud, but at night became horrors of flesh and blood. Many bizarre rock forms were attributed to this malevolent race (and indeed, once in the Rake a brutish face was noticed in the rock wall, though later climbers were unable to locate it). These legends also explained why sheep who had ventured out after dark were supposedly found torn to shreds in remote locations.

One hoary old climber – a former 'leading edge man' of the 1950s and 1960s – doesn't laugh at such superstition. He wished to remain anonymous, but wrote: "There's no obvious reason why the Rake should be haunted. People have died up there, but not in great numbers. There were no battles, no political assassinations. The Vikings explained it by saying the chilling cries you often heard were trolls calling to one another. They also blamed the supernatural for unexplained rock-falls, calling them attacks on unwanted intruders. I put these things down to geological explanation myself, but it's easy enough if you've made a solo climb up there to be so oppressed by the gloom and the blustering wind, and the long, deep shadows of the crags, to imagine that you're not quite alone."

ALONG LIFE'S TRAIL
Gary McMahon

It was the last day of the holiday and Murray was lost.

Well, he *called* it a holiday – they both did – but in actuality it was merely a short weekend break. Two days in the Lake District, seeing a part of the country neither of them was familiar with despite living less than a hundred miles away in Newcastle and having spoken about taking a trip to the Lakes for years.

It had been Polly's idea, of course – these things always were. She often got it into her head that it would be good for them to get away and breathe some fresh country air rather than the usual pollution and exhaust fumes they had to deal with in the city.

Murray stood at the top of the hill he'd just briskly climbed, staring down at the broad expanse of rough valley moorland below. He'd thought he was walking part of the Bowfell route, but his surroundings didn't look anything like the landscape he remembered from yesterday. It was barren countryside, this; mile upon mile of green scrubland dotted here and there with fists of purple heather and punctuated by rocky peaks and outcroppings. It had its own kind of beauty, raw and untamed, and despite his habitual disdain for all the New Age back-to-nature nonsense Polly had recently taken an interest in, he had to admit that he felt as if the trip really was doing him some good.

Polly had insisted that he make one final trek out into 'the Wilds' (as she'd called it) before they left for home later that afternoon. Due to a minor set-to the night before caused by his over-consumption of real ale in the *Old Dungeon Ghyll Hotel*, Murray felt that it might be a good idea to put some space between them. Just for a little while: at least until she'd taken down the sodding tent.

"Just so you don't miss out," he said to his absent wife as he took the digital camera from his cagoule pocket to snap off a shot of the view.

As the camera clicked, he noticed an appealing sight about a mile away, back down the hill and off to the left. It looked like a pub: a small country hostelry, standing invitingly at the side of a narrow blacktop road; one of those ancient stone buildings that proliferated in the area, and probably dated back centuries. Yes, there was even a wooden sign dangling from a metal cross brace over what seemed to be the entrance … he couldn't quite make out the name, or the image depicted on the sign, but it was definitely a pub of some kind.

Consulting his laminated Ordnance Survey map, Murray deduced that the road might in fact be one which could lead him back to the campsite in the ravine of Dungeon Ghyll, where Polly was even now packing up the tent and the provisions. It would be nice to sink another smooth pint of local brew before heading off back to pretend to help her. If he was lucky, she might even have finished stowing away their stuff in the boot of the car, and he could take a nice nap while she drove back to Newcastle.

Just then his mind was made up for him. Spots of rain began to appear on the sleeves of his cagoule, creating dark splotches, and when he glanced up, at the previously blue sky, it was now bisected by thick wedges of grey cloud.

Quickly, Murray began to make his way down the side of the hill, pushing the map into his pocket and hunching his shoulders against the oncoming downpour.

By the time he was close enough to the building to realise that it was derelict, the rain was already coming down too heavily for him to care. The sound of it thrashing against his hood was like that of pebbles being thrown against a tin roof. His face was wet; the exposed parts of his trouser legs were soaked. Thankfully his walking boots protected his feet, but still he knew that shelter was a priority. If he couldn't get a drink, he'd at least use the pub to keep dry. Surely even an empty establishment would offer him that slender amount of hospitality.

Murray jogged towards the ruined structure (he could see clearly now that it was indeed a ruin: the roof had partially collapsed, the windows were without glass, and the front door had been kicked or blown in). There was shelter beneath the overhanging eaves at the side of the building; for some reason he was reluctant to set foot inside. He stood there and gazed out across the empty moors and fells, watching a heavy grey shadow fall slowly down to cover the landscape. It was a spooky sight, and he was glad that it was still early in the day. He couldn't stand the thought of being stuck out here after nightfall.

Looking for a distraction from the weather, Murray turned and examined the wall against which he stood. The blocks that made up the structure were huge, probably local stone quarried nearby. Moss had grown in the joints and some of the stone had crumbled away, but the construction still looked sound. They built things to last back then – whenever 'back then' was.

180

Walking along the side of the pub, Murray noticed something on the ground, near the base of the wall. At first he thought it was a puddle, caused by rain water gushing through the broken eaves or guttering, but the eaves above that location were intact. He looked again, peering at the stain – for that was what it was: a stain in the grass – and suddenly realised that he was looking at a pool of blood.

Murray was suddenly very cold. It was not the rain, because that was warm; no, this chill came from within.

The blood formed a long trail, leading around the building. Not really thinking about what he was doing, Murray followed it. He walked along the wall, then around to the rear of the pub. The dark red trail stopped at a closed and barred wooden door. This, he thought, must be the back entrance, where tradesmen and beer deliveries had been dealt with. In fact, buried beneath the straggly grass that grew at the base of the walls, was a wooden hatch that must lead down into the cellar. The blood seemed to stop at the hatch: the trail ended there, forming yet another pool of liquid, this one larger than the first and clotted in the grain and joints.

The rain soon began to ease off, and Murray, glad of this turn of events, stepped back from out of the shadow of the building. As he did so, he could see the trail almost in its entirety; the way it bent around the corner of the building, as if a wounded animal had crawled along the base of the walls, looking for a place to die.

Murray's hand was in his pocket, clasped around the digital camera. He took it out, focused on the trail, and took a photograph. It would be something to tell Polly about later: a slightly exciting anecdote that might break the ice during their return journey up the motorway.

He walked back around to the front of the building, where the crude road passed by the remains of the facade. Just as he was about to turn and walk away in the direction of the camp site, he caught sight of a plaque bolted to the front wall, to the left of the door. It was one of those English Heritage information signs, offering tourists gaudy historical details of various sites up and down the country.

Murray stepped closer to the door, being careful not to stumble inside – the floorboards in there looked unstable, and he was sure that the rest of the roof might come down at any minute. He squinted from beneath his hood and read the text on the plaque:

The Fellwatch Inn

Hereabouts is the site of the murder of Mr.
Thomas Daldry, an unpopular landlord of this
esteemed establishment.

Late in the evening of October 17th 1806, Mr
Daldry was murdered whilst investigating a noise
outside his public house. His body was found
early the next morning, at the end of a bloody
trail, torn to shreds at the rear of the building.
Either Mr. Daldry had crawled around there,
away from the front entrance in an attempt to
draw attention from his concerned wife, or his
body had been dragged by his attacker.

The authorities blamed a wild animal as the
wounds on the corpse were so vicious that no
man could have inflicted them, but locals spoke of
something else – a mythical spirit with "the body
of a wild cat, wings and talons like an eagle, the
face of a young maiden and the teeth of a wolf".
This hideous entity was said to protect the
"sacred valley" from unwelcome outsiders, and
Mr. Daldry had only recently moved into the area
to take on the tenancy of the inn.

Murray felt cold again; his hands went numb and his face
prickled from what felt like an icy breeze. Usually he enjoyed this
kind of folklore – local colour, as he liked to call it – but here, now,
standing beside the pub after seeing the trail of blood, it no longer
seemed so entertaining.

He took a few steps, moving away from the front of the building,
and leaned around the corner, where he'd first noticed the blood. The
grass, where the pool of blood had been visible, was clean. No trail
led from the spot, and as Murray followed the line of the trail with
his eyes, he could see no other sign of the lengthy mark.

It was gone. Not a hint of it remained.

Murray pulled his cagoule tighter around his torso and set off
along the road, keeping to the verge in case a vehicle came along.
Nothing much had occurred, not really: just his imagination playing
tricks. But he felt afraid, as if he'd just stepped off a known trail and
entered strange new territory, where he was not entirely welcome.

An hour later he was entering the campsite, and the sight of the trail of blood was nothing but an unpleasant memory, something he could pretend he had not really seen. Polly was standing beside the car, smoking a cigarette. She'd told him that she'd given up months ago, but this was not the first time he'd caught her having a sly puff.

Murray slowed his pace, giving her enough time to see him and conceal the cigarette (he didn't want to embarrass her), and his mind drifted back to the *Fellwatch Inn* and the vanishing trail of blood. *It must have been water*, he reasoned. *The rain*. His traipsing across the area must have inadvertently cleaned it up. This argument was not too convincing, but he was eager to pin an explanation on what he had seen – or thought he had seen. It was good enough for him. Good enough for now. He'd think about it again later, once they were safe back home.

"Where did you get to?" Polly had somehow managed to dispose of her smoke, and was standing facing him, hands by her sides.

"What's that?" He increased his pace, keen to reach the car now that he didn't have to pretend he had not seen her smoking.

"You've been gone ages. I thought I'd lost you." She smiled, but Murray was unable to tell if it was one of humour or sarcasm. Perhaps it was both.

"Well, I'm back now. I see you managed all by yourself." He took off his cagoule and put it on the back seat, ruffling his hair with his fingers. The dark skies had cleared and sunshine was once again piercing the clouds.

"That nice bloke from the camp shop gave me a hand. He did all the heavy lifting, seeing as you waltzed off and left me." She shifted her position, assuming what looked to Murray like a gladiatorial stance.

"You've got some nerve." He didn't like the man from the camp shop; he was sleazy, shifty, and always talked to a woman's chest instead of her face. "I offered to stay here and help, but you wouldn't have it."

"Oh, get in," Polly said, shaking her head. "I'll drive."

He felt oddly emasculated by her insistence upon driving. It never usually affected him in such a way, but today things felt different. Perhaps it was the scare he'd experienced during his walk, or the fact that the bloke from the camp shop was watching from his doorway … there must be some simple reason why he was building things up like this, blowing them out of proportion.

As Polly guided the car along narrow country lanes, Murray felt the need to reach out and rest his hand on her thigh. It was almost a reassertion of his position in the relationship, and Polly glanced at him sidelong when he did so. "Feeling affectionate today?" Again, the unreadable smile, the unfamiliar look in her eye.

Murray said nothing. He just watched the hills and lanes unfurl beyond the windscreen. He gripped her knee, feeling like he wanted to keep on squeezing; but when the car took a sharp left turn he took away his hand and rested it in his own lap instead.

They did not say much during the rest of the journey home. Murray was trapped inside his own vague thoughts, and Polly seemed distracted. He thought it best that they sit in silence, enjoying the view. There'd be time for talk later, once they were back on familiar ground. The dispute (it was barely substantial enough, really, to be called an argument) from last night was still echoing around the car, filling the space between them. The silly thing was he could barely even remember the reason why they'd had cross words. They'd both been drunk, and a lively conversation had become bogged down in some kind of innuendo.

But the silence stretched even when they got home. They unpacked the car and Polly ordered a takeaway. When Murray opened a bottle of wine, she declined, saying that she was getting a headache – Polly's shorthand for "leave me alone".

"Sorry about last night," he said later, when she was carrying the dinner dishes though into the kitchen.

Polly stopped, turned, and looked at him. "Sorry for what?"

Murray, unable to give her a straight answer, shook his head. "Just…sorry. That argument we had."

"It wasn't your fault," she said, walking into the kitchen. "We were both full of booze and, well, I still don't really know what the hell we were arguing about." She smiled; a tired, worn-out expression.

"You should go to bed."

Polly nodded. "I think that's a good idea. G'night."

Alone in the lounge, Murray tried to rid his head of the fug that had been gathering there all day. He felt strange: tired and heavy-limbed, as if the exercise had been too much for him. His mind, however, was buzzing, and the wine slipped down far too easily.

The lounge was gloomy, with only the corner lamp providing illumination. Murray was sitting in the armchair by the window, facing into the room, and as he stared at nothing in particular, he began to see a shadow forming on the floor ... no, not a shadow: a stain. But even that wasn't quite right, because it was a trail.

A dark trail traced a line across the lounge carpet, turning at the wall to follow it along below the skirting board and towards him. It was the same as the trail he'd seen earlier that day, outside the old pub: dark red in colour, with neat edges. A trail that led back to the Lakes.

Murray stood, taking a step forward, and as he moved away from the chair the trail seemed to vanish, becoming part of the pattern on the carpet. He blinked deliberately, trying to clear his vision, and only when he was sure that there was nothing there to concern him did he walk away. Turning off the lamp, he left the room and went upstairs. He was trying so very hard not to think of what he had just experienced, and certainly not to link it with the valley, the crags, and the rundown pub, but it was difficult to dampen the feeling that something was wrong here. Not wrong in the normal sense, at a natural level, but deeply wrong: *unnaturally* wrong.

Murray climbed the stairs, heading for the bathroom. It was dark; he had left off the light, ostensibly because he knew his way in the dark, but he couldn't shake the realisation that he'd also done it because he didn't want to see too clearly. At the top of the stairs he turned around. He couldn't help it: the compulsion was much too strong to fight.

He bent his head and stared down the way he'd come, and saw a dark trail leading up the stairs, snaking up each riser, across each tread, and following in his wake.

"No." He said it out loud just to hear his voice in the dark, to impress his humanity upon the situation. "Impossible." He closed his eyes. Kept them closed for a long time. When he opened them again the trail was gone.

Feeling like a stranger in his own home, a tourist inside his own head, Murray went to the bedroom, closed the door, and lay awake until sleep finally claimed him.

*

He woke before the alarm the following morning, desperate to void his bladder. The wine was sitting heavily inside him, and he needed to get rid of it before he could even think about getting dressed for work. He blinked at the room, trying to focus his vision. Sliding his legs out from beneath the covers, he slipped off the mattress and set his feet down on the floor. The soles of his feet were wet; he must have knocked over the glass of water he always kept by the bed. Still blinking, he turned and stared down at the floor. His feet were resting in a pool of thick red fluid, and a trail stretched across the room and out of the door, where it led away along the landing.

Murray felt a scream rising in his throat. He did his best to swallow it, but could not halt its progress for more than a second.

Polly came abruptly awake at the sound of his screams. "What's wrong? What is it?" She crawled over to his side of the bed, leaning across his body and looking down at the floor, where he was staring. "What?" she said, her voice rising in pitch.

"Look at it! The blood! The trail!" He pointed down, and then across the room at the open door.

"There's nothing there," Polly said. "I can't see a thing."

*

Despite her protestations, he managed to convince Polly to go to work – she had a training day, so wouldn't be back until late. She kissed him at the doorway, unwilling to let him go. It seemed that their recent tensions had been forgotten. Murray's hallucinations were bringing them closer together.

Hallucinations: that was what she insisted they were when he told her. And, of course he'd agreed with her; he'd also let her telephone the doctor to make an emergency appointment for later that afternoon. He wouldn't go, of course. He had more important things to do. Somewhere else he needed to go.

As soon as Polly disappeared from sight, her thin form blending into the greater mass of the commuter crowd gathered at the bus stop, Murray went into action. He packed a rucksack and grabbed the map they'd used the previous weekend – the one marked with the route they'd taken to Greater Langdale. He was sure that he could find the ruined pub again; the only thing he was uncertain of was what he would do when he got there.

He drove fast, breaking the speed limits whenever he hit a stretch of road without any speed cameras. Once he got on the motorway, and the morning rush hour was over, he made good time: two hours from Newcastle to the Langdale Valley. If he was lucky he'd be back home before Polly returned from work, and she would never have to know where he'd been. He refused to think beyond that; if his vague plan to confront the source of his fear was unsuccessful, he would simply have to come up with another option.

The sky was clear; clouds were thin and bright, like blown glass. The weather report had promised sunny spells, so at least he knew that it would be bright when he got there, and what could possibly scare him in broad daylight?

The radio lulled him with its mindless tunes and empty chatter. Before long, he found himself on a familiar road that dipped into the valley – one he thought might be the narrow one-way stretch that led directly to the *Fellwatch Inn*. He passed stone cairns and broken-down timber fences, tumbled dry-stone walls and acres of green and brown ground flecked with tired purple patches. The Langdale Pikes stared down at him as he dropped towards the valley bottom. They were craggy and impassive – some boring old crone in the pub on their first night here had told Murray each of their names but the only one he could recall right now was the Pike of Stickle, because at the time it had made him laugh.

But he wasn't laughing now.

The *Fellwatch Inn* came into view just before lunchtime; it sat at the roadside like a portent of doom. But no, that was all in his mind. It was just a derelict building, and his business here was to be quick and decisive. There really was nothing to be afraid of.

Murray parked the car at the side of the road a hundred yards away from the old pub. For some reason, he did not want to stop the vehicle too close to the building, in case its influence reached out to damage the engine and keep him here. It was a stupid thought, of course, but now that he was here, in close proximity to the place, he decided to humour his own delusion.

He walked the rest of the way, keeping to the side of the road and watching out for ruts and holes in the verge. The sky was powder blue; birds flew in formation high above his position; the air was soundless, like he was stuck in a bell jar. The Pikes hemmed him in.

Something skittered off to his right: he told himself it was a rabbit or hare running across the open ground, heading for its burrow. A slight breeze lifted the swathes of heather and gorse like wigs on half-buried heads that were merely small hillocks. Murray was far too aware of his own breathing; the sound was almost deafening.

He stood before the pub, staring at the shattered front door and the dusty darkness within. Sunlight knifed through the holes in the roof, slashing at shadows. He could see clearly the interior of the *Fellwatch Inn*: the single room was empty, with not even a table or chair remaining inside. Everything had been stripped out, taken away.

He crossed the patch of land in front of the building and turned at the wall, following it around. There was no trail of blood this time; just the tufts of grass moving in the breeze and a fresh animal carcass – probably that of a small vole or field mouse. He stared at the spot, unsure how to progress. Part of him had been certain that he would see the trail, and convinced that if he could somehow clean it up he would be free of its bloody influence.

Murray clenched his fists. He closed his eyes and opened them again. What should he do now?

The air was restless. The grass whispered in the breeze.

Murray turned around. This was stupid. He should get back to the car, keep his appointment at the doctor's surgery and then discuss everything again with Polly that evening.

He stopped, staring in disbelief that turned swiftly to acceptance.

The neat trail stretched away from him, right back to the car, where it had smeared the door and painted it a deep shade of red. It had followed him even as he was heading towards its source, as if mocking him. It began at the car door and then ended about ten yards from his current position, forming a small shallow pool in the sparse grass. He stared at it, and watched as the end of the trail began to nudge closer, closing the gap between them. The grass at his feet turned dark red; the soil became sodden.

"No," he whispered, taking a step back. "No. Please." He did not know who or what he was addressing, but he was sure that something was listening. It had to be.

"Please stop … I haven't done anything wrong." He kept back-peddling, his feet shuffling across the hard ground. He raised his hands, as if warding off a blow, and then stumbled, going down heavily on his backside, his feet scrabbling in the compacted dirt.

Panicked now, he tried to scramble to his feet, but the syrupy red trail was closing in … the blood touched his boots, climbed his legs, and made its slow, inexorable way up towards his trunk. Murray spun on to his back, scrubbing at his pants, at his shirt; trying to cleanse the blood even as it stained him. The trail was alive; it was hungry. He watched in terror as it consumed him. The Langdale Pikes, silent onlookers as they were, passed no comment or judgment.

Then, painlessly, wounds began to open up across Murray's body, as if he were being attacked by some invisible beast: slices and slashes in his stomach; gouges across his chest; a deep gash at his throat. The blood moved in reverse, entering these wounds instead of pouring out of them, linking the previously disembodied trail to his physical form in a way that he could not comprehend.

Murray tried to scream, but his ruined throat would only produce a moist hissing sound. He reached for his face, felt cuts open up on his cheeks, and wondered when he would get to feel the pain. Turning once again onto his stomach, he began to crawl, heading away from the road and towards the rising fells. He had no specific direction in mind; his convulsing body was moving purely on instinct, trying to escape this valley and the terrible history that had stained it.

It was a moment before he noticed the shredded shape as it moved clumsily towards him across the ground, crawling from out of the shadow of the derelict pub. There was an *eagerness* about the tattered form that was terrible to witness. Its progress was gradual, as if each movement brought with it an indescribable agony, but there was no doubt that it was heading straight for Murray and it would not stop until their paths met. The two were on a collision course, and neither of them seemed physically capable of moving aside.

Murray could barely lift his head to watch the thing, but how could he be expected do anything but stare at such an implacable vision of horror?

It had once been a man, of that much he was sure, but the sheer ferocity of its injuries had rendered it inhuman. It was simply old bones wrapped up in strips of meat, a slow-moving nightmare of blood and damage and decay. Behind the figure, and stretching right back towards the exact same point on the wall at which Murray had stood and stared a few days before, was its wide, wet red trail: a trail that matched his own.

He crawled forward to meet the slowly approaching figure of the *Fellwatch Inn's* murdered landlord. His hands and arms were now shredded beyond repair, but he hoped there might be enough left of him to sit up and beg for mercy.

Then, from out of the corner of his eye, Murray saw the blurred motion of something with a sleek pelt and flapping wings. As it raced towards him along the flat, stony ground, he knew that whatever had killed Thomas Daldry had now followed the trail back to him.

THE BLACK HOUND OF SHAP

The whole of British folklore is riddled with stories of ferocious black dogs appearing through the midnight mist as portents of doom, but few stories are as blood-curdling or as attested to by so many reliable witnesses as the mysterious Black Hound of Shap Fell.

In many ways this tale follows the classical pattern. On a lonely stretch of country lane, a terrifying bogey creature – a dog-like apparition formed from the moorland mist – is said to approach unwary travelers, snarling and slavering. Though described as a dog it in fact resembles no dog known to Man, for it is the size of a donkey, covered in a thick, shaggy pelt, and has glowing embers for eyes. At least, this was the creature described in versions of the story from prior to the nineteenth century. In that respect, it stirs memories of the Barguest, another Lakeland demon, or Gytrash, the Lancashire hell-hound whose hunting ground is located sixty miles to the south. In all cases, it was said, the appearance of this monstrosity would presage a disaster of some sort.

Origins of these black dog stories go back to the Middle Ages. There was even a belief among medieval scholars that such evil spirits had been brought to Britain by the Danes and unleashed on the frightened populace as Dark Age weapons of mass destruction. They are not uncommon in any part of the country, and yet the particularly strange thing about the Black Hound of Shap Fell is that sightings of the brute have been reported as recently as the 1980s.

That may sound astonishing, but nowadays the A6 road passes through this locality. In severe winters it is a notoriously difficult and dangerous route, and there have been a number of serious and even fatal accidents. Stories have made it into the local press that some of these collisions were caused by the appearance of a spectral dog. The monstrous proportions described in lurid folklore are absent from this modern variant, though the more recent apparition was still said to be black in colour and to have emerged literally from nowhere. To add further credibility to these startling tales, in 1937 a series of very detailed sightings were made over several nights and these also featured in local newspaper reports. The 1930s dog supposedly ran alongside vehicles at night, and then leapt over a low wall, beyond which was a drop of nearly 300 feet.

In daytime, Shap is a beautiful and sedate corner of Cumbria, famous for being part of the scenic 'coast to coast walk'. But at *night, when the mist comes down and blankets a landscape which is already almost impenetrably dark thanks to a lack of artificial light, it is all too easy to believe that evil, supernatural beings are abroad.*

STRIDING EDGE
Reggie Oliver

I am not generally afraid of heights, but there are some high places which make me afraid. They are pitiless and apart; they seem to mock at the futility of your ascent. And when the mist blows across them in vagrant drifts, like idiot ghosts, they can be dangerous. That has always been my feeling about Striding Edge, the rock-fanged ridge that takes the fell walker by the most spectacular route to the summit of Helvellyn. I know that it does not strike everyone like that, and I will admit that my feelings about it have a good deal to do with Derek Shorecliff.

You see, the first time I was ever on Striding Edge I met him there and he was about the last person I expected – or wanted – to see. It was barely two years since we had been at Okeham Grammar together, but the distance between school and college is a huge one. To me in my first summer vacation from Morchester University, he seemed part of a remote and rather dingy past.

*

My parents lived in Suburban London from which, in the long summer vacation, I looked for any opportunity for an inexpensive exile while I studied my books. (I was a swot in those days.) One offered itself in the shape of my godmother Vanessa who, with her friend Gwen, a journalist and one-time Labour MP, had decided in their latter years to withdraw to the Lake District and run a little sweet shop in a village called Urnthwaite not far from Keswick. What drove them to this course of action, or what brought them together, I never really knew. There is always a fundamental mystery about the lives of others, a mystery that on the whole I like to preserve. I accepted with gratitude their kind invitation to spent part of the summer there.

So, one afternoon in the early August of 1973 I was picked up from Penrith station. Vanessa, like Gwen in her late sixties, was a gentle soul and had once been a beauty. I understood from my father that she had long ago endured a short unhappy marriage to an alcoholic and had never tried it again. Gwen, an eternal spinster, was the more forceful character: short, compact, given to decisive pronouncements. I sensed in her a reserve towards me, but also a genuine attempt not to seem disobliging. In my turn, I tried to make it clear that I would be as much help and as little trouble to them as I could be. I read in the mornings and bicycled about the country in the afternoons. It was my first time in the Lake District and, though I liked the look of it, I felt somehow uninitiated into its particular splendours. One evening over supper I tried to express this rather nebulous feeling and Gwen immediately took me up on it.

"Right then, young man," she said, "tomorrow afternoon, I shall take you fell walking. Throw you in at the deep end. I think we'll try Helvellyn. It's a very sporty peak," I had no idea what she meant by the last remark but I tried to respond with enthusiasm.

The following day, after an early lunch, Gwen drove me into Patterdale, leaving Vanessa to mind the shop. There, on Gwen's instructions, I bought a pair of fell walking boots and a copy of Wainwright's *The Eastern Fells* while she invested, for both of us, in several slabs of Kendal Mint Cake, a delicacy of which I had never heard until that date. From there we made the short journey to Glenridding where we parked the car, put on our boots and began the trek to Helvellyn.

It was a bright day and despite this and the lines of blue and red anoraks that were threading their way up the stony track to the mountain ahead of us, I felt daunted. Helvellyn had a savage shape which no amount of hearty hikers could dissipate. In fact, I felt that, given half a chance, it would gobble them up in mist or batter them to death on its scree-strewn slopes. I kept these fears to myself though, because I sensed that Gwen would be scornful of them.

The first part of the walk across Birkhouse Moor to the Hole in the Wall was easy enough. We walked quickly, passing several more grizzled and leisurely hikers. Gwen always greeted them with some cheerful remark about the weather and walking conditions. I sensed that she was trying to impress me with her expertise which touched me.

After the Hole in the Wall the way became a little steeper as we began to ascend to the ridge known as Striding Edge.

We had just reached the top of the slope where Striding Edge proper begins when I saw Derek Shorecliff. He was standing just off the main path in the midst of a group of about a dozen young boys aged between eight to thirteen. Shorecliff, like me, was nineteen at the time. Accompanying him was a man I guessed to be in his early forties whom I did not recognise. The whole party seemed to have halted in order perhaps to wait for someone.

There was no escaping the fact that Shorecliff and I had

193

recognised one another, so I greeted him and we performed the introductions to our respective companions.

"Fancy seeing you here," said Shorecliff. I could have said the same.

*

At school Shorecliff had been one of those people who, for no obvious reason, are generally disliked. In this instance I was one with the majority, even though I was not usually the sort to go with it out of convenience or inclination. Even as I try to analyse it now I cannot find a completely convincing explanation for my aversion. He was not rude or sarcastic, nor, apparently, a bully. He was fairly clever and moderately good at games. He played the clarinet in the school orchestra.

Nor was there anything in his appearance that marked him out as a pariah. He was rather tall and bulky with slightly blunt features and the kind of pale, fine hair that prophesies the early onset of baldness. He smiled rather a lot in an apparently meaningless way, but that is not a major offence. People, for no very good reason, called him 'a creep.'

He always seemed to be on the margin of things. When a group of us were gathered together, Shorecliff could often be observed nearby, smiling enigmatically. We suspected him of listening in on private conversations, though there was no evidence that he made use of information garnered by such activity. When his own views were canvassed on any subject he would either give an evasive, ambiguous reply, or he would parrot the opinions of the last person to have spoken. He was an unknown quantity; that, I suppose, was the sum of it.

He had no particular friendships, except for one, and that was an odd one. There was a junior boy called Nelson, some two years below Shorecliff and the two could often be seen together. Nelson wore thick spectacles, had a muddy complexion, and permanently greasy hair. He was not especially clever and his parents were neither rich nor famous. Nelson and Shorecliff both played the clarinet, and that may have been a bond of sorts.

If Nelson had not been such a notably unattractive boy, some kind of homosexual liaison between the two might have been suspected, but that seemed to the rest of us wildly improbable. Most teenagers are aesthetic snobs, and the idea of less than perfect physical specimens engaging in any kind of amorous activity is absurd to them. Though I have since modified my prejudice, I still think that sex between Nelson and Shorecliff was unlikely.

Nelson's most unappealing trait was the way he cleared his throat. He did this with a long stertorous snort and a sort of gargle at the back of his throat, as if he were gathering all the snotty detritus from his nasal passages and then swallowing them wrapped in a sticky coat of mucus. It was a repulsive sound and he made it often. In fact he gained a reputation for it, of the kind that otherwise quite undistinguished individuals can acquire in a school environment. There used to be unofficial competitions among us as to who could produce the most lifelike and disgusting imitations of 'Nelson's gurgle,' as it was called, at the end of which someone would nearly always say:

"God! Imagine doing it with him and then having him clear his throat in the middle of it all."

To which everyone else would respond: "Oh, Christ! Yuk! Please! We don't want to know!"

Shorecliff belonged to an organisation, not affiliated to the school, called 'The Greenwood Folk'. We knew about it because he was always making strenuous efforts to recruit Okehamians to it, but, unsurprisingly, with very little success. From the leaflets he distributed, I gathered that it was an association, akin to the Boy Scouts but less militaristic, dedicated to healthy outdoor and rustic pastimes. If I am not mistaken I caught a whiff of pagan mysticism from some of the Folk's literature. Apart from camping out, the activities included folk dancing, country crafts and ceremonies conducted around trees. Green was the predominant colour of the Folk: green flannel shorts, green shirts, green woollen socks, even, I believe, green shoes.

Shorecliff's only successful recruit to the Folk was, of course, Nelson. I remember that towards the end of my time at Okeham he and Nelson turned up at a major school sporting event dressed in their Greenwood Folk costumes. Nelson wore the plain green shorts and shirt of a Greenwood Folk novice, but Shorecliff, who had obviously acquired some foothold on the organisation's ladder, wore a yellow flash on his arm like a lance corporal's stripe and a green cape piped with scarlet. The rest of us did not mock these strange apparitions, we simply avoided them. For some reason they made us feel uneasy.

*

Shorecliff was wearing the same uniform that day on Striding Edge, except that there were two yellow flashes on his arm instead of just the one. The young boys with him were also dressed in the green shirt and shorts uniform and were introduced by Shorecliff as "our Greenwood Goblins," apparently a junior branch of the Folk, like Cubs and Brownies. Goblins was not a bad name for them. They were pasty-faced, hollow eyed creatures, and, to judge from their accents, had been recruited from some of the more insalubrious quarters of an inner city.

The older man who accompanied Shorecliff and the Goblins was tall and ugly, with a bald head, spectacles and a bushy reddish-brown beard. Shorecliff introduced him to us as "Colin, our Grand Wizard of the Greenwood." He wore roughly the same uniform as Shorecliff except that his shirt was emblazoned with all kinds of badges and insignia and his cape was not green, but purple and had a hood. Thick white knobbly knees were visible below his green shorts and above his green woollen stockings which had three yellow bands around their tops. Despite this rather ridiculous get-up, he managed to convey an air of authority. Instinctively I bowed as I shook hands with him. Gwen did not shake hands; she remained quite still and stared at this peculiar specimen.

Rather reluctantly, I told Shorecliff what I was doing here and he responded by telling me that he was a trainee chartered accountant, but that he also did a lot of work "for the Folk, especially with young disadvantaged people." He gestured vaguely towards the Goblins who stared back at him with round-eyed inscrutability. It sounded meritorious, if rather condescending. I had nothing as worthy to respond with, so a silence followed in which I searched for something to say. Eventually I came up with the fatuous: "I thought you concentrated on living in the woods. I didn't know you went up hills as well."

Colin replied: "Our Temple is the Greenwood, but the Mountains are our gods." He spoke these words like an incantation, in a high-pitched nasal voice. For all his apparent absurdity, there was something powerful, even threatening about the Grand Wizard.

"I see," I said, and there was another pause. Then I heard a sound which brought back my schooldays with Proustian immediacy; it was the sound of someone clearing their throat in a peculiarly disgusting way. It could only be Nelson, and indeed, up the little track from Birkhouse Moor, we saw him struggling to reach us. He wore the Folk's green uniform and was sweating profusely in the unclouded sunlight. I noticed that he had put on weight since I last

196

saw him, a change that had in no way enhanced his physical appeal.

"And about time too, fatso," said Shorecliff, as Nelson puffed up towards us. "Where have you been? We have been waiting for you, you know."

"Sorry, Derek, sorry, Grand Wizard, sorry, folks," said Nelson. "I suddenly felt ... I had to ... Oh, hello!"

He waved to me in recognition and I waved back, but I had no desire to pursue the reunion. I said something about "pressing on" and that maybe we would meet at the summit. I realised how false I sounded, as if I were an experienced fell walker; but I had to get away, so Gwen and I set off along Striding Edge towards Helvellyn. Gwen, tactfully, made no immediate comment on our encounter, and for some minutes we trod the stony track in silence. A combination of my youthful fitness and Gwen's toughness and experience put a considerable distance between us and the Greenwood Folk which made me feel easier.

After a while we paused to stare down the treacherous scree on our left towards Red Tarn, black as a pool of ink in a lonely hollow, some two hundred feet below us.

"My God," said Gwen after a decent silence, "I didn't know *they* were still going strong."

"Who?"

"The Greenwood Folk."

"You've come across them before?"

"Oh, yes. Just before the war when I was a Labour Councillor in the East End of London. The Folk had what they called a 'Mission' down there; used to take the poor city kids out on country rambles, that sort of thing."

"Sounds rather admirable."

"Yes. It was okay, I suppose. But some of them had pretty weird views. Pagan stuff. Dancing round the maypole, herbal remedies, corn dollies and folk songs, you know. Which is fairly harmless, I know. But then we found out that a number of the Folk were recruiting the boys to Mosley's lot."

"The Blackshirts? The Fascists?"

"Yes. There was a bit of a stink about it. We were pretty close to war with Hitler by then, you see. Well, somehow the Folk managed to clean up their act. I believe quite a few of their members did pretty well in the war: commando stuff and that kind of thing. And after it they managed to find the name of their organisation on some sort of Nazi black list, so all was forgiven; but I haven't heard of them for some time. I thought they had just died out. Evidently not."

We pursued our way along Striding Edge. If it weren't for Gwen's dogged confidence, I might have turned back. One false move either way and I'd have been tumbling down a stony slope; I felt I was walking a tightrope, or dancing along the blade of a gigantic knife. Experienced fell-walkers will read these lines with contempt, I know; but you have to remember that it was my first time.

There was, I admit, exhilaration too. Despite the presence of other walkers, the world up there felt savagely, bracingly lonely. Sun glittered on stone and moss, wind blew off the heat of the day, leaving one feeling clean and pure. It was like a pilgrimage.

When we reached the summit we sat contentedly with our backs against a dry-stone wall, sheltered from the wind and ate shards of Kendal Mint Cake. I am not myself very excited by views from mountain tops – I prefer to look up rather than down – but as such views go, it was a fine one. We could have lingered to savour the moment, but then I saw the column of Greenwood Folk approaching the summit over the last broken teeth of Striding Edge. I thought I spotted the awkward figure of Nelson stumbling along in the rear.

I did not want to involve myself again with Nelson or Shorecliff; in fact I felt suddenly and passionately averse to such a re-encounter, so I suggested to Gwen that we start our descent. Gwen gave me a quizzical glance, but she agreed. We came down by Swirrall Edge and the silent waters of Red Tarn, and so returned to the car park in Glenridding. I did not look back to see how the Folk were faring.

The rest of the day was bathed in the virtuous glow of strenuous exercise well taken, and I noticed that Gwen's attitude towards me had changed. She became less formal, more companionable. Before that day I had attributed her reserve towards me to a constitutional dislike of men, but I now began to suspect something more complex had been at work. Her Puritan Socialist heart had been uneasy about me, her partner's godson. She had probably considered me to be a spoilt Southerner, a milksop, perhaps even a secret Tory. However my conduct on Striding Edge had convinced her that I was made of the right – or perhaps the left? – stuff. I had passed her test: that is what I like to think. My view of her had changed too.

As we drove home Gwen talked for the first time freely about her time as an MP in the Atlee Government, evidently the high point of her life. When we got back to the shop my dear godmother Vanessa greeted us like returning adventurers.

That evening, after an early evening meal, and while it was still light, there was a ring at the door. Vanessa went to see who it was and came back to say that it was an old friend of mine who wanted to see me. My feelings of contentment evaporated almost instantly. I suspected that the person who had erroneously described himself as "an old friend" was going to be Shorecliff, but it was not. It was Nelson.

Gwen and Vanessa made him very welcome and offered him a glass of beer which he nervously accepted. Conversation in their little sitting room above the shop was rather stilted, and presently Gwen and Vanessa said they would "leave us to it" while they went to the office to do some accounts.

Their absence did not appreciably untense the atmosphere, but we managed a rather awkward exchange of personal information. I asked Nelson how he had found out where I was and he said that Shorecliff had told him and that he and the rest of the Folk happened to be camped in a little stretch of woodland just below Urnthwaite. He informed me that he had left Okeham and was studying at a sixth form college for his A Levels with a view to reading biochemistry at Exeter. It seemed to my arrogant young mind just the sort of dim activity he might be engaged in.

"So," I said, changing the subject slightly, "you're still with the Folk." Nelson shrugged disconsolately. He did not seem to be too happy about it.

"I didn't do the Helvellyn climb well enough today," he said. "Derek is very disappointed in me. He said even the Goblins did better than me. He told me the Grand Wizard was very angry about my behaviour, so Derek has given me this stone as a punishment." He took out of his anorak pocket a smooth flat stone – tarn pebble at a guess – on which a drawing of a tree had been crudely scratched. I recognised the logo of the Greenwood Folk.

"Funny sort of punishment," I said.

"No," said Nelson, suddenly becoming agitated. "You don't understand. I've got to go off tomorrow morning before dawn, taking one of the Folk's bicycles to Glenridding, I've got to climb Helvellyn again and put this stone on top of the cairn on the summit at sunrise. Later someone will come and see if the stone's there to check that I've done it. That's my punishment."

"Bloody hell! That's awful. You can't do that!"

"I've got to."

"Tell the bastards to get stuffed."

"Easier said than done."

I took a deep breath: "Look, why don't you stay here for the night. I'm sure we can put you up somehow. Then in the morning, we can drive you into Penrith and you can take a train back home."

Nelson looked terrified. "No! No! I couldn't possibly do that! It's very kind of you, but that's just ... out of the question."

"Why?"

"I can't explain. It just is." To my shame, I was immensely relieved. Much of my schoolboy fastidiousness about him had remained intact. "Look," said Nelson, "I've really got to get back to camp. I shouldn't even be having this beer. Alcohol is forbidden. I must go."

"I'll walk you back then."

To my surprise he agreed gratefully to my suggestion. It was a beautiful evening as we set off down the hill from my godmother's sweet shop. We walked in silence. I felt I had shot my bolt as far as persuading Nelson to leave the Folk, though I have since wondered whether I gave up too easily. As we came down into the valley Nelson pointed to a belt of fir trees across a stream.

"There's our camp," he said.

As we approached I began to see lights among the trees which flickered and moved. We climbed over a gate into the field which was separated from the camp by the stream. Just as I began to see what was happening in the trees Nelson stopped me.

"Actually, you'd better not come any further than this," he said, then added half apologetically: "if you don't mind."

A number of dark green canvas tents had been set up in a small clearing among the fir trees. They surrounded a central camp fire which burned bright, illuminating the faces and limbs of anyone who came near it. Most of the Greenwood Goblins had picked up burning brands from the bonfire and were threading their way among the trees in single file. From a distance it looked as if a long, fiery snake were weaving its way around the copse. The Goblins were moving in rhythm, almost dancing, and their high treble voices were raised in a chant. When I asked Nelson what words they were intoning, he reluctantly told me:

"All hail to the Gods of Greenwood and Hill! All Power to those that live under the Will!"

He added: "The Greenwood Folk are said to 'live under the Will'."

"Whose will?"

"Nature's will," said Nelson. I was not so sure.

In front of the fire, arms folded across his chest in a hieratic pose, stood Colin, the Grand Wizard of the Greenwood. The hood of his purple cloak was up, so that, in the flickering shadow of the leaping flames, his great bearded face was sometimes revealed, sometimes darkened. At his feet crouched Shorecliff, wrapped in his green cape.

"I'd better go back now," said Nelson. "I shouldn't have been away so long."

That was the moment when I ought to have made a last appeal to Nelson to leave the Folk and come back with me, but I didn't. Reason, of course, told me that the Folk were a harmless bunch of cranks and that, in any case, it was none of my business. That was the mantra I repeated all the way back to my godmother's, but it didn't entirely convince me. I knew that I had felt fear, even from a distance.

When I returned to the shop, Vanessa greeted me apologetically. She said: "I'm sorry we left you alone with him, but we simply couldn't bear that foul way the poor boy cleared his throat. Has he got sinus problems or something?"

Two days later there was a paragraph in our local paper, *The Lakeland Messenger,* about a missing boy. His name was Keith Nelson, age seventeen, and he had last been seen in the vicinity of Helvellyn early on the morning after he visited me. There was no photograph, but it must have been him. I felt dread and guilt at the same time. I wondered if I should go to the police and tell them about my conversation with Nelson on the night before he vanished, but what had I of relevance to tell them which was not known already? The truth is, I did not want to be involved. The paper had told me that extensive searches were being conducted: there was nothing I could contribute. Guiltily I kept an eye on the *Messenger* for any further news, but the story seemed to peter out. Perhaps, after all, he had been found alive. If he were dead it would surely have been reported.

On the day I read that first newspaper report I had gone down to the Folk's camp among the fir trees, but it was no longer there. There was a disc of grey ash where the camp fire had been, but otherwise you would not have known there had been anybody living and sleeping in that place.

*

Three years passed during which I got my degree and began to train to be a teacher. Then, early in 1976, I heard from Vanessa that Gwen had died from a heart attack. Later that year, in August as it happens, I went to stay with my godmother in Urnthwaite. She was giving up the shop and was coming back to live in a small flat in London. I was to help her pack up and move.

My task was not arduous and I had time to reacquaint myself with Lakeland. Occasionally I would borrow Vanessa's car and drive off to see the sights. I had not quite forgotten about Nelson and his disappearance, and occasionally I felt the pull to revisit Helvellyn to see if ... what? I really did not know. There was no chance all these years later of discovering some clue to the mystery, but I felt, obscurely, that I owed it to Nelson to go there and see. Eventually, shortly before the end of my stay, I yielded to the urge and went.

It was not the best of days. The sky was full of ragged cloud and there was a threat of rain. Not surprisingly there were few walkers about. I parked the car in Glenridding, put on my boots, slipped Wainwright into the pocket of my anorak and set off up towards Striding Edge.

The more I think about it, the more terrible the coincidence seems, but at the time it was barely a shock at all. He was there. I met Shorecliff at the start of Striding Edge in exactly the same place as I had encountered him three years before, but this time he was alone. There were no Goblins or Grand Wizards with him and he was not wearing the uniform of the Greenwood Folk. He wore a plain green anorak and had one of those maps in transparent plastic cases hanging around his neck.

He seemed a lot older than the last time I saw him. I noticed that his expected baldness had come upon him.

"Hello," he said. "Fancy seeing you here." But he did not seem particularly surprised to see me.

We compared notes about our respective progress. Shorecliff told me he was now a fully fledged chartered accountant; I gave away a little about myself but he didn't appear to be very interested.

I said: "Do you still belong to that weird organisation, the Greenwood People, or whatever they call themselves?" (I knew the real name, of course, but I just wanted to annoy him.)

"Folk," said Shorecliff huffily. "May I give you a piece of advice? In the words of Bob Dylan: 'don't criticise what you can't understand.' "

I don't know quite why this sounded so false and pompous, but it did. Perhaps it was because I would never have associated a buttoned-up individual like Shorecliff with Dylan.

"As a matter of fact," he said frowning down at me, "I am about to become a Wizard in the Folk."

"Does that mean you get to wear a purple cloak?"

"That's right." My conjecture about the cloak had been, I thought, a rather brilliant guess, but Shorecliff had taken it for granted, as if we were all expected to know such things. I was beginning to gauge the extent of his egoism and I wanted to puncture it.

"Did you ever find out what happened to Nelson?" I asked.

"No." Shorecliff seemed quite undisturbed.

"I mean, he can't have just disappeared."

"Apparently he did." Again there was total indifference.

"How sad. I mean, how did his parents feel about it?"

"I've no idea."

"You were his best friend, weren't you?"

"These things happen."

"I mean, didn't you feel guilty about sending him up Helvellyn that morning?"

"How did you know that?" For the first time Shorecliff seemed shaken. I told him about Nelson's visit to me the night before his disappearance.

"You've got it all wrong," said Shorecliff. "Nelson did what he wanted to do. He went his own way. He may be still alive for all we know."

"Don't you care?"

"Life goes on. Nelson was weighed in the balance and found wanting."

"What the hell do you mean by that?"

"If you don't understand what I mean, there's no point in explaining."

I turned away from him towards Striding Edge and Helvellyn.

"Are you going to go on?" He asked. "There's beginning to be a lot of mist about. There could be some rain. It won't be too safe. I'm going back down. Care to join me?"

"No thanks." There was nothing I would have liked less. Shorecliff smiled at me, and then suddenly I saw his face change. There had been a shock to his system. He looked around wildly.

"Something the matter?" I asked.

"No. Did you hear anything just now?"

"No. What sort of thing?"

"Never mind. Well ... Ciao!" He flickered his right hand at me in a perfunctory farewell, then turned and began to walk down the slope towards Birkhouse Moor.

Shorecliff was right. Great ragged sheets of mist were beginning to roll in over the Edge. I could barely see ten feet in front of me. The air was damp and chilly. I should have followed his example and gone down, but something in me rebelled against it. I would go on and damn the consequences.

Very soon I was surrounded by white fog. Reality had shrunk to the few feet of stony track in front of me. The steep slopes of scree on either side of me had vanished. They could still be there; they could have been replaced by deep chasms going down infinite depths to black Hades. I walked on.

The mist was greyer and blowing faster across my path carrying spits of sleet which stung my cheeks. I kept my eyes down, fixed on the tiny visible space of track in front. To turn around was unthinkable; it was no more dangerous to go forward. My progress was slow, so slow that time and space meant little to me now. At any moment I could slip or take a wrong turn and then I would be falling.

The silence was immense: not the silence of a small room, secreted from the outer world, but the silence of infinite space. Then, as I listened hard, it seemed to me that it was not quite silence. There were little specks of noise in the atmosphere like the transient grains of sleet that burned my face. Of course it was my imagination. I stopped and tried to listen but though the sounds were there, they had become fainter.

I moved forward again and the sounds became more distinct, though still very far away. They were little splinters of noise like high pitched squeaks as if one sound had been shattered like a glass bulb and I was touching its sharp, glittering fragments. Put together the noises might have been the laughter or mockery of children in a playground. The sounds were now behind me urging me forward. I looked round and thought for a moment I could see little shards of green in the mist, like tiny disembodied limbs. I turned and did not look back again.

I was now moving along the path quite quickly, conscious that I was trying to escape from something, but that that something may not actually have been behind me. The little squeaks of sound were now about my head like a cloud of midges. "There are green things following me," I found myself thinking. A second later I was sweating with fear, not so much because I was being followed as because the mad thought of being followed by green things had entered my mind. I was going insane. I could not stop. I pressed on.

By now, I was stumbling through the mist in a kind of daze. I tried to slow down but found I could not. Then suddenly a great noise struck me like a physical blow and stopped me. It was a vile noise, a horrible noise, like a great sticky snort from the mouth of a giant. I knew it. It was Nelson.

I stood there swaying while the mist eddied around me and then, for a brief moment cleared from the way ahead. I had come to that point almost at the end of Striding Edge where there is an unexpected drop: one has to scramble down and then up again. In normal circumstances it is, according to Wainwright, "a little awkward"; in these conditions it might have been fatal. "Nelson's gurgle" had saved me.

I made the last part of the ascent to Helvellyn with infinite care, untroubled by noise of any kind. When I came out onto the slopes of the summit the mist was clearing and weak, pale sunshine began filtering through the clouds. I looked around. I was alone, for once the solitary lord of Helvellyn.

I remembered then why I had come there. I wanted to see if by any chance Nelson had got to the summit that morning three years ago. I walked over to the cairn to see if the pebble with the tree scratched on it was in the pile. I spent nearly an hour searching for it, but it was not there.

I scrambled down via Swirrall Edge, still alone, and wandered back to my car past the waters of Red Tarn, ruffled into hammered pewter by a light breeze. No birds sang.

*

It was about a year later that I read of Shorecliff's death. I came across it quite by accident in my *Guardian*, attracted by the headline: STRIDING EDGE MYSTERY.

Shorecliff had been conducting a summer camp near Patterdale for, as the paper put it, "esoteric Back-to-Nature movement, the Greenwood Folk" when, one morning, he disappeared. The authorities were alerted and the following afternoon his body was discovered by some ramblers below Helvellyn. It was lying at the bottom of the Northern slope of Striding Edge on the shores of Red Tarn. He was wearing the green uniform and the hooded purple cape of a Wizard of the Greenwood Folk. It had probably been an accident. The possibility of foul play was investigated and then discarded. He had gone out on his own in the early morning to climb Helvellyn, became disorientated in the mist and lost his footing on Striding Edge. It happens.

Nevertheless the tragedy had its puzzling aspects. Fragments of human bone had been found spread around Shorecliff's body. Analysis showed them to be the bones of a boy in his late teens. How long they had been there could not be determined. They might have been there for ages, and probably had been. But it was odd that while most of the bone fragments were beneath Shorecliff's body, a few shards appeared to have been scattered over the corpse.

In the hood of Shorecliff's purple cloak was found a pebble on which the shape of a tree was crudely scratched.

SOURCES

All of these stories are original to *Terror Tales of the Lake District*, with the exception of *Devils Of Lakeland* by Paul Finch, which first appeared in Enigmatic Tales #2, 1998, *Above The World* by Ramsey Campbell, which first appeared in Whispers #2, 1979, and *Jewels In The Dust* by Peter Crowther, a different version of which first appeared in *Haunted Holidays*, 2004; the version appearing here is original to this book.